LOVE FEAST

Books by Frederick Buechner

Novels

Non-Fiction

FREDERICK BUECHNER

LOVE FEAST

Atheneum   *New York*   1974

C. 2

For my mother

LOVE FEAST

CHAPTER ONE

THERE WAS A TIME when it was out of sight out of mind. A day, a week, a year ended, and when it ended, that was the end of it. But then they invented home movies. Before we left for Europe one summer, my father-in-law, Leo Bebb, gave me a Bell and Howell super-8 with a zoom lens and an optronic eye, and for anyone with a piece of equipment like that, the past may drop out of mind the way it always used to but out of sight never. It is always around to sight any time you feel like sighting it, thousands of feet of it wound up in reels and stowed away in cans. Baby's first steps, the picnic on the beach, some lilac bush tossing its dowager plumes in the spring breeze someplace—even if you don't take it out and look

at it very often, you know it's available. Bebb's septua-
genarian paramour and traveling companion Gertrude
Conover, who is a Theosophist, claims that this reflects a
cosmic truth. Maybe so. What I can attest to is only
that, cinematically speaking if not cosmically, the song is
over but the melody lingers on.

My father-in-law Leo Bebb, my wife Sharon and I at
the Eiffel Tower, for instance. For all the ground we
have covered since and will go on covering for better or
worse until finally the ground covers us, there we continue to stand on that first platform the elevator lands
you at, the one where the restaurant and the souvenir
shop are. It is one of the best shots I got that summer.
Bebb is leaning against the guard-rail with an ice cream
cone in his hand. His bald dome glints like a second
Sacré Coeur against the clear Parisian sky. His firm, fat
face looks fussed and sweaty. His gaze is aimed straight
at the optronic eye, and he is gesturing at it with his ice
cream cone. His mouth is snapping open and shut like a
change purse. My Bell and Howell has no sound attach-
ment, but I remember his words anyway. Not surprisingly they are from Scripture. "Forget not the congregation of the poor forever," he is saying. I zoom in on his
face until it all but fills the screen. His trick eyelid
flutters half way down, then up again. "For the dark
places of the earth are full of the habitations of cruelty."
His text and my fifty feet run out almost simultaneously.

What happened next I had no film left to immortal-
ize, but I remember it well enough. He gave the ice
cream cone an upward swipe with his tongue and said,
"Antonio, you've got to hand it to these Frenchies. They
don't say flavor like we do, they say perfume, and they're
right. Without you can smell what you're putting in

4

your mouth, it might as well be pencil shavings." He must have worked the ice cream loose with his tongue and the gesturing because as the three of us stood there looking down, he tipped the cone inadvertently, and the ice cream fell out. It hit one of the diagonal struts on the way down and hung there. It gave me a queasy feeling in the groin to watch it. Bebb was in a pensive mood. "It looks like a blob of pink spit," he said, "and below it . . . Down there below it lies Paris, France, spread out like a crazy-quilt. The City of Lights." Part of the ice cream slid down the strut and fell off onto the next one below. "It's got a long way to go before it makes the City of Lights, Antonio," Bebb said. "We all of us do."

Holding onto the rail with both hands, Sharon straightened her arms and pushed back away from it as if she was pumping on a swing. She said, "There's a sermon in that, Bip."

Evangelist, Founder of the Church of Holy Love, Inc., and of the Open Heart Church, International President of Gospel Faith College, which offered ordination through the mail ("Put yourself on God's payroll—start working for Jesus NOW"), ex Bible salesman, ex con.— Bebb was as eager as the next man to believe that to get away from things for a while was with luck to make them disappear, and when he invited Sharon and me to go to Europe with him that summer, we leapt at it with no less optimism. God knows there was plenty to get away from. There was Open Heart for one thing, the church Bebb had started in a barn near where Sharon and I lived in Sutton, Connecticut, with our baby son Bill and my dead sister's two teenage sons, Tony and Chris.

5

Open Heart had never panned out, at least not the way Bebb hoped, and he knew it.

He said, " 'When two or three are gathered together in my name, I will be with them' saith the Lord, and I don't doubt for one minute that he keeps his promises. He was with us at Open Heart, all right, but he was with us in a special way. The Good Shepherd doesn't always just stand around and let the sheep graze wherever they take it into their heads. Sometimes he drives them on to greener pastures, and that's how it was at Open Heart. He was there the whole time only he was there telling us to move on out to a place he would show us. He hasn't showed us that place yet, but he will. He's never let me down yet, Antonio." So for Bebb our European summer was a matter of getting away from the black help, the cousin of Harry Truman, the lady with the gerbil in the cage and the handful of others who gathered together Sundays to hear him preach the Kingdom in the wrong place and at the wrong time. The right place and the right time would turn up when they would turn up. Bebb had no doubts about that. He said, "It's like Christopher Columbus, Antonio. To discover the New World, you got to scrap the Old."

As far as you could name it, I suppose what Sharon and I were getting away from was Tony, the younger of my two nephews who was named for me—that muscle-bound jock as Sharon called him in one of their turbulent encounters, that seventeen year-old track star and Lothario who glittered in the waters of our domesticity as harmless as a beach ball until you touched him the wrong way, or the right way, and he went off like a mine, scattering wreckage for miles. It was late one night when I unlocked the door to let him in from some spring adventure that he told me that he and Sharon had become lovers, and later in her own way Sharon told me too. It had happened by accident apparently, catching both of them by surprise no less than it caught me. Neither of them had any plans to let it happen again, but even a little adultery goes a long way and although our marriage survived, it survived barely. With the hull stove in, the engine room flooded, and Bebb at the bridge, we limped to Europe for repairs. Tony and his brother Chris plus our son Bill were packed off to spend the summer with Charlie Blaine. Charlie Blaine was the father of my two nephews, a nap-taking valetudinarian who during his waking hours wrote scripts for educational TV and waking and sleeping both was looked after by Billie Kling, a big-busted Florence Nightingale with a voice that could lance boils.

And then there was the death of Bebb's wife, Lucille. We were all three getting away from that. Poor Lucille. The dead, by and large, are harder to get away from than the living. I see her at the Manse in Armadillo, Florida, sitting in front of the color TV with her black glasses on and a Tropicana at her side—half gin, half orange juice —the way she'd been when I first met her. I see her listing down the aisle of Open Heart in her French heels and Aimee Semple Macpherson gauze. I see her laid out in Bea Trionka's dress with her hands crossed at her breast so that the wrists she'd spilled her life out of wouldn't show. I don't suppose her name was mentioned more than a half dozen times all the weeks we toured southern England in Gertrude Conover's rented Daimler, and yet the silences between us were again and again hers—those long, askew silences that had always been her primary means of communication, that slight ·

dropping of her lower jaw that was her smile. I wondered often what she would think of Bebb's romance with Gertrude Conover, and there were times when I had the strong sense that she was telling me. Bebb and Gertrude Conover at the rail of a Thames ferry with Traitors Gate looming dark behind them. Bebb and Gertrude Conover in the maze at Hampton Court, Gertrude Conover with her Baedecker in hand reading to Bebb through the box hedge the secret of how to get out. What did Lucille think? *There*, I all but heard her saying with a deflection of her black glasses toward them. *You tell me.*

There was no getting away from any of the things we were trying to get away from, but somehow the trip worked anyhow. When we took the Golden Arrow for a final week in France before sailing home, we left Gertrude Conover behind in London, and Bebb moped around for a while, missing her, but Paris restored him. We stayed at the Hotel Voltaire where according to a plaque Jan Sibelius, Richard Wagner and Oscar Wilde had all preceded us. I pictured them arriving as a three-some, standing there together at the concierge's desk. Our rooms were in front, and the noise of the traffic that went on all night made it like sleeping in the Lincoln Tunnel, but the view was spectacular. From our shallow balcony you could have tossed a croissant over the book stalls into the Seine, and directly across on the right bank was the Louvre. From the start Sharon had disliked London. She took it personally. "Those crazy English," she said, "they're too damned hung up on history. All their old churches and castles and beat-up you-name-its, they remind me of those things they used to make out of dead people's hair. Luce had one had been her Grandma Yancey's, a whole lot of wreaths and flowers that the moths got into. The French, they've got as much history as anybody else has and then some, but they can take it or leave it." Paris, unlike London, met with her full approval, in other words, and it was she who showed us the sights. She got a lot of circulars from American Express, and there wasn't much we missed.

The day before we sailed for home we took the train to Versailles, and if I had to choose one moment to stand for the best that happened to us that summer, Versailles would be the moment. The precariousness of our marriage, the failure of Open Heart, Lucille's death, as always they were as inescapably part of the gear we carried with us as Bebb's binoculars, my Bell and Howell, and Sharon's *Guide Bleu,* but Versailles taught us something about how to carry them. The little grotto where Marie Antoinette hid when she heard that the women of Paris were marching out to storm the chateau. The room where Louis XV died in a stench of gangrene. The *Salle des Glaces* where the treaty was signed that solved nothing in particular. The past clung to the place all right but as a proud and even festal garment—history not as mould but as glitter. Sharon wangled us tickets to the *Jeu de Son et Lumière* in the evening, and although the *lumière* was less than what my optronic eye needed to operate at top effectiveness, there was enough to let it record at least some of the more incandescent moments such as the grand finale when all the fountains were turned on full force which even in their heyday were put into action only when the Sun King was known to be coming around the corner. Great floodlit plumes pulsed high into the dark from pool to pool all the way down the whole range of terraces, light bursting apart into water, water falling apart into light. Over the loud-speaker system came the *son* of Charles Boyer's narration against a background of the *Marseillaise* sung by a chorus of thousands with drums, trumpets, cannons, and I don't know what-all else. Behind us, with only its foundations in shadow, the great chateau floated a few feet off the ground.

Bebb sat there like something carved out of soap with the binoculars pressed to his eyes. Sharon was between us in a sleeveless dress, her long, straight hair dividing over her ears the way it always did when it needed washing. I had my arm over the back of her chair, my hand on her bare shoulder where I could feel both the coolness of her skin and the warmth of her life beneath it. There wasn't one of the three of us who didn't wear some kind of cockeyed crown.

Several weeks after we got home, when all my twenty-odd reels of film finally came back processed from Eastman Kodak, I sat down to the task of editing and splicing them. It was the first time I had had the chance to see them, and my fingers literally trembled with apprehension as I set about cranking them through my viewer. My fingers trembled because although I had every reason to believe that our trip had been a success, I couldn't escape the fear that if for some reason the movies didn't turn out, it would prove that with all its deadly accuracy the optronic eye had seen dark things that I had failed to see or that the bright things that I thought I'd seen had been only the fictions of my longing for bright things.

Nothing is ever clear-cut, of course. The movies had good parts and bad parts both. For every successful shot like Bebb with his ice cream cone on the Eiffel Tower or Sharon and Gertrude Conover on a fallen lintel stone at

Stonehenge, there was a failure—the Queen's Horse Guard blowing across the screen like autumn leaves because I'd panned too fast or a sunny morning of feeding the pigeons at Trafalgar Square turned into a dim and moonlit swirl of ghosts because I'd inadvertently switched the exposure control knob to manual.

So far all the preservative powers of cinematography, in the long run maybe the past is just as elusive as it always was. I snipped out all the bad parts and with little bandages of splicing tape mended what was left into an unbroken sequence of good parts. The worst is lost forever. Only the best remains. With possibly one exception.

As the Q.E. 2 steamed up the Hudson toward New York Harbor, it looked for a crazy moment as though the great stacks couldn't possibly clear the Verrazano Bridge. My movies end with an overexposed view of Bebb on the open deck bracing himself for what seemed inevitable catastrophe. His plump fists are clenched at his sides. His tipped-up face is a bright and featureless blur. You can't go home again said Thomas Wolfe. What my parting shot seems to say is that, at your own risk, you can.

CHAPTER TWO

WHEN WE GOT BACK from Europe, we found that Open
Heart was gone. The barn that housed it had burned
down so completely that there was nothing much left
but some charred beams. One day Bebb poked around
through the wreckage for a while in the hope, I suspect,
that he might find his big preaching Bible miraculously
preserved from the flames, but of course he didn't.
Everything was gone including the murals Bebb's friend
Clarence Golden had slapped up all over the walls—a
kind of Sistine comic-strip that told the story of Bebb's
life as Mr. Golden had come to know it during the time,
years before, when they had been cell-mates. Bebb had
pled innocent to a charge of indecent exposure behind a

seafood restaurant in Miami, but he had been convicted and sentenced to five years anyway. What Mr. Golden had been convicted of, I didn't learn till later. In fact I was still open to the possibility that as Lucille had often darkly hinted, Mr. Golden was a creature from outer space.

Bebb had a theory that the world was full of creatures from outer space—they were what Scripture referred to as angels, he said—and more than once Lucille had suggested that Bebb himself was one of them. Except at occasional odd moments, I was never able to take this charge seriously, and I find it hard to believe that Lucille really did either, but Mr. Golden was another matter. He didn't look like an angel. He was a wide, flat man with a wrinkled, beardless face and a girl's sweet smile who could have been either remarkably well preserved for an old man or prematurely old for a relatively young one. He wore a windbreaker and a pork pie hat. He said he suffered from bladder trouble. But like an angel he had a way of turning up at unexpected times and unexpected places, and when he turned up at the time of Lucille's death, Bebb told him he could stay in the Open Heart barn for a while. Then Bebb moved in with Sharon and me. It was during that period that Mr. Golden had painted his pictures on the walls. Then Bebb had taken us off with him to Europe, and when we returned, Open Heart and Mr. Golden were both gone.

The same day we found out about the fire, we found a note left under the kitchen door. It read:

Friend Leo, in Hebrews 12:29 it says by FAITH they passed through the Red Sea as by dry land so when you land back safe and sound from the other side you know what you got to thank for it is the same as what we all of us got to thank for everything we have or ever HOPE to have worth more than two pins. My sugar is back down where it belongs, and when I wasn't wrestling it out with Guess Who I had a real rest cure at your place. Thanks for the hospitality. Its the wide blue yonder for yours truly now and there is no telling the next time our paths will cross, if not in this world then in a better world to come, Amen. Leo let the dead bury the dead. You got your work cut out for you down here like we all do and don't you worry but what without ceasing I will make mention of you always in my prayers same as I count on you making mention always in yours of your fellow sinner in Jesus and old chum without ceasing, F. P.S. Remember Bull Litton? He's signed me on as night watchman so whatever happens you'll know I'm there watching. Smiles.

Bebb said, "I'll tell you one mistake he made. Anybody knows Scripture knows it's Hebrews *eleven* is the big chapter on faith. It was Hebrews eleven twenty-nine he ought to put down, not Hebrews twelve twenty-nine. He ought to know better than that."

Sharon said, "I'll tell you another mistake he made. His name is Clarence Golden, and he signed it F."

Bebb said, "Fats. Back when I first knew him, a lot of them called him Fats. So that's no mistake. F is Fats Golden. But the other one, that's what you call a mistake. Hebrews twelve twenty-nine. Who'd have thought Clarence Golden would go and make a mistake like that?"

Later on with nothing else to do except unpack her bags, get food in for supper, arrange about bringing the baby back from Charlie Blaine's and so on, Sharon took out the rusty Gideon I had acquired somewhere and checked Bebb out. She said, "That Bip, he sure knows his Scripture. The part about the Red Sea *is* eleven twenty-nine."

"Just for kicks," I said, "see what it says in twelve twenty-nine."

I remember she was sitting on the stripped mattress of our bed with one bare leg crossed over her lap in what looked like one of her Yoga positions, the Gideon propped against her calf. She said, "Jesus, you're never going to believe this. You know what twelve twenty-nine says?"

She kept her finger on the double-columned page, but she looked at me as she read it. She said, "It says, 'Our God is a consuming fire,' that's what it says. Before Open Heart burned down, Fats Golden wrote us our God is a consuming fire."

I said, "*Maybe* that's what he wrote us."

"Smiles," Sharon said.

I said, "I wouldn't tell Bip if I were you. He's got enough on his mind."

She said, "Listen, we've all of us got enough on our mind."

Even at that early point maybe part of what we both had on our minds was the knowledge that for better or worse something was coming to an end between us.

Charlie Blaine was a hypochondriac, and it always surprised me that he had as much time left over as he did for his educational TV. What kept him busy was not so much his various sicknesses themselves—as far as I know, not one of them ever seriously incapacitated him —but trying to work out in his mind how to describe his symptoms to the doctor. He told me once that to put a pain into words for somebody who has never felt that pain is as much of a challenge as to put the colors of a sunset into words for somebody born blind. I suppose that trying to put his pain into words was the story of his life. Maybe it is the story of all our lives.

Not long after his wife, my twin sister Miriam, died of myeloma, a form of cancer that attacks the bones, Charlie thought he had it. Even assuming it was contagious, he could hardly have caught it from Miriam since they had been divorced for several years before her death and such communication as there was between them had taken place almost entirely over the telephone. But Charlie was sure he had it anyway. Because I had seen a lot of Miriam from the early stages of her sickness right up to the end, I knew as much about it as anybody, and on a number of occasions Charlie tried out on me various ways of desribing his symptoms. The pain was not localized, he told me; in fact he suggested that maybe *pain* was too much of a word at that point although *sensation*, on the other hand, didn't strike him as quite word enough. But whatever you called it, he said, it seemed to affect him all over. He told me how once when he was a child there was a strange and apparently sourceless rumbling sound in his family's house that led them to believe for a while that they must have a ghost until they discovered eventually that what they had was a community of squirrels in the hot air ducts of the furnace. What he felt was something like that, he said. The problem was to locate those fatal ducts of his being where the squirrels had taken up residence. He also told me that whenever he got up out of a chair or sat down in one, a peculiar thing happened. He could feel his muscles doing all the things muscles do when you get up or sit down, only then, as soon as they had finished doing it, he could feel them doing it all over again like a kind of echo. It was as if he had two bodies, he said, a substantial one and an insubstantial one. Death like a ghostly comedian was following him everywhere, aping each of his most basic and life-like movements. Or maybe it was all in his mind. Even Charlie was sometimes willing to admit that possibility.

The symptoms of my failing marriage were no less obscure and uncertain, and even at that early point my attempts to describe them, if only to myself, were no less time-consuming. Something was rumbling in the hot air ducts. We went through the motions of our life together much as usual, Sharon and I, but I sensed that in the background, dimly, we were perhaps also going through the motions of our death together.

How did it all start? When did I first become aware of the sensation if not then the pain? Many times I tried to trace my way back to the earliest symptoms. Maybe it started when Bebb moved out of our house a few months after we all got back from Europe and it didn't do much good for any of us let alone for Bebb himself.

Moving out was his own idea. He left his portable TV in the small third floor room he had been living in, telling Tony and Chris they could go up and use it any time they felt like getting away from things. Everything else he owned he managed to squeeze into two dog-eared suitcases with straps around them, relics of his days on the road as Bible salesman. Sharon said they looked like the kind of suitcases you find torsos in in vacant lots.

Bebb the far-darter. I remember him standing at the airport in his Happy Hooligan hat and tight-fitting black

raincoat saying goodbye to us. He said, "I'd as soon drive
a nail through my thumb as go up in one of those things,
but then I ask myself what am I saving myself for,
Antonio?" It was a November afternoon, raw and wet.

He said, "I've got something here to remember me
by. Luce, she run it up for me on her machine to use
at Open Heart, but seeing how there's no such place as
Open Heart any more I want you to— Here. It's a keepsake." Out of his raincoat pocket he produced a brown
paper bag. In it there was a piece of white linen which,
when unfolded, turned out to have the words OPEN YOUR
HEART TO JESUS stitched in red along one edge—an altar
cloth—and as he stood there in the drizzle holding it out
for us to see, a small contingent of demonstrators happened to come off the air field toward us. They carried
banners and placards with peace signs and anti Viet
Nam slogans, and a boy with a pony tail and a Robert
Louis Stevenson moustache spotted Bebb's keepsake and
came over.

He said, "Man, that's where the whole thing's at. You
a Jesus Freak?"

Bebb said, "I'm behind Jesus a hundred per cent, and
I've been called a lot worse things than freak in my day if
that's what you mean." His trick eyelid did its trick. He
said, "What can I do you for, son?"

"We surely could use that flag in our army," the boy
said. "We'd fly it high and wide for peace."

"Jesus was for peace," one of the girls said. She had a
World War II overcoat that reached almost to her
ankles and a Day-Glow headband.

Bebb said, "Honey, Jesus is the Prince of Peace.
Where there isn't any Jesus, there isn't any peace worth
a nickel."

Lucille's altar cloth must have been about six feet

wide. The girl took it by one corner, and Bebb still had hold of the other, so they stood there with it spread out between them. The air was chilly enough to see their breath in.

"Go on and give it to them, Bip," Sharon said. "We don't have any place for it home."

They called Bebb's flight number over the loud-speaker, and his face went as pale as the cloth either from the necessity for a quick decision or the imminence of his departure.

Finally he said, "I'll tell you one thing. I don't go in for dope or you-name-it sex or walking the public streets got up like Hallowe'en and knocking the U.S.A. every chance you get, but I believe in Jesus and I believe in peace so if you'll treat this thing with respect and do like what it's got written on it, you can have it and welcome."

So in the end all we got to remember him by was the brown paper bag. At the gate his last words were, "Even rigged out like crazies and hair all over their faces, there's no two ways about it. They're beautiful. They're beautiful and they're young, and it's like the Book says, 'It shall come to pass that your sons and daughters shall prophesy and your *young* men shall see visions.' That's how come I let them have it, Antonio."

As he walked up the steps to the plane, he bent over with his handkerchief to his mouth, and Sharon said, "Sometimes even before he gets on board he pukes."

Although the reason Bebb gave for going back to Houston and Holy Love was that it was time for him to rejoin the laborers in the vineyard, even then I had a feeling that the real reason was that he sensed the ghostly rumbling in our marriage and thought we might stand a better chance of exorcising it without him. I think he knew perfectly well before he got there that the vineyard at Herman Redpath's ranch had all the laborers it needed.

When he had moved north to found Open Heart, he had left his assistant, Brownie, in charge of Holy Love, and Brownie had everything well in hand. He had put in air-conditioning. He had installed a more powerful caril-lon in the tower so that there was no part of the ranch beyond the Sunday strains of *The Old Rugged Cross* and *I Need Thee Every Hour*. And Herman Redpath had left Holy Love such a handsome endowment in his will that not even Bebb's remarkable money-raising skills were needed. So for the better part of a year after Bebb left us, he rattled around down there among all those Indians who lived on the Red Path Ranch. He got Brownie to let him preach once in a while. He helped the two fat Trionka sisters put the files of Gospel Faith College in order and read some of the 8½ x 11 book summaries submitted through the mails for advanced theological degrees. He signed diplomas. He helped ar-range such tribal festivities as what Maudie Redpath claimed was her hundred and tenth birthday at John Turtle's Tom Thumb golf course. But his heart wasn't in any of it. Nobody down there really needed him the way Herman Redpath had, and he knew it. Gone were the days when two or three times a week he was summoned to lay his hands on the scalp of that geriatric Geronimo and call down upon him the potency of years long past.

So Bebb ended up leaving the ranch and joining forces with Gertrude Conover in Princeton, New Jersey. He became a world traveler. Over the course of three years or so they visited together every continent except Australia, and some of them they visited more than once. They went on a photographic safari in Kenya and sent back snapshots of themselves in pith helmets sitting side by side on the mountainous rib-cage of a drugged elephant. After a cruise through the Greek Islands, they spent a week at Delphi where through theosophic channels Gertrude Conover established contact with the ancient oracle whom she had apparently done business with in an earlier incarnation.

One spring they went to Egypt and took a boat trip down the Nile. According to Gertrude Conover, one of the earlier lives during which she and Bebb had known each other had occurred when she had been Uttu the Pharaoh's ward and Bebb had been a priest called Ptahsitti. Bebb said that only once while they were in Egypt did he have any inkling of having been there before. They had taken a taxi out to see the Sphinx, and as they stood there between its paws, Bebb said that for a moment or two he had a feeling that this was not the first time he had gazed up into that great ruined face. But then, he wrote, "It come over me in a flash the reason the face of the Sphinx looked so familiar was it was a dead ringer for the face of George Washington on the front of every dollar bill I've had in my hand for going on sixty-some years. If the two of them aren't one and the same, they're identical twins. When I told that to Gertrude Conover, though, she asked me what it was put it into my head that the U.S.A. was the first country George Washington was the Father of."

In between trips Bebb returned occasionally to the Red Path Ranch and once in a while visited Sharon and me for a few days in Connecticut, but when not traveling he spent most of his time with Gertrude Conover at Revonoc in Princeton. Revonoc was a large whitewashed brick house with stone lions at the entrance to the drive and a broad terrace in back that looked out over a sweep of putting-green lawn and a heated swimming pool protected on three sides by a yew hedge. Whatever some people said, you couldn't accuse Bebb of using his friend for her money. With most of the hundred thousand dollar bequest from Herman Redpath still intact, he had all the money he needed. And he was no toady either. He was always interested in finding out more from her about her theosophy, but he gave no signs of believing much of it himself. He made no attempt to be like her Princeton friends. He kept on wearing the same kind of gents furnishing suits and pointed shoes and painted ties he'd always worn. He didn't try to improve his grammar. Often he would take the train into New York by himself on errands that she knew nothing about. There was no sense in which he seemed to have sold out to Gertrude Conover and the placid rhythms of Revonoc, and yet I couldn't escape the feeling that those years with her were somehow lost ones for him.

I remember seeing him once when he didn't know I was anywhere around. It was during a weekend I spent at Revonoc one winter. I was walking down Nassau Street on some errand or other when I suddenly happened to notice Bebb walking slowly along in the same direction on the other side of the street. It was late afternoon and snowing. On my side, the lights of the shops made everything look comforting and Dickensian, but on Bebb's side there was only the massive stone shadow of the Firestone Library dimmed by the tumbling flakes. Bebb had on his habitual black raincoat with a lining buttoned in which made it look even tighter than usual but which probably wasn't enough to keep him warm. He had on his small, neo-Tyrolean hat but no galoshes, no gloves. He looked somehow diminished walking along through the winter, and the sadness I felt as I watched him was mixed with a sense of disillusion.

He moved independently enough through the landscape Gertrude Conover provided him, but it wasn't his landscape any more than the snow was his snow. Bebb belonged closer to the sweaty heart of things. He belonged where the lions were not stone like the ones at Revonoc but hairy, horny, cantankerous like the ones I had seen him stand unafraid among on the scrubby plains of Lion Country near Armadillo. He had let down the congregation of the poor he had talked about half way up the Eiffel Tower, had let himself down, and I had the feeling Sharon and I were somehow to blame.

If she and I had been more each other's, Bebb would have been more ours, more his own—not that he would have necessarily stayed on living with us, I suppose, but that, humanly if not geographically, we instead of Gertrude Conover would have been the base he operated out from. And with us as his base, I felt he would have operated more in his own peculiar way, toward his own peculiar ends. Instead of making it easier for us to exorcise our ghosts by leaving us, he became one of our ghosts himself. We were haunted by the Bebb he used to be, the Bebb who except for us he might have kept on being.

CHAPTER THREE

IN WHAT WAY wasn't Sharon quite mine in those days? Maybe she had never been quite mine from the beginning and it was only when we were left alone together that I began to notice it. Bebb and my nephew Chris cleared out within a few months of each other, and Tony cleared out within a few months of that, so that within the space of about a year the house was empty except for Sharon and the baby and me.

Chris, that pimply, pale, and stage-struck boy who was endlessly exploited by Sharon as resident baby-sitter and maid of all work. After graduating from Sutton High, where I taught English, he was accepted at Harvard, where he went with every intention of becoming Elia

Kazan if not Tennessee Williams only to become instead Merrill, Lynch, Pierce, Fenner and whoever it is rolled into one. He started a typing service his freshman year, branched out into Xeroxing as a sophomore, and by the time he was a junior was earning more than his tuition and switching his major from Drama to Economics. Vacations he took to spending with his father and Billie Kling and summers he worked as runner for a Wall Street brokerage so that Sharon and I rarely saw him. His complexion cleared up, his hair grew thinner, his neck and shoulders filled out enough to take away some of his Bunthornian willowiness, and by the time of his graduation he could have been taken for an assistant dean or successful young alumnus. "I want to make the theater my life," he had said once to Bebb in the accents of *Mary Noble, Backstage Wife*, and maybe Moneymaking Prodigy was only a role he was trying on for size. What sneak previews were going on behind that dim, well-organized face were anybody's guess. Sharon's guess was simplicity itself. "What that Chris needs," she said, "is to get laid."

Tony had no such problem, but he had others. He graduated from High School the year after his brother and partly through disinclination and partly through poor grades didn't go to college. Instead, he joined me on the staff of Sutton High the fall after his graduation in a variegated capacity that included helping coach track and swimming, running the manual training shop, and doing such grounds work as operating the snowblower in the winter and one of the power mowers in the spring. "A jock of all trades" was what one of the faculty wags called him, and after the dazzling spring of his senior year when he broke three school records in track and virtually singlehanded brought Sutton out ahead of Port Chester, Rye and Greenwich, his return that fall was like Lindbergh's coming back the next morning to sweep up the ticker-tape. He let his dark hair grow thick around his ears and down the back of his neck so that he looked more than ever like something out of the Elgin Marbles when, stripped to the waist, he would work out with his weights in the back yard to keep himself in shape; but with no more records to break or cups to win, he must have asked himself the question what he was keeping himself in shape for, because after a while he gave the weights up and spent most of his free time in his own room playing his cassettes with the door locked.

Except for the night he confessed to me about himself and Sharon, the only time we ever risked touching directly on the subject again had been one spring afternoon just before we left for Europe when I remember his saying to me that he would do anything if he could only make it as if it had never happened, and my answering him—for lack of anything else to say—that maybe we could at least make things happen around it that would make it not matter so much. Actually we did a better job of it than I had any reason to hope, and the reason was that by some miracle of grace the kind of things we made happen around it were pretty much the same kind of things we'd been making happen always. Tony and Sharon went on fighting the same wild battles they'd been fighting since he first moved in with us—his slovenly room versus her slovenly housekeeping, his nocturnal adventures that kept him out till all hours versus her yoga, speed-reading, guitar lessons that kept her from—and so on. In between such assaults there were as usual the equally passionate truces when they would sit together in front of the Late Show red-eyed at Paul Henreid leading Rick's bar in the *Marseillaise* right under the nose of Conrad Veidt and his Nazis, or at Leslie Howard, fresh from the arms of Ingrid Bergman, seeing the child he had abandoned for her struck down by a car as she ran toward him across the street. And in much the same old ways I went on being me with them and they themselves with me until finally among such familiar happenings it came to seem to all three of us that nothing so outlandish as a man's wife cuckolding him with his nephew could possibly have happened except perhaps on the TV screen. Thus it was not by taking pains with each other that we saved the day, or almost did, but by being as shiftlessly congenial and inconsiderate as ever. The slightest gesture of sympathetic understanding, the faintest effort toward some sort of civilized accommodation, would have spelled our doom.

I think it was that locked door that spelled it finally or at least the early stages of it. Doom like the mystic syllable Om is not just the part in the middle that you hear but the silent parts at either end. Tony would come back from school in the afternoon and maybe polish off a can of beer or some unnamable thing Sharon had left in the ice-box. He might fool around with our son Bill for a while or tell us about something that had amused him that day like the time he was taken to task for saying to somebody that an affable senior named Bruce Hurley was the biggest prick in school when what he'd actually said was the simple locker-room statistic that Bruce Hurley *had* the biggest prick in school. Then he would thump up stairs in his disintegrating loafers held together with adhesive tape and put on the Stones or the Airplane or whatever. From below you couldn't hear the tune very well, just the beat, but you could hear him shut the door. And if you listened, you could hear him lock it.

Every time it happened, it sent Sharon up the wall. "What's he do in there all the time with the latch on, play with himself? Does he think we want to break in and watch him for Christ sake?" I remember the first time she said that, I thought of Brownie for some reason, Bebb's seraphic assistant with the china teeth and Little Merry Sunshine approach to even the darkest places of life and Scripture both. I thought of how Brownie might have said that if we would go in and really watch him for *Christ's* sake, maybe he wouldn't have to play with himself any more but would come out and play with us, play and make merry before the Lord. *Dear*, Brownie would have said. He called everybody dear. Sharon said, "He doesn't need to lock it. I wouldn't go into that hole if he paid me, the way he leaves it. You could cut the air in there with a axe."

The bed unmade, the pajama pants accordioned on the floor where he'd stepped out of them. There was a wedding picture of his parents on the dresser—Charlie in his Navy whites, my sister Miriam with a little too much lipstick, a little too much lace, looking very Italian, at his side. There were his track shoes, a framed award Charlie had received for some TV series, a brassiere hanging down from the ceiling light. There was a button the size of a butter plate with *Kiss a Toad Tonight* on it. There was a stack of old *Playboys* and a picture of Jesus Bebb had given him which had eyes that looked closed until you looked at them hard and they opened. There was his cassette player. "That poor bastard," Sharon said once, standing in the midst of it one morning when he was away. "Maybe he's not locking anybody out. Maybe he's just locking himself in with his treasures." But the next time he locked it, she carried on the way she always did although never to him for a wonder, only to me, as if I were the one who locked the door or it was because of me he locked it. Maybe it was, for all I know—Ulysses chaining himself to the mast when the sirens sang, because one of them happened to be, after a manner of speaking, his aunt. Anyway, his locked door prepared the way so successfully for the day he told us he was moving out that we weren't even surprised when it happened. He'd rented a room in a boarding house on the other side of town, he told us. He didn't give us any special reason why, and we didn't ask him because to all intents and purposes he'd of course moved out already.

Bebb walking along through the snow down Nassau Street. Chris turning into J. Paul Getty in Cambridge and not coming back for vacations any more. Tony off on his own at a boarding house. Looking back at the early symptoms of what went wrong between Sharon and me, I have the feeling that with each departure there was, if not a pain, a sensation at least of something lost beyond the loss of the one who had departed. Life went on as usual in our increasingly empty house, our schedule or lack of it continued basically unchanged, but as in the case of Charlie's musculature, there began to be an echo. Even making love at night we were both who we were and also who we either could have been or maybe never could.

Then, not long after Tony left, Sharon started a health food store with her guitar teacher, a grizzled little marmoset named Anita Steen. They called it the Sharanita Shop and handled the regular line—variants by the dozen of every known vitamin and combination of vitamins, seeds and seaweeds, yoghurt and brown rice, everything so unrefined and natural that even the paperbacks of Adele Davis, Sakurazawa Nyoti and Euell Gibbons were such, Anita said, that if you got tired of reading them, you could always eat them. Anita took care of the business end and the ordering, and most of the time Sharon ran the shop. She would leave in the morning when I did, taking Bill with her, and often she didn't get back until just in time to throw something together for supper. From the start business boomed. There were days when we hardly met except in bed.

Whatever the fatal disorder was that we'd caught, though, there were periods of remission, and out of bed as well as in it we continued to have good times. There were afternoons on the beach with a length of clothesline attached to Bill's harness so we didn't have to keep an eye on him every minute as he staggered around after the sandpipers. We had people in. We went out. We had a few evenings in the city. Sometimes Bebb and Gertrude Conover, in between voyages, would come in from Princeton to have supper with us. We had our good times, Sharon and I, and to have heard us together, even when we were alone together, nobody would ever have guessed that anything was wrong any more than most of the time either one of us guessed it. But it wasn't what we talked about that told the tale. It was what we didn't talk about.

First what we didn't talk about was the sad things that had happened like poor Lucille's death and not seeing Tony and Chris much any more and Bebb's losing most of his bounce off there somewhere with Gertrude Con-over. Only then by a process no less subtle than the process by which a sensation turns almost imperceptibly into a pain, it got to where what we didn't talk about was no longer the sad things that had happened but the sad thing we both of us more or less knew was getting ready to happen next. Little by little the silences be-tween us changed their shape the way clouds do with an upheaval so vast and furious and slow you hardly notice it.

One evening in October Sharon asked Anita Steen for supper, and in place of the usual corned beef hash or frozen chicken pies, she put together a real meal for once which we ate not in the kitchen but in the dining room with wine and candles. After supper, with a girl from school to clean up and put Bill to bed, Sharon and Anita set up a card table in the living room and got down to the business of the evening which was to go over a month's worth of sales slips and check them off against the last inventory. I had a batch of themes to correct which I set about doing at my desk in the same room. There was a wind, and you could hear it stirring through the dead leaves at the side of the house.

I remember the way the two of them looked sitting there at the card table by lamplight—Sharon in a peasant skirt and low-necked, puff-sleeved blouse, Anita in her usual grey flannel slacks with a white shirt that had frilled cuffs and ruffles down the front like a matador's. I remember the grey crew-cut and bullet head of Anita Steen and that stunning cascade of wrinkles that was her smile, that flaring of nostril and baring of teeth like a horse on a merry-go-round. Her sharp yellow pencil, her half-moon spectacles, her king-sized cigarettes—everything she touched seemed part of a trick proving that her hand was quicker than every eye except her own, those quick brown eyes of Anita Steen's that were always busy with something other than whatever was busying the rest of her.

And Sharon. I remember Sharon sitting there with her elbows on the table and her chin in her hand, the way looped at the wrist her long hair fell, the shadow of her eyes as she gazed down, lazy and bored, at the record of all the good health she'd sold that month. I remember that Renaissance face always so somber and deadpan until with a sudden Bojangles grin she let the cat out of the bag and made even her sternest judge her partner in crime. The gaudy crime of Sharon's smile. She hadn't lost her summer tan, and you could see the low-cut boundary of it still, could see down to where it turned pale and freckled like thrushes' eggs. Sitting there looking at her with my red pencil in my hand and those feckless themes, I could see in my mind the whole cool and moonlit landscape of her flesh as I had come to know it the first time we made love together at the Salamander Motel in Armadillo. It was the landscape where I had lost my way never really to find it quite again, or her either, and I thought how the way I would describe my symptoms as I sat there watching her would be to say that it wasn't exactly a pain but it wasn't a picnic either. It kept changing: sometimes a choked feeling when I started to speak, sometimes more like a lump in the throat, sometimes just the shiver you get when a rabbit runs across your grave.

She said, "Go get Shorty and me a coke, will you,

Bopper? You don't look like those papers are grabbing you anyway," which God knows they weren't, the usual catalogue of plane crashes, suicides, drugcrazed knifings I was used to getting from my tenth graders who always stirred a strong mixture of death into their literary efforts to make up for what they knew was a fatal absence of anything much like life.

Anita Steen said, "Get it yourself, you spoiled beauty," and then to me, "You better take this brat in hand," only taking her in hand herself, catching Sharon's neck in the crook of her arm and pulling her over sideways till for a moment their heads just touched and Sharon popped her eyes and tongue out at me, strangling to death, then *Shit* as she knocked a week's worth of sales slips off the table with her bare arm. As she ducked down under the table to pick them up, the eyes of Anita Steen and my eyes met roughly at the place where Sharon's face had been, and instead of meeting there as enemies, we met for the first and only time in our lives as old war comrades coming together in an empty place where some crucial battle had taken place while both of us were looking the other way. Anita Steen tried flashing her brigadier wrinkles at me, but for once they failed her, just rocketed like tears from the outer corners of her eyes and fizzled out in the shadowy no man's land where her smile should have been. Sharon was the prize we both were battling for, and with our eyes we told each other we both had lost.

After she left that night, we had a battle about her, Sharon and I. Sharon was lying on top of our bed in a pair of my pajamas and I was still in the bathroom where through the open door I said something mostly fatuous about how anybody could see the whole Sharanita enterprise was just an elaborate maneuver for getting Sharon into the sack with her, and Sharon said if I couldn't accept Anita Steen for what she was, it was time I wised up and stopped being such a tight-assed square. I said I could accept Anita Steen for what she was without much sweat but didn't know whether I wanted to accept the way Sharon led her on, getting all fancied out for her plus candles and wine and letting her paw her whenever she felt like it, and Sharon said anybody thick enough to think Anita Steen wanted to play grab-ass with her was thick enough to think she wanted to play grab-ass with Anita Steen. She said Anita Steen had long since leveled with her about what she was but had told her she didn't have to get up-tight about it because Sharon wasn't her type, and I said if I was Anita Steen that's just what I would have said too.

My accelerated pulse and labored breathing, the sense I had that my vision must be going back on me because the air between us had somehow gotten bent and what I was seeing was not Sharon herself but some refracted image of Sharon—all my symptoms grew to the point where I could no longer believe they were just in my mind because they were sure as hell working now on my vital functions themselves so that what had been up to then only a sensation had turned into a five-star, technicolor pain that even Charlie Blaine could have been proud of.

There was Sharon, my heart's desire and shipmate, stretched out like a *Playboy* center-fold in a pair of my drip-dry pajamas on that six by eight raft that was the bed where we had ridden out many a dark storm, clinging on to each other for dear life; and the pain I felt as I saw whatever my failing eyes could see of her there had nothing whatever to do with Anita Steen or any impossible fever-dream of that puckered little castaway clambering aboard to find haven in the sea-cool, salt-sweet flesh and ingenious, yoga-supple games which all too well I knew that flesh could play. It was Anita Steen we were yelling at each other about above the high wind that filled my mouth, but at the heart of our howling there was a silence as at the eye of the storm a failure of breath, and that was where the pain came from, the unbreathed knowledge in both of us that this time it was Davy Jones almost for sure and that part of what we were howling at each other for was help.

No help came until such as there was in Sharon's finally rolling half over on her side to grab a cigarette from the night table and light it behind the veil of her hair as at the same time my drip-drys pulled apart enough to show her tanned belly and she said through a lamplit puff of smoke, "Jesus, Antonio, why don't you get your balls out of here," which if not a life-line was at least a line to leave on. Just as I was, with only a towel wrapped around me and the toothpaste still unrinsed from my mouth, I went upstairs and spent the night with a group of dead flies in the stuffy third floor room where Bebb had left his portable TV. He had also left a copy of Billy Graham's *The Jesus Generation*, but I couldn't keep my mind on it and spent most of what was left of the night watching the wind in the telephone wires and the leaves.

Breakfast the next morning went normally enough. The Cream of Wheat boiled over, and Bill kept up a steady patter which like bad handwriting you could understand only so long as you didn't stop to figure out any particular word. Sharon and I had no more and no less to say to each other than we usually did at that hour, and whatever it was we said was neither more nor less historic, but the air I saw her through was still bent air and the sound of her voice came to me from across water. That afternoon I let my tenth graders out of class early and drove downtown where I made arrangements to rent a room for myself and my balls both at my nephew Tony's boarding house.

Among the paperbacks you could buy at the Sharanita Shop was one called *Sweet and Dangerous: the new facts about the sugar you eat*. Sharon had left on the kitchen table the copy of it that she was reading, and I propped my note against that rather than pinning it to the more traditional pincushion upstairs. I said that if too much sweet was dangerous, maybe too little sweet was dangerous too. I told her where I was going and how to get hold of me in case she needed me. I asked her to tell Bill that I would come back to see him the first chance I got. I signed it with just the single initial A, that letter that in one form or another has haunted me for years. A as the shape of the cast my poor sister died in with most of her bones broken, and as the shape too (quite unintentional on my part—it was my old girlfriend Ellie Pierce who first pointed it out to me) of the outsize wooden mobile I'd made and with Tony's help hung from a tripod in the back yard where it had weathered to a silvery grey covered with bird droppings. A as the Eiffel Tower where the ice cream had fallen out of Bebb's ice cream cone marking for him no less than for Sharon and me the end of one era and the beginning of another. A for Adultery, *Andiamo*, Amen. A for A *rivederci*, Antonio. I signed the note, packed my bag, and left the house with a kind of dazed efficiency.

36

It was only when I was in the car driving toward town through the Hallowe'en-colored maples that I found my face wet with tears almost as if it was somebody else's tears and somebody else's face. A for delayed Adolescence. A for that deep-drawn ah-h-h of mingled regret and relief with which we tend to greet the death of even the people we love most; maybe even, in the last analysis, the death of ourselves.

CHAPTER FOUR

POOR BEBB. The news of Sharon's and my separation hit him hard, coming as it did at a time when he was in so many ways separated and at loose ends himself. He drove up to Sutton when word first reached him and saw us both. Separately. With Sharon he tried prayer. He told me about it later. Right there in the same kitchen where I'd left my note, he laid his plump hands on her head as in the old days he'd laid them on Herman Redpath and tried, in his phrase, to raise the whole mess to the Lord.

I have seen busboys in restaurants do much the same, crouching down by the service table to get their right shoulder and the palm of their right hand underneath a tray piled high with dirty dishes, then struggling to their feet under the weight of it and trying to make it out to the kitchen without losing balance and dropping the whole thing. Bebb must have risked a spiritual hernia straining to get us off the ground with his prayer—not just Sharon and Bill and me but Tony and Chris and in some measure himself too as they were all involved in our mess with us. I picture the sweat running down his bald head and his eyes bugging out as step after precarious step he tries to make it to where the Lord can take over in the Big Kitchen Up There and wash us all clean in the blood of the Lamb.

Bebb ascribed the flop of his prayer not to any lack of interest on the part of the Lord but to Sharon. He said, "Antonio, she didn't even let me get as far as—why I'd hardly more than shifted out of second before she busted in. She said, 'Bip, I might just as well lay it on the line. Whoever you think you're talking to, I've never seen him or heard him or felt him, and I've never tasted or smelled him either. As far as I'm concerned, you're just beating your gums.' Antonio, it pulls the rug right out from under a prayer to have somebody come out with a crack like that. To be honest with you, I feel like I've had the rug pulled out from under me in more ways than one. I don't have the zip I once did. When a miserable thing like that happens, I don't snap back like I used to."

With me, he didn't try prayer; in fact he seemed to lose track of his mission of reconciliation altogether in a fog of melancholy reminiscence. He talked about the old days in Armadillo and about Holy Love and how maybe he and Lucille would be there still if only he'd played his cards differently. Oblique as it was, it was the first reference I'd ever heard him make to the event that had led to his sudden departure from Armadillo—the ordination of Herman Redpath where at the climax of the ceremony, with his Ojibway ordinand kneeling in front of him, Bebb had raised his arms heavenward and like the high priest rending his garments had rent a certain portion of his sufficiently to empty Holy Love of every last Indian plus the Methodist youth choir and their parents in little more time than it took the photographer from Fort Lauderdale to flash a couple of shots, none of which, thanks largely to the intervention of Herman Redpath's head, showed all they might have. Sitting there in my empty classroom in front of a map of the United States with red pins stuck in to mark such literary shrines as Concord, Massachusetts, and Hannibal, Missouri, Bebb went on as far as to say, "When a man does things he can't rightly account for, there's two possibilities. One, the Almighty's behind it. Two, Satan's behind it. If it was Satan, I believe the Almighty wouldn't never have kept on doing business with me like he has all these years. That's what I *got* to believe, Antonio."

With the mark of Sharon's lipstick on his cheek, he stared out at the grey sky, looking as though maybe he could believe it and maybe he couldn't. In any case, he drove back to Princeton that evening with no reason to think that he had done any good at all in coming to see us. All he took back with him for his pains was the knowledge that Sharon had cut loose not only from me but from whatever it was Bebb had thought he was praying to in the kitchen as well.

I think that in many ways it may have been his bleakest hour up to that point because whereas five years

in the pen and the débacle of Herman Redpath's ordination and even Lucille's suicide had all been events he
could steel himself to, this new phase of his life was
hardly an event at all but more just a falling apart, a
gradual gathering of darkness. It was Gertrude Conover
who caused the light to shine for him again, a light that
for a while blazed down as hot and bright as any Bebb
had ever sweated under before.

She was pushing eighty at the time, but you would
never have known it to look at her. She had blue hair
and weathered blue eyes and her color was washed-out,
but there was something very female about her still,
something almost seductive. She was on the short side,
wiry, and when she walked, she had a way of tilting her
chin slightly down toward one shoulder so that she
seemed always to be coming at you sideways. It was as if,
although the general drift of her life was in another
direction altogether, she was nonetheless determined to
tack her way somehow to you, and when she got there,
you had the feeling not only that there was nothing of
herself left behind or gone on ahead someplace else but
that she wouldn't settle for any less than all of you
either. She had a way of smiling dimly while you talked
as though what she was smiling at was not what you
were saying but who you were and who she was and the
curious fact that with all the worlds there were to get
born into, the two of you happened to have found your
way to this particular world at this particular time.
Theosophically speaking, it might be eons before such a
fluke happened again, and it would be ridiculous not to
make the most of it while you could. There was no telling in what quaint ways you might be useful to each
other. She herself told me months later how it came

about that she was able to be useful in rescuing Bebb from the dark night of his soul.

The two of them had returned from shopping one November afternoon, she said, and since there were too many packages to carry into the house all at once, Bebb went back to the car to get the ones that were left. When he hadn't reappeared after a half an hour or so, she got worried about him and went out to see what had happened. She found him sitting in the front seat of the car with the packages forgotten in his lap and staring out the window with such a morose expression, the light through the tinted glass giving him such a grim pallor, that she asked him what on earth was the matter. When Gertrude Conover asked you what on earth was the matter, you felt it was more than just information she was after, and instead of ducking the question, Bebb more or less answered it.

"He said he was homesick," she told me. "My dear, he sat there all crumpled up over the groceries, and his voice sounded as though it was coming out of a deep hole. I asked him what he was homesick for, and he said, 'Gertrude Conover'—because you know I'm never just Gertrude to him but always this Southern thing of both names together—he said, 'Gertrude Conover, I don't know. I'm homesick, but I don't know what I'm homesick for any more than you do.' Poor soul. He was so blue. What does a person say? I said everybody gets homesick like that sometimes. I quoted Wordsworth about how the soul that travels with us, our life's star, hath had elsewhere its something and cometh from afar. He's always quoting Holy Writ to me, and I like quoting *The Oxford Book of English Verse* back at him, but you could see he wasn't listening. Blue? I've never seen him bluer. You get so you can actually see the color of it, you know. The astral body. So I tried another approach. I said, 'Come out of it, Leo. Think of other people for a change. Thanksgiving's only a few days off, and the University's full of young people who won't be getting home for it.' I said, 'For all their long hair and so forth, they're probably every bit as homesick in their way as you are in yours.' I said, 'Why don't you think about what you can do for *them?*' You know, it worked like magic. He said to me, 'Blessed art thou among women, Gertrude Conover,' and right there in the front seat of the Lincoln he blossomed like a rose.''

Suppose that there had been no second load of packages for Bebb to go back to the car for, or that it hadn't been that close to Thanksgiving, or that Gertrude Conover had just quoted Wordsworth to him about his homesickness and let it go at that. On such slender chances hang the destinies of us all, unless Gertrude Conover is right that there is no such thing as chance. Anyway, Bebb caught the ball that she tossed in his direction and for all I know may somewhere, somehow, be running with it still. His astral body shifted from blue to a positively sunrise pink as he decided the thing to do was throw a free turkey dinner for any Princeton undergraduates left on campus who wanted to come, and Gertrude Conover helped him for all she was worth as at that point she would surely have helped him for all she was worth if he'd wanted to stage a mass baptism in her heated swimming pool behind the yew hedge.

As for my own Thanksgiving, Charlie Blaine asked me to come out with Tony for the weekend, but not feeling up to the window-rattling cordialities of Billie Kling, I had reconciled myself to staying at the boarding house alone when Bebb phoned and invited me to Revonoc, describing his plans for the free turkey dinner with such

43

enthusiasm that I couldn't resist being on hand to watch them unfold. I drove past our house on the way out of town and saw Bill riding his tricycle on the driveway. I thought of stopping by for a moment to make sure Sharon was keeping an eye on him from inside, but considering the risks both ways, I decided against it. I thought at one point that Bill had seen me, and I waved at him out of the car window, but he must have been looking at something else. He had on a rainbow-colored tam with a pom-pom, and his small, fierce face was thrust out over the handlebars as he charged a pile of dead leaves.

I arrived at Revonoc the day before Thanksgiving and was given a full description of all the preparations that I wasn't there in time to observe for myself. Bebb showed me one of the posters that he had put up at the U Store, Murray Dodge, Freshman Commons, and other strategic spots all over the campus. He and Gertrude Conover had lettered them themselves.

The Rev. Leo Bebb, Evangelist, and Mrs. Harold Conover invite you to join them in giving Thanks at a Turkey Dinner at 1 P.M. Thanksgiving Day at No. 17, Gouverneur Road (off Bayard Lane). Sign up below and Come as you are. BLESSED ARE THEY WHICH DO HUNGER AND THIRST AFTER RIGHTEOUSNESS FOR THEY SHALL BE FILLED (Matthew 6:5)

Bebb had made the rounds several times a day to check on how many had signed up, and the results were somewhat disappointing. Not counting Chairman Mao, Mary Poppins, Angela Davis and Judas Iscariot plus others that were either illegible or the work of small children, there were only about twenty-five signatures all-told; but Gertrude Conover checked with friends at Nassau Hall on the number of students who were expected to remain on campus over the holiday, and she and Bebb decided that there would be a good deal more than twenty-five who would probably come whether they bothered to sign up ahead of time or not. By some occult formula they arrived at a figure between seventy-five and one hundred.

Trestle tables were set up in the spacious front hall of Revonoc with several extra ones in the adjoining solarium in the event of an overflow. On the landing of the main staircase chairs were placed for a four-piece orchestra. A caterer provided china, glassware, silver, and white tablecloths twenty feet long. Frozen turkeys were rounded up. Extra help was signed on. From an old family recipe Gertrude Conover personally prepared an enormous claret punch that called for *violettes de Parme*, which she had to send to New York for, and Appollinaris Water, for which she substituted Saratoga Vichy. Chrysanthemums, white, yellow, and copper-colored, were arranged in vases all over the house. The tables were decorated with wicker cornucopias of vegetables and fruit waxed and rubbed to a high polish. The whole house was cleaned from the billiard room in the cellar to the maids' quarters on the third floor. The gravel drive was raked. The stone lions out front were hung with wreaths of laurel around their necks. Signs were put up at either end of Gouverneur Road bearing the single word REVONOC plus an arrow, a heart, and, in an effort at contemporaneity, the circular peace symbol with the upside-down Y inside.

The preparations reached a crescendo around ten

Thanksgiving morning when the tables were being decorated and the caterer's truck arrived followed shortly by the waiters and the four musicians with their instruments. Bebb in shirtsleeves helped carry the small, nightclub-sized piano to the landing, and I remember him standing there staring down over the bannister at all the activity he had precipitated. His face was flushed and his eyes almost feverishly bright, and I thought how different he looked from the time he had watched his ice cream fall slowly down toward the City of Lights. Solid and compact with his thick shoulders and bare forearms, he looked as though he might have carried the piano up there single-handed, and when he caught the eye of Gertrude Conover, who was supervising the decoration of the tables, he raised one hand to her in a small clipped gesture which suggested by its very economy vast stores of energy still in reserve. "He's really come into his own," I said to her, with a bowl full of raisins and mixed nuts in my hands, and she turned to me with those weathered blue eyes and said, "Let's hope this time his own will receive him" not as if she thought they wouldn't but as if, thumbing back through the earlier lives of Leo Bebb, she had come upon some times when they had and other times when they had not, and she hoped that this time in Princeton, New Jersey, would be one of the former. Behind Bebb on the landing, the pianist was giving the violinist a note to tune up by.

By one o'clock only about a dozen students had arrived. One of them must have been close to seven feet tall with a bad case of acne and an Abe Lincoln beard. There was a fat, effeminate boy who turned out to be the grandson of somebody Gertrude Conover had known as a girl in Cleveland, Ohio. A pair of blacks arrived to-

46

gether, one of them wearing a striped black and terra-cotta kaftan and the other a grey flannel suit with a Tattersall vest and a large Afro. There was a boy who said he was there to do a story for the *Daily Princetonian* and a girl in vinyl slacks who had come with the understanding that there was to be a peace rally. There were also two or three of the kind that I suppose Bebb had dreamed of—fresh-faced boys straight out of Pepsi Cola ads with their pink cheeks and strong white teeth.

Bebb and Gertrude Conover greeted them all as they straggled in. The claret punch was passed around, and most of them accepted it except for a few like the black in the kaftan who declined on the grounds that he was a Muslim and a swarthy man in a jump-suit who looked ten years older than the rest of them and asked for a dry martini. The orchestra on the landing played things like *Tea for Two* and *Smoke Gets in Your Eyes*. White-coated waiters who almost outnumbered the guests moved among us with trays of canapés. Gertrude Conover, looking small and older than usual in a green wool dress with pearls and several of the yellow chrysanthemums pinned at her waist, tried to keep conversation going among the few who had gathered around her, and I did the best I could with the ones around me except that I kept losing track of what we were talking about in my effort to see how Bebb was making out.

He stood near the foot of the stairs with a group that I was glad to notice included the Pepsi Cola contingent, and although I thought I was able to catch him glancing at the front door from time to time to see if any more were arriving, there was nothing in his manner to suggest that he found anything wrong. He was doing most of the talking himself, everybody listening with what seemed more than merely polite interest, and I remember thinking that whereas there is nothing but faith to support Gertrude Conover's theory that a person lives many lives both before and after this one, the fact that a person lives many lives *within* this one is not only incontrovertible but in its way no less extraordinary. Bebb the only son of a disabled father and a relentlessly religious mother, first learning about death from a crated coffin he saw waiting for shipment at the Spartanburg, South Carolina, railroad depot, and about sin from peaches rotting along the roadside where they had been dumped to keep the price up. Bebb the Bible salesman spending nights in drummers' hotels all the way from Memphis to Tallahassee while at home in Knoxville Lucille was developing a taste for Tropicanas and one night while he was on the road found their baby dead in its crib from a beating that in her lonely and savage despair she couldn't even remember giving. Bebb spending five years with Clarence Golden in a cell where they told and retold each other the stories of their lives until they found it hard to be sure sometimes whose life was whose, where they played games like imagining their way down the whole list of Howard Johnson ice cream flavors to see who would be the first actually to taste each one as it came along—banana, black raspberry, fudge ripple. Bebb among the Indians. Bebb at Versailles. And now Bebb in the Ivy League at last—Bebb as Nicholas Murray Butler or William Sloane Coffin, Junior.

Given that the mind and body both are continually changing right down to and including the last living cell, what if anything of a person carries over from one year to the next let alone from one life to the next? What if anything makes the man who begets a son, say, the same as the man who waves at him, unnoticed, from a car window? Were the Bebb standing there among the undergraduates and the Bebb who had once stood unarmed and unafraid among the lions of Lion Country, the selfsame Bebb, or was Gertrude Conover right that the self is a will-o-the-wisp and the carry-over from one moment to the next as indefinable and insubstantial as whatever carries over when one candle is lit from another? Such metaphysical speculations as these together with my attempt to hear what Bebb was talking about made it difficult to focus very satisfactorily on the future of the Prospect Street eating clubs which as nearly as I can remember was the subject my group was tossing back and forth. I know only that by about two o'clock there can't have been more than at most twenty people waiting with increasing restlessness to start eating a meal that had been prepared for four or five times that many. When I saw Bebb climbing the stairs and gesturing to the orchestra to stop playing, I was sure that he felt the time had come to settle for the ones who were there, write off the ones who were not, and give the signal to start digging in.

As soon as the music stopped, the talking stopped too, and everybody looked up at Bebb on the landing. His breast-pocket handkerchief was folded into five neat points with the B showing. His tie was a metallic silver shading down into midnight blue. His round, white face was packed tight with confidence.

He said, "Welcome to Revonoc, folks. In case anybody hasn't noticed it yet, Revonoc is Conover spelled backwards because this place where you're standing is the home of Mrs. Gertrude Conover, who is the salt of the earth backwards and forwards both and has a heart so big it must wear her down sometimes just carrying it around. The two of us, we're real glad you college students have come out to return thanks with us today, in fact you're part of what we got to be thankful for most. I know there's lots as don't go in for your long hair and your beards and all that, but like I said to Gertrude Conover the other day, Gertrude Conover there was a time the boys used to go around looking like cowboys and moving picture stars. Nowadays they go around looking like Jesus. Boys, I'm here to tell you for my money that's a change in the right direction."

You could smell the turkey. Several waiters had come in with water pitchers, and you could hear the velvety rattle of ice against silver. Gertrude Conover stood beside the black in the striped kaftan. She held her head a little to one side, and from the back her slip was showing. I wondered if Bebb was just making it all up as he went along.

He said, "Friends, I know you're all waiting for me to wind this up so you can sit down and start piling it in, but first let me unload something I've got on my chest. I'm going to be open and above-board with you, and the long and the short of it is this. Gertrude Conover and me, we expected a bigger turn-out today, a lot bigger. There's no point in the world trying to pretend different. Why, we got gobbler and gravy and candy yams out there enough to feed this pack for a week and still have enough left over for a church supper. We got ice cream in special that's made like turkeys and pilgrim hats. We got pots of coffee keeping hot that's enough to float this piano if you poured it all in one place. Even if we all was to eat up till it started repeating on us something wicked, it wouldn't hardly make a dent on what's been

50

laid out here today. What a waste of good food! What a waste of a warm and loving heart like Gertrude Conover's who put this spread on! Most of all, what a waste of a day the Almighty made on purpose for sharing together the bread that strengtheneth man's heart and the wine that maketh it glad."

Bebb took a quick, deep breath, and I thought I saw something falter inside his face as if for the first time since he had started, he didn't know what he was going to say next—or do next—and for one moment, out of the same cackling abyss from which laughter threatens to break out at funerals, there arose within me a vision of Bebb doing as he had done in front of the children at Miami Beach and in front of the Indians at Holy Love: there on the baronial staircase of Revonoc exposing his final secret—opening, sharing, shriving himself down to the naked and nethermost truth to the Pepsi generation. His eye-lid fluttered, but that was all.

He said, "There's a story in Scripture Jesus told. Every one of you know it. It's a story didn't come into my mind till just now while I was standing here. It seems like someways the—there's times you least expect it when the Spirit himself maketh intercession for us with groanings which cannot be uttered.

"You know the story I mean," Bebb said, wiping the back of his neck with his handkerchief. "It's the story of the great supper. Luke fourteen sixteen. Jesus, he told it. He told it one Sabbath at a Pharisee's house. The way Jesus spun it out, seems there was a man once that decided to throw a big do. He invited everybody he could think of and some others he'd never of got round to thinking of without he wanted to make sure there wouldn't be a soul left off the list by accident. He got in the food and fancied up his house. He hired a band to play through dinner. Finally the day come round just like this Thanksgiving day did, and the man waited for the company to start turning up. Only it never did. All that turned up was a batch of excuses. There was one sent word he couldn't make it on account of he'd bought him a herd of cows he had to look after. There was another couldn't make it seeing as how he'd just got married and the bride didn't want him to leave her high and dry on the honeymoon, and so on. So the man took all that kind of thing he could take, and then he just flared up. He called in his servant, and he told him to go out into the streets of the town and haul in whoever he saw didn't look like they had anything better to do. The servant went and did it only even after everybody had sat down the man still saw empty chairs around the table, so this time he sent the servant out into the country and told him not to bother coming back till he found enough people to fill every last chair even if the ones he found were the down-and-outest specimens you can imagine. The servant did like the man said, and you never saw such a pack of lame ducks and has-beens as he brought back with him, but there was party hats and snappers to go round, and everybody had the time of their life. That was how the great supper finally come off.

"Friends," Bebb said, and he was glistening now where his sideburns would have been if he'd had sideburns, and his mouth was snapping open and shut like a slot machine hopper when the jackpot starts shooting out. "Friends, there must be ninety and nine places in this room with nobody to sit down in them, and Princeton, New Jersey, must be full as any town of people who don't have a place on earth to go for Thanksgiving. So what are we waiting for? Brothers and sisters, if we shake the dust off our shoe-leather and take off all of us in different directions, we can be back here inside the hour with enough folks to polish off everything down to the Pope's nose.

"Come," said Bebb, spreading his arms so wide that his jacket strained at the single button that held it. "Come and gather yourselves together unto the supper of the great God."

If it was partly the power of Bebb's oratory that made the thing catch fire, it was partly also the power of Gertrude Conover's claret punch. One cup packed the wallop of two martinis, and during the long wait before Bebb's speech many cups had been emptied. Bebb deployed us like J. Edgar Hoover—some to the campus and some to the Seminary and the Westminster Choir School, some to upper Nassau Street and some as far down as Jugtown, others to Witherspoon, Mercer, Prospect, and so on. Even the musicians and several waiters volunteered to join in the search. Bebb took as many as Gertrude Conover's Lincoln would hold and dropped them off at their appointed beats along the way before proceeding on by himself to cover the hospital, the Junction, and God knows where-all else. Those with assignments closer by went off on foot, some of them running. The reporter from the *Daily Princetonian* stood out on the front steps getting action shots. Gertrude Conover stayed behind to see if she could round up anybody by telephone. Somehow the turkeys were kept warm.

As for me, I ended up by the Palmer Square tiger full of claret and half convinced that either I was dreaming the whole thing or was having a nervous breakdown. The supper of the great God, Bebb had said, with his jacket button almost popping off but everything else mercifully buttoned up, zipped up, in place; and I thought how that made me some kind of apocalyptic wino almost certain as I accosted total strangers to be taken for a middle-aged degenerate or con artist. How did you invite people to a parable? Whom did you invite?

I had the dream-like feeling that anybody might show up including the dead and that if the dead showed up there on Palmer Square, it would turn out as it sometimes does in dreams that there had been some complicated misunderstanding and they weren't really dead at all. As I stood by the tiger wondering how to proceed from there, I half expected to see old Herman Redpath padding up from the Post Office in his chocolate brown suit and broad-brimmed circuit-rider's hat, or Lucille in French heels and a furpiece that had seen better days. I could even imagine coming on my twin sister, Miriam, not at the age she was when she died but as she was when we were children together in New York and used to sit at the window of our apartment watching the home-bound traffic move slowly up Park Avenue through the winter dusk. I don't think for years I missed her as much as I did then, and if I could have called back any ghost out of history to Bebb's party, it was Miriam's I would have called.

There's been this mix-up on Gouverneur Road . . . There's this rich lady named Gertrude Conover . . . I know it sounds crazy, but . . . . One after another I tried out various approaches in my head as I started off down the square. November, that bleakest of all months—in October Englishmen shoot grouse, in November themselves, as the grim French jest goes—and never was it much bleaker than just then with the streets virtually empty and the raw, grey air. There was a family of three coming down the steps from the Nassau Inn—a mother and a father and their teen-age son—but using the excuse that they looked as though they'd just had their dinner, I decided against approaching them. On a balcony over one of the shops a woman in a polo coat was setting out two pots of dead ivy, but she had disappeared inside by the time I got close enough to call up to her. There was a man sweeping the floor inside the liquor store and I knocked at the window, but he thought I wanted to come in and buy something and shook his head at me. Farther down, a boy and a girl were standing in front of the Playhouse reading the announcements of coming attractions. The girl had a long orange and black scarf wrapped several times around her neck, and the boy had hair down to his shoulders and was holding a fox terrier on a leash. I tried to explain to them what I was after, but they got it turned around somehow, or I did, with the result that they thought I was asking for a hand-out instead of offering them one, and although they were very nice about it, they indicated they were broke themselves. It wasn't until I reached the big parking lot at the bottom of the square that I finally succeeded in getting my pitch straight, and of all the people in New Jersey I might have found to make it to, the one it turned out to be was Nancy Oglethorpe.

It is as hard for me to believe there was a time in my life when I had never heard of Nancy Oglethorpe as it is to believe there was a time in my life when I'd never heard of religion or sex. It is also hard for me to understand why—if, as Gertrude Conover maintained, even such unpromising specimens as myself are capable of precognition—I didn't feel the slightest vibration or astral twinge of things to come when Nancy Oglethorpe came into my view for the first time.

Maybe it was because she came into it backwards. She was climbing into one of the parked cars so that the first view I had of her was of a pair of fat legs seen from behind with the stockings rolled up six inches or so above the knee. She had on a poison green coat with fur collar and cuffs, and she was carrying an enormous black patent leather purse. She had some kind of black scarf tied around her head and under her chin, but in the process of getting into the car, she knocked it off and it fell to the ground. Stepping back out again, she picked it up and placed it between her teeth while she dug in the big purse for her keys. When she turned around to do this, she still had the scarf in her teeth, which meant that my first impression of her frontally was of a woman with a luxuriant black beard. It was only when she removed the scarf from her teeth that I could see her face.

Those soft, dark, football shaped eyes, that great Babel of a nose, that small scarlet seam of a mouth and milky skin, it was pure Mesopotamian, the face of some Sumerian soubrette or Babylonian beauty queen. Her black hair was teased up into a giant beehive except where silken sideburns descended flat about her ears. Even under the folds of her green coat the hanging gardens of her bosom jutted verdant and proud, her hips swelling like the bass fiddle at Belshazzar's feast, and yet for all of this, she tapered down to surprisingly shapely calves and ankles and a pair of almost dainty patent leather feet. Lachaise could have sculpted her or Michelangelo laid her on over eight square feet of Sistine ceiling, but to do her full justice it would have taken some ancient near-Easterner working on a sun-baked wall in Ur. I was about to speak to her through the braided wire parking lot fence when in a voice that sounded as though she might never have been nearer the ancient near east than Canarsie she spoke to me instead. "Pardon me for asking," Nancy Oglethorpe said, "but do you happen to know if there's any place still serving lunch?"

"It's a funny thing you should ask," I said, "because it just happens that—" and so on, with the chill breeze swaying her behive and making my nose water while in the background the dreaming towers of Princeton went on with their grey November dream. It was almost too easy, and as soon as I'd finished explaining Bebb's problem to her, she made it easier still.

She said, "This is positively providential, and I accept with pleasure I'm sure. I was supposed to meet a gentleman at the Nass, but he didn't show, and by the time I decided to go in without him they told me the dining room was closed, wouldn't you know it. We can take my car if you want and maybe pick up some others on the way. Believe me, this town is full of displaced persons."

And so it was that I ended up in Nancy Oglethorpe's Chevvy with the shocks gone and a tubercular rattle under the hood, looking for strangers to fill out the ranks at Revonoc. She drove, and I looked. We cruised down Witherspoon as far as the hospital, then threaded our way back through a lot of narrow side streets. After hearing me bumble my way through the first couple of solicitations, Nancy took over the talking. An old Negro inching his way along John Street in an aluminum walker, a woman with a child coming out of a laundromat, a graduate student with a bad stammer whom Nancy Oglethorpe turned out to have done some work for once, a pair of nuns who were attending an ecumenical conference at the Seminary—her approach with each of them was the same. She would pull up to the curb, roll down the window, and then make a brief statement of which the opening gambit was "Do me a favor" and the closing one "Do yourself a favor" and sandwiched between them a synopsis of the situation on Gouverneur Road presented with such breezy eloquence—those Assyrian eyes, that hanging garden—that by the time we hit Nassau Street again, we had a full car.

Most of the others had returned before we did, and the hall of Revonoc was crowded with people. By three thirty or four the somber afternoon had started deepening to twilight, and lamps were lit, the chandelier that hung down from the top of the stairwell seeding the waxed fruit and polished glasses with pearls of light. The orchestra went back into business with musical comedy—*Hello Dolly, The Rain in Spain, Vilia.* The punch bowl was replenished. Young and old, black and white, town and gown—"Antonio, it's Noah's ark," Bebb said to me at some point. "We got two of everything, only here it's the clean and the unclean both." He was in his element, standing near the door to greet as many as he could when they first came in. *The heart of Gertrude Conover's as big as all outdoors. You young people are the hope of the future. It's a great school, a great town, a great time to be alive.* Bebb's cheeks swelled out as if with the effort to hold all his phrases in his mouth at once while he popped them out one by one like watermelon seeds. *Praise the Lord, brother, Halleluiah, sister,* and chattering in the overexcited cadence of flood victims in a Red Cross soup kitchen they eddied around through the turkey-laden air. Gertrude Conover had had some success on the phone, and there was a fair sprinkling of blue hair and pearls among what was a mostly young to middle-aged miscellany with the young predominating and decidedly more Elizabethan than Edwardian, more Woodstock than Gouverneur Road. Ants and anteaters, cats and dogs, lambs and lions, they were all stabled together there in uproarious harmony while outside the chill sky darkened. The elation of Bebb was contagious as he moved around like the bouncing ball in the movie house sing-alongs of my youth. He was pulling something off and he knew he was and everybody there would know it if they stopped to think back on it later. I knew it myself except that maybe from my Italian mother, maybe from a sour stomach, I inherit a possibly fatal taste for doom so that even at the height of carnival it is always the valediction that ends up drowning out the carnality, the sense of old time a-flying that keeps me from savoring as I only wish I could even the choicest rosebuds that come my way for gathering. There at Bebb's finest hour I could not help thinking that once the punch bowl was empty for good and the food ran out, we would all go back to our accustomed diet, which was each other. And I couldn't help thinking too of how even the supper of the great God was a less than adequate substitute for the supper of my small son and estranged wife sitting in Sutton with the TV on top of the icebox going, the breakfast dishes still unwashed in the sink, and a combination of smells in that cluttered kitchen that were like no other smells on earth because

59

they were for better or worse the smells of my own life.

In a way Bebb spoke to this when the time came, among the other things he spoke to. The time came more or less when the ice cream did, the turkeys and pilgrim hats Bebb had mentioned earlier, only starting to go a little soft and shapeless by the time they finally made it to the table. Bebb rose from his seat and spoke from there rather than climbing up to the orchestra landing as before. On one side of him sat the old black whose aluminum walker we had managed to squeeze into the trunk of Nancy Oglethorpe's Chevvy, on his other side a man in a Norfolk jacket who presumably had come with one of the blue-haired ladies.

Bebb talked a long time—it must have been five years since the last time he had had a congregation that big and who knew how long it would be before he had one as big again—but they listened to him, you could tell—listened to him partly, I suppose, because what he said, he said in his high style and partly because although as a teetotaler he hadn't touched a drop of Gertrude Conover's claret punch, he was drunk on the occasion and spoke in such a disconnected way that you had to listen if only to hear what he was going to bounce to next. I remember in fragments what he said because he said it in fragments.

He said, "The Kingdom of Heaven is like a great feast. That's the way of it. The Kingdom of Heaven is a love feast where nobody's a stranger. Like right here. There's strangers everywheres else you can think of. There's strangers was born out of the same womb. There's strangers was raised together in the same town and worked side by side all their life through. There's

60

strangers got married and been climbing in and out of the same fourposter together for thirty-five or forty years and they're strangers still. And Jesus, it's like most of the time he is a stranger too. Even when he's near as the end of your nose, people make like he's nowhere around. They won't talk to him. They won't listen to him. They keep their eye on the ground. But here in this place there's no strangers, and Jesus, he isn't a stranger either. The Kingdom of Heaven's like this."

He said, "We all got secrets. I got them same as everybody else—things we feel bad about and wish hadn't ever happened. Hurtful things. We're all scared and lonesome, but most of the time we keep it hid. It's like every one of us has lost his way so bad we don't even know which way is home any more only we're ashamed to ask. You know what would happen if we would own up we're lost and ask? Why, what would happen is we'd find out home is each other. We'd find out home is Jesus loves us lost or found or any whichway."

The room flickered like the scratched print of an old newsreel, the hands of Bebb jerky as Woodrow Wilson laying a wreath on the tomb of the Unknown Soldier. Shadows. Faces. Afros like puff balls of dust under beds, more air than hair. Grainy, light-struck blizzarding of old film.

Bebb said, "Eating. Feeding your face. Folks, I've eaten my way 'round the known world. I've eaten snails out of their own shells in Paris, France. I've eaten octopus in Spain and curry in India so hot it makes your eyes water and the skin on your head go cold as ice. I've eaten hamburgs pitiful and grey like the sole of your shoe in greasy spoons from here to Saint Joe. I've eaten the bread of affliction, all of us has. We got to eat or—

61

food, it's life, but all the food in the world, all the turkey and fixings plus your ice cream the shape of hats, it's not life enough to keep you alive without you eat it with love in the heart.

"Dear hearts," Bebb said, "we got to love one another and Jesus or die guessing."

Bebb said, "I wasn't born yesterday. I'm not kidding myself what we got going here is a hundred percent guaranteed to last forever. There's nothing in this world lasts forever. That's the miserable sadness of it. Time will be when the party's over. Time will be when all the good times of our life is over because they are like grass which in the morning it flourisheth and groweth up and in the evening is cut down and withereth. Time is the enemy, and the tick of the clock is the sound his toenails make pattering up on us for the kill. Friends, while we're still sitting here feeling good let us promise to remember how for a little bit of time we loved each other in this place. Even when the party's over, let us remember the good time we had here with Jesus."

Where did Bebb's speech begin? Where did it end? The whole gathering was Bebb's speech, his parable, and everything that happened and was said there by anybody was in a way part of what Bebb said. I don't know who started the singing, but there was singing. There was *Onward Christian Soldiers* and *Going Back to Nassau Hall* and *We Shall Overcome*. There was *Swing Low Sweet Chariot, The Orange and the Black, Roll out the Barrel,* and *Blowin' in the Wind*. There was a toast to Gertrude Conover proposed by Bebb and followed by a great deal of whistling and table-thumping during which Gertrude Conover stood up in her green dress like a small, lopsided Christmas tree. There was Bebb's saying that before we got up from the table we should all join hands and sing *Praise God from Whom All Blessings Flow*. When this worked as well as it did, he proposed that we follow ancient procedure and exchange with the neighbor to our right the kiss of peace.

There was a moment's hush, a silent passing of the angel of death over our heads, and then Bebb turned to the old Negro beside him. He took that black face between his hands, held it for a few seconds like a mirror he was studying his own face in, and then tipped it forward until at some particular point in time which for all I know was a point appointed before the world began, those tight, relentless lips and that corrugated black forehead met. Then everybody got into the act.

If you added together all the hugging and squeezing and shoulder-pounding that have taken place on Gouverneur Road since the Continental Congress sat in Nassau Hall, I doubt you would have come close to what took place at Revonoc during the next five minutes or so. Boys who looked like Jesus kissed blue-haired ladies and girls out of Charles Addams cartoons, kissed other boys who looked like Jesus. Old tigers with prostates and hearing aids kissed short order cooks and retired policemen. Nuns kissed Daughters of the American Revolution and stammering grad students. Jump-suited martini drinkers and teeny boppers with fly buttons down the outside of their flies kissed Abe Lincolns welted with acne, Midwestern fairies, and vestals from Miss Fine's and Westminster Choir. Seen from the landing it must have looked like some ancient Roman orgy as filmed by D. W. Griffith, a writhing Bacchanal with lions roaring from the arena below and Claudette Colbert taking a bath in mother's milk. The band played ragtime, as unknown to the merrymakers the great ship slowly started to go down.

Nancy Oglethorpe. Somewhere out of the maelstrom Nancy Oglethorpe rose up in white and gold like an iceberg, and at the sound of her voice the room grew still. "Jesus . . . *Jesus!*" she called out. She made it sound as though Jesus was taking his time in the washroom and a taxi was waiting outside with the meter on.

There were people long afterwards who said that Nancy Oglethorpe was a plant and that she and Bebb had cooked the whole thing up ahead of time. I do not believe that. On the other hand what happened couldn't have worked out better for Bebb if they had cooked it up. With her eyes lowered, her towering beehive tilted slightly forward, she looked as though she was saying a prayer except that she seemed to be saying it to us rather than to Jesus and in a voice that sounded less like Saint Thérèse of Lisieux than like a New York telephone operator. There was something of the TV commercial in the way she did it: first the real-life scenes of irregularity —the headache, the irritability, the loss of pep—and then the helpful friend with the knowing smile and the family-size remedy.

The first thing Nancy Oglethorpe did was tell her story. She said she was thirty years old. She was unmarried. She had to work for a living. She had started out as a public stenographer at the Pennsylvania Hotel in Manhattan, but she was attracted to Princeton because of its rich cultural opportunities and decided to try her hand there instead. I remember thinking of her immersing

64

herself in the rich cultural opportunities of Princeton like Bathsheba settling down into the tub where King David first laid his eye on her: Nancy Oglethorpe signing up for the chamber music series at McCarter; Nancy Oglethorpe auditing a graduate course in cultural anthropology; Nancy Oglethorpe in flat heels and a corduroy jumper exchanging views on Kafka and women's lib at faculty cocktail parties.

She said that as time went by she found that the greatest call for her services came from the Grad School —dissertations to type, footnotes to check, bibliographies to compile—and since much of this required the presence if not of her employers themselves at least of their books and index cards, she made it a practice of coming to their rooms to do her work. Like Florence Nightingale moving through the wounded with her lamp, I pictured Nancy Oglethorpe entering the kind of academic squalor I remembered from my own university days—the unmade bed and mad scientist desk, the glutted ashtray, the petrified coffee at the bottom of plastic cups—and there in the midst of it Nancy Oglethorpe standing in a cloud of patchouli with those eyes as sweet and dark as stewed prunes. She unties the scarf from around her head and pats the beehive back into shape. She removes the poison green coat like the seventh veil and drapes it over the back of an eviscerated armchair.

At this point in her narrative Nancy Oglethorpe paused, and the level of silence in the great hall of Revonoc clicked up a notch. You could hear it. All those faces turned toward her. That whole hymn singing, yam-stuffed mob frozen in their tracks like the court of the Sleeping Beauty. Bebb with his neck twisted like a cruller so he could see her over his shoulder. A lady with pixie glasses and a harelip. Prince Valiant smoking a joint. Uncle Remus in a sheepskin Afghanistan vest trimmed with sequins and yeti fur. The dowagers of Gouverneur Road and Lilac Lane.

"I was a mere child," she said. "I didn't know what I was getting into. The flesh is weak." Nancy Oglethorpe not dry behind the ears yet, those ears that glittered now with jewels like spoonfuls of fruit salad. The flesh of Nancy Oglethorpe weak as moonshine on the Euphrates or the breeze that wafted the scent of Susanna to the elders' ravening nostrils, that same flesh that rose among us now in all its chryselephantine prime.

"I started having affairs," Nancy Oglethorpe said. "I have been leading an extremely promiscuous existence ever since to say the least." Affairs with Nancy Oglethorpe. It would have needed Solomon himself to sing the song of them, I thought. Her navel like a round goblet which wanteth not liquor, her belly like a heap of wheat set about with lilies, the smell of her nose like apples. I pictured her on that unmade scholar's bed like a great mound of yoghurt, her electric typewriter forgotten on the littered desk.

"But that's all a thing of the past now," she said. "I'm making a clean breast of it to you. I'm making a clean breast of it to Jesus." The breast of Nancy Oglethorpe clean as a hillside of new snow, a Beautyrest made up with fresh linen. I tried to imagine Jesus watching her the way I was watching her as she stood there in the glitter of Gertrude Conover's chandelier. In the event that he had answered her summons and was present there on Gouverneur Road with the rest of us, would he see whatever the bees inside that hive were up to that had prompted her to this public confession? And how

66

would Nancy Oglethorpe see Jesus, I wondered, remembering from catechism class a homily to the effect that if Shakespeare were to walk into a room, everybody would automatically stand up whereas if Jesus did, everybody would automatically kneel down—Nancy Oglethorpe melting to the floor like ice cream, the nuns melting, the Afros, all of us.

Nancy Oglethorpe was saying, "I haven't been able to look myself in the eye for seven years. I wanted to sever connections with the past and make a fresh start, but psychological factors having to do with long-term patterns of behavior and the unfortunate reputation I have acquired in certain circles plus the fact that my professional work is constantly exposing me to situations that are too much for me to handle, these have all contributed to making it problematical at best that I could ever change. I have been like a rat caught in a trap. Then out of the blue I got invited here. I've never been a religious person vis-à-vis church and Jesus et cetera, but right here in this room it hit me like a bolt out of the blue."

Nancy Oglethorpe paused and smiled. It was the first time I'd seen those tiny teeth. Her zeppelin eyes were so charged with whatever she was smiling at that they looked almost goiterish. "Frankly," she said, "what did Jesus ever mean to me before this? All this rhubarb about the blood of the lamb and what have you, to be perfectly frank I never related to it."

Her voice got smaller and more precise then as if she was working on a stencil and didn't want to have to go back and make corrections.

She said, "The gentleman I had a luncheon date with today didn't have the common courtesy to show up. It's like cold water in the face when a thing like that happens. There I was, dressed up in clothes appropriate to the occasion only to have the props kicked right out from under me. Then this total stranger appeared and asked me here, and I confess my motives in accepting him were extremely mixed, to put it mildly. But it's like Reverend Bebb has so well expressed it. Nobody's a stranger. That stranger who came up to me in the parking lot was no stranger. He was Jesus, as it were. Jesus sent him there to pick me up."

She clasped her hands at her bosom as though she was going to sing the rest. "Jesus has come into my life to stay," she said. "I am through with the past. I am through with not daring to let my right hand know what my left hand is up to. Jesus did it for me, and I want to give him and Reverend Bebb some small token of my appreciation. I want to give thanks, and I think I have found the way. I think the way is we should go on having get-togethers like this on a regular basis. I think we owe it to Jesus to share with other persons this salvation-type experience we have had here today.

"I think," said Nancy Oglethorpe, slowly sweeping the room with her glance, "I think we should try to make Princeton, New Jersey, one big love feast for Jesus."

There is no power on earth, they say, that can stop an idea when its time has come, and there at Revonoc that November afternoon there was no power that even tried to stop it. After the failure of Open Heart, the burning of the barn, and those four sad and footloose years that followed it, Bebb had finally managed to open a heart to Jesus, and partly because the time was ripe but partly also because the heart he opened was Nancy Oglethorpe's heart, history was made that day on Gouverneur Road.

68

CHAPTER FIVE

LIFE MUST GO ON, so they say, and by the same token I suppose death also must go on, the two of them hand in hand like old playmates. Life was Bebb, it seemed to me then—Bebb launched on a brilliant new career with Nancy Oglethorpe and Gertrude Conover both beside him at the tiller, Bebb poised to evangelize Princeton, New Jersey, to set up the Supper of the Lamb in the groves of academe. And death was me returning to Mrs. Gunther's boarding house in Sutton, Connecticut, was me driving to school past the house where my wife and son lived as if I had died there. As a ghost I was more haunted than haunting since if either of them marked my spectral passing at about quarter to eight every morning, they gave no sign of it. If from deep inside the house they saw me, I had the feeling that what they saw must be as transparent as the reflection of my own face in the car window that I searched for them through. My arrangement with Sharon was that for the time being we would not see each other, but in my case anyway that seemed a redundance. Even if she had wanted to, I couldn't believe there would be enough of me for Sharon to see. I was free to see Bill whenever I liked, but it was weeks before I felt substantial enough even for that.

Tony and I had rooms side by side at Mrs. Gunther's and shared the bathroom with one other boarder, a retired schoolteacher named Metzger, who spent most of his time in his room watching television. Metzger lived in fear of having a heart attack and made arrangements with Tony and me that if ever he was stricken, he would summon our help by pounding three times on the wall. He tried it on several occasions in the middle of the night just to see if we were on our toes, and it was after one of these false alarms that Tony and I found it possible to talk for about three minutes about something more than what was new at Sutton High.

In T-shirt and undershorts, he sat smoking a cigarette on the foot of my bed and said, "Honest to Christ, Tono, I feel awful about you and Shar. If I thought it was my fault, I'd shoot myself," and I said, "Save your ammunition."

He said, "Are you ever going to get back together again? I mean like this way it's not either one thing or another. It's a real nothing situation."

I said, "I wish you'd tell me," and I remember thinking maybe he could—my own flesh and blood telling me about my own flesh, my own blood; this boy whom my sister had named after me and who, having lived with us since the beginning, not to mention having bedded my wife, was the world's greatest living authority on our marriage, impressed upon it like a seal and with its seal impressed upon him. If anybody could enlighten me, I thought maybe he could.

He said, "It must take real guts."

"Being married," I said.

"I guess," he said. "Being married to her. Only being here like this too, living in this dump all by yourself after all those years of having her to live with. It must take guts. I couldn't do it myself, I mean having had it all once and then not having it any more."

"Having somebody to live with and having nobody to live with. You're right," I said, wanting him to be right, wanting somebody to be right. "I suppose it takes guts both ways."

"Having somebody to live with," he said. "And having somebody to sack out with," and I remember the little jolt of almost schoolteacherly satisfaction I felt, as if he was in my English class and had spotted something in a book that I hadn't spotted myself: the guts it took literally to sack out, *sleep*, by yourself, to let yourself drift alone into dreams, pass unaccompanied into the night where Mark Twain said no man is ever entirely sane.

"Sometimes I get horny as hell," he said, sitting there with his cigarette in one hand and his bare foot in the other, and my schoolteacherly satisfaction vanished as I suddenly saw that all he had meant was that it must take guts to have nobody to have sex with, which was the least of my worries as of course it was among the worst of his. I could hear old Metzger flushing the can across

the hall while before my eyes my wise friend and coun-
selor turned into a child dressed up to look like a man
with hair on his chest and the muscles working in his
stubbly jaw as he avoided my glance by looking down at
the bare floor.

"You should try cold showers," I said. I had never felt
more alone. I was a middle-aged man surrounded by
children and death.

Death was there not only in the form of Metzger
ready to thump three times on the wall any minute—
maybe his flushing was a signal for all I knew—but death
was downstairs too, laid out in glass cases for me to walk
through on my way out of the house every morning,
death spread out on the tops of every table and shelf in
sight. Our landlady, Mrs. Gunther, was the widow of an
undertaker who, following the custom of his trade, had
over the years accepted payment in kind for his services
so that Mrs. Gunther had gone into the antique business
with a house full of the lockets and brooches, the beads
and spoons and assorted fripperies of the bereaved.

Children also surrounded me—not just Tony, whom I
saw every day, and Bill, whom I saw more clearly for not
actually seeing him at all, but the children I taught
whatever it is you try to teach in English—why Brutus
joined the conspirators, the difference between a mixed
metaphor and a dangling participle, how to use the
language of Shakespeare and Milton more like a preci-
sion tool than a blunt instrument. But such matters as
these can be dealt with for only so long at a time, and
then there you are with maybe half your fifty minutes
still left to fill up with something else. If you're good at
it, you hold your tongue and wait to see what the class
will fill it up with themselves. You let a silence endure

until one of them can't stand it any more and says something out of the depths of his discomfort and then another says something else if you're lucky, and before you know it who can tell what queer and instructive thing may happen. But I have never been good at silences myself. In the classroom I am always the uneasy host to whom the absence of chatter spells disaster, and there is no end to the disastrous things I have said just to keep the party going, things that later I could have bitten my tongue for saying.

Not long after the fateful Thanksgiving at Revonoc, for instance, I remember going on at excessive length to a group of ninth graders about what *irony* meant. I think most of them understood it well enough before I started, but just to keep the silence at bay I rattled on about it anyway. I talked about outer meaning and inner meaning. I said that an ironic statement was a statement where you said one thing but to people who had their ears open said another. I explained that when Mark Antony in his funeral oration called the Romans who had murdered Caesar honorable men, he was being ironic because his inner meaning was that they were a bunch of hoods, and when that remark didn't seem to get anything started, I waded in deeper still. I said that in addition to ironic statements you also had ironic situations. Their silence deepened. I remember then a small, fat boy named Stephen Kulak. He was young for the ninth grade and looked it with a round, pink face and the judicious gaze of a child. He said he saw how something you *said* could mean two things but he didn't see how something that *happened* could, so I reached down into my own silence and pulled out the first example that came to hand. I said suppose you had a bride on her wedding day. Suppose she was all dressed up in her white dress and veil, and then on her way back from church a car ran into her and she was killed. That was an ironic situation, I said. It was ironic because on the same day that she started out on a new life, her life stopped. Two things. Now did he see what ironic meant? I remember watching him as he sat there at his desk in a Red Baron sweat-shirt trying to puzzle through my lugubrious illustration until finally in some dim and memorable way his pink face seemed to change and he said, "I get it now. It's a kind of joke," and I could see that he really had gotten it, that there in a classroom with the Pledge of Allegiance framed on the wall and Christmas wreaths made of red and green construction paper Scotch taped to the window panes, Stephen Kulak had learned from kindly old Mr. Parr, who had a hard time keeping his mouth shut, what irony was, and jokes, and life itself if you made the mistake of keeping your ears open. Once you get the reading and writing out of the way, I suppose what you teach children in an English class is, God help you, yourself.

Death ready to thump on the wall or flush the can whenever you least expected it, and Mrs. Gunther, that blondine pelican whose cry was "You don't find them like that much any more," meaning the mortuary napkin rings, lapel watches, christening mugs and souvenir spoons from Grand Rapids, Niagara Falls, the Chicago World's Fair, that she sold in the front parlor directly under the room of that lonesome, horny child who was my nephew. Death leaping out of my own mouth like the frog in the haiku, PLOP into that primeval pond of dozing innocence that was Stephen Kulak. You never knew when death would come at you or from where.

The children at least you could usually see coming. But not always.

I did not see Laura Fleischman coming, for instance, and I suppose there was a certain rightness about it. You do not see the first day of spring coming either. Sharon forwarded me a printed notice from the dentist that it was time I showed up for my annual prophylaxis, and I went for the appointment resigned to yet another meeting with Darius Bildabian, whose chairside manner is perhaps best represented by the way he would wait till you had your mouth full of spit-drainers and cotton wadding and then as you were mumbling with pain under the repeated blasts of cold air that he shot into the living heart of your cavity would say to whoever his nurse happened to be at the moment, "What do you suppose Antonio is trying to tell us, Miss X? Maybe it's something funny that happened in school today," his own exorbitant teeth flashing above you terrible as an army with banners.

Waiting in his outer office that December afternoon, I was deep in an article on diseases of the mouth which included the color plate of a tongue covered with matted, black hair when I was summoned into one of the treatment rooms to discover that the hygienist who was to do the preliminaries was Laura Fleischman—a child whom I had not only failed to see coming but whom there would probably have been no way to prepare for even if I had.

She had graduated from Sutton High the same year as Tony, and I had had her as a student in senior English. She was a shy, dark-haired girl with high cheekbones and something fragile about her smile, like a nun on holiday. The year that she was my student, we had met by accident once in a bar at Grand Central, and in my mind at least, certain things had become possible that day—certain doors had half opened which, I suppose because we had not passed through them, had never fully closed so that in a way some shadow of me had stayed waiting in front of them ever since. Sometimes the things that do not quite happen in your life count for more than the things that do.

I had not seen her since the day she graduated, and there she stood now in a white dress and white stockings with her hair caught back in a silver barette. The first thing she did was anoint the corners of my mouth with a fingertip each of some white lubricant that made me feel like the Tin Woodman when Dorothy oiled his hinges to keep his tears from rusting them, and such conversation as we had took place for the most part with her hands in my mouth—the little whirring wheels of rubber and emery, the gritty pink dentifrice, the squirts of tepid Lavoris. She had seen my name in the appointment book so she was ready for our meeting as I was not. Was *King Lear* still my favorite play? Did I ever see so-and-so or so-and-so from her class? What did I think were Sutton's chances in track that spring? How were Mrs. Parr and the baby? She had come with questions enough to see her through the whole session whereas I was empty-handed of course and with my mouth jacked open and my eyes fixed glassily on Darius Bildabian's dental school diploma hanging on the wall considered telling her the truth about Sharon and me but decided not to, said just that Mrs. Parr was still every inch herself but the baby was no longer a baby. None of us was. The one question

I could think to ask her in return was about Carl West, the boy she had been going steady with when I'd last known her, a handsome, laconic basketball player who according to Tony was making out with her in those days any time he felt like it, which I could only imagine was often.

"Oh, I haven't seen him for ages," she said, "not since we broke things off my senior year." She had turned to get something out of a drawer when my question stopped her. The silver barette held her hair away from her head in back, and as she stood gazing down into the drawer for whatever she would start looking for again when she remembered what it was, the nape of her neck looked bare and vulnerable. She said, "I wrote you a letter about it. You were in England, and I wrote you things were over between Carl West and I. I wrote you on my eighteenth birthday."

I said, "I remember," not remembering. I wondered if I had ever answered the letter.

Out of the drawer she took a long-handled dentist's mirror that caught the light like a star in her hands as she turned back to me. "Carl always said I had a schoolgirl crush on you," she said.

With pick and mirror she poked her away around my lower jaw while I watched her face for signs of what she was finding. At twenty-two she could have been my daughter, I thought, could have made me in my forties a grandfather by now as for all I knew maybe she already had although she wore no ring. I wondered if Tony had been right about her and Carl West. She frowned as though she was reading my teeth like a palm, my character as well as my cavities lying open before her, my future as well as my past. I dreaded the moment when she would remove her mirror long enough to tell me that she had seen the first tell-tale signs of fuzz on my tongue, a suspiciously soft spot near the gum line of my marriage. I could see the pulse at the base of her throat, the open white collar and shoulder straps of her white slip as she leaned over me. "Rinse," she said, handing me a pleated paper cup of warm water which I tried to spit out with the urbanity of a wine-taster.

"Did you?" I said as she came at me again, and it stopped her mirror in mid-air.

"I'm sorry?" she said as though I had caught her attention wandering in senior English.

"Have a crush," I said.

"All the girls did," she said. "Open, please," hurrying back from the spree of her smile to telling my teeth again like beads. She made a pencil mark on the chart of my lower jaw. "Everybody thought you were out of this world, your name being Antonio and everything. You know how girls are at that age. You seemed so much younger than the other teachers. You didn't treat us like a bunch of dumb kids like most of them did. Remember the time you spent the class before the prom showing the boys how to tie a bow tie? We thought—" Sharp as a needle, her pick had found something to reckon with in one of my back molars. It kept getting stuck in it as though the molar was made of wax. The edge of her hand was cool against my lip. She said, "Naturally we knew we didn't have a chance, I mean the girls. We used to see your wife when she came out to watch track practice. Everybody said she looked like a Hollywood star. Carl West said—" Some fragment of the molar suddenly chipped off and the pick hit pay dirt with a squill of hot pain that I could feel down to the soles of my feet.

"You'll need Novocaine for that one," she said as she marked it down on her chart.

I said, "I'll need last rites," and there was death again because every pain is a kind of rehearsal, I suppose, for the final pain, the loss of each snag of tooth, each inch of hairline, a foretaste of loss itself as John Donne knew, that grim wag with his puns on dying: dying as death, dying as orgasm, because every time you fire forth the stuff and substance of life, your life itself is somehow less, somehow lost a little. Death, sex, a child named Laura Fleischman, all staring me down together as I reclined there with a rubber bib under my chin and Darius Bildabian's fluorescent klieg bright in my eyes. CASTLE, it said on the light—the seige perilous.

"Mrs. Parr and I," I said. "Maybe you've heard. We're not together right now."

"Golly, Mr. Parr. I didn't know," Laura Fleischman said. Golly . . . gee whiz. . . "I'm awfully sorry."

I'm sorry. It had been Tony's phrase the night he had told me through chattering teeth that he and Sharon were lovers, burying his face in my shoulder, his salt-stiff hair, and saying it over and over again. When a child says *I'm sorry*, the sorrow becomes yours to hear the child have to say it. It was Stephen Kulak all over again—the sorrow mine for having exposed inner meaning to a child for whom outer meaning was puzzle enough. Irony is a game primarily for grownups. A form of solitaire. Laura Fleischman waited beside me in first communion white as I looked for some way to make light, to make white, of the whole thing. I said, "You know it may be for the best. You fall in love and get married and have kids—all of it in such a blind rush the way things go. Maybe somewhere along the line there's got to be a pulling apart so you can pull back together someday with your eyes open.

I haven't given up by a long shot."

"You mean it's not a legal separation or anything," Laura Fleischman said.

I said, "Separation is always illegal as hell."

She was looking down at the lilypad tray where her instruments lay and the chart where she'd marked down the worst. She said, "They say it's always darkest just before the dawn."

I said, "There are always lots of good things like that left to say."

" 'The worst returns to laughter,' " she said. "When Carl and I split up, I wrote you that was my favorite line in *King Lear* because it was so hopeful. I never dreamed I'd be using it someday to cheer you up."

I said, "You've cheered me up already."

Once in my life I had held Laura Fleischman's hand. It was the time we had happened to meet in the bar at Grand Central, and with a couple of martinis under my belt I had done it then almost by accident, before I knew what I was doing. This time I was dentist chair sober and knew what I was doing what seemed centuries before I got around to doing it. My hand was still holding the arm of the chair it had grabbed onto when the pick struck home, and her hand was near enough mine for me to feel the little warmth of air between them. In distant cities mothers unaccountably gathered their children to their skirts and stray dogs showed their teeth as I reached out and took her hand in mine. I said, "You've given me back my Pepsodent smile."

The *irony* of the thing as I look back on it, the outerness and innerness of what took place there in Bildabian's office. What was outer was the hands themselves, was the diploma on the wall and the jet of water circling in the basin at my elbow, was those white stockings and trig white nurse's dress she wore, with her dark hair gathered back at her neck, and my grey flannel legs stretched out at full length, my scuffed cordovans toed out on the footrest. What was inner was not just the puzzlement of flesh our hands had failed to solve—in the comic-strip balloon of my forty-three year old fancy I saw her of course not in white but in nothing, the slimness of her fragrant and shy as John Skelton's midsummer flower, gentle as falcon or hawk of the tower. What was inner was mostly the sense of history, her history and mine, the history we were making. The irony of the present is that it has a future. The irony of a hand is all it stands both to hold and to lose.

"Poor fool and knave," I said, like Bebb quoting Scripture, "I have one part in my heart that's sorry yet for thee."

Darius Bildabian said, "Long time no see, young fella. What's the bad news?" He pushed through the curtained door with a round mirror strapped to his forehead like a miner, the sound of his voice cleaving our hands like a pick. He took the chart from Laura Fleischman, studied it, humming, and then pushed the mirror down to where he could peer through the hole in the middle and see into the open secret of my mouth. Later, when the drilling started on my back molar and I lay there making strangled noises at the sheer metaphysics of the thing, he said, "Maybe it's the one about the traveling salesman, Miss Fleischman. Maybe it's one Antonio picked up in the locker room at Sutton High," and when I stood up eventually to leave—he had his arm around my shoulder and part of my face was dead and cold—Laura Fleischman said, "I'm still living with my mother in the same old house, so if you ever feel like a home-cooked meal, you just let us know," which meant among other things that before I left the office, I had to explain everything to Darius Bildabian, or almost everything.

My face was just starting to come back into its own when later that same day of death and children I drove over to Sharon's to pick up my son Bill and take him to a restaurant for supper, just the two of us. It was to be our first meeting since my departure some three weeks before, and I had arranged it with Sharon over the telephone. It was also the first time I was to see her, or so I assumed until I rang the doorbell—how did the stray dogs of the world respond as I stood there on my own doorstep wondering whether to ring or just walk in?— and it was answered not by Sharon but by Anita Steen. It was like taking a drink of ice-water only to discover it isn't ice-water but Gordon's gin. Or vice versa.

Anita Steen looked like a kind of child herself in a way, a short, wrinkled child in velvet slacks and a frilled shirt, a child grown old before its time trying to get somebody to adopt it. She said Sharon had had to stay late at the shop and Bill was still upstairs finishing his bath. She asked me to come in and sit down while I waited. She offered me a drink, which I accepted. She leaned forward with her elbows on her velvet knees and talked to me through the smoke of her king-size Winston.

She said, "Big boy, I'm going to give it to you straight. I don't like what's going on one bit. This kid you're married to is going through hell. She'd shoot me if she knew I was saying that, but I'm saying it. When you brought her up here from Squatville, Florida, did you ever stop to think what you were letting her in for? Did you ever stop to think *who* you were bringing up here, for God's sake? Maybe she's picked up how to look like Westchester County, but she's straight corn pone just the same. She doesn't say manure, she says horseshit. She doesn't read *The New Yorker*, she reads *True Confessions*. If her tail itches, she scratches it, and she wouldn't call it her tail either. I don't mean she doesn't try like hell. What do you think all these lessons are about—speed reading lessons and yogi lessons and studying Adele Davis as if it was the holy damn Bible? Why do you think she came to me for guitar? The point is it doesn't work. She's a fish out of water. You name me three friends she's made up here on her own. I don't mean people you know together. I mean people she knows all by herself. She's made one friend, and you want to know what her name is? Her name is Anita Steen, and that's not exactly what you'd call hitting the jackpot."

She said, "Listen, it's time you learned something about loneliness from an expert. If I was the bad fairy at the christening, you know what I'd leave by the cradle all wrapped up in pink ribbon? I'd leave loneliness, that's what I'd leave—the straight, hundred proof, bonded stuff. I'm going to tell you something. That bourbon you're drinking isn't any of the stuff you left here when you pulled out. I happen to know you left three fifths of Jack Daniels when you pulled out, and that's not one of them because the last of the Mohicans was carried out of here feet first days ago. Somebody told me this morning just breathing the air in the Sharanita Shop was enough to give you a buzz. Maybe she's not off the deep end yet, but she's climbing up to the high board. And I'm going to tell you another thing before Buster Brown gets down here. I'm going to tell you the time your pants get hottest is the time you've got time on your hands. All right, so you knew that anyhow, and so I wouldn't be laying it on you this way if I was cold sober myself, but you can thank your lucky stars Anita Steen's not cold sober. Take it from me. Time on your hands is time that burns hot as the hinges, and you don't have to be sweet sixteen either. You can be pushing sixty and sour as hell."

She said, "I'm going to tell you one more thing, and then I'll shut up. You better make *mucho* big effort to patch things up between you two or it's going to be too late. For Christ sake, come down off your high horse, Antonio Parr, because pardon my French, but don't you believe you're the only thing in pants that's rung this doorbell since you left, and I'm not referring to Anita Steen either." Whereupon, as if on cue, my five year old son arrived. He was wearing corduroy overalls the color of tomato soup and an Irish sweater put on backwards so that it crowded him under the chin. His feet were bare and lobsterish from the bath, and he was carrying his sneakers in his hands. He said, "Guess what, I made a pee in the tub and nobody even knew a thing."

CHAPTER SIX

DURING THE WEEK, I lived in Sutton—lived in my room at Mrs. Gunther's where I corrected papers, slept and ate my solitary breakfasts of tap-water instant coffee and dry cereal wet down with milk kept cold on the windowsill, lived in my classroom at school, lived in the diner down by the station where I had supper sometimes with Tony or Metzger but usually alone. Tony went his own way, and I leaned over backwards not to pry because the same footlooseness which was purgatory for me was a kind of potential paradise for him, the first time in his life he had been on his own, and I didn't want him to think he had to carry his uncle on his back. Most of the time I didn't know much about whom he saw or where he went, knew only that he kept late hours. Once in a while I would happen on him talking over the phone under the stairs when I came in. At my approach his slow murmur always turned clipped and informational, and no matter how many steps at a time I tried to make it up to my room, he had invariably hung up by the time I got there. Metzger had no such involvements as far as I knew, but supper time, he explained to me, was prime time with Perry Mason leading on to Walter Cronkite leading on to Truth or Consequences and thence to the crescendo of Dean Martin or Laugh In so most of my suppers I ate by myself.

I spent the weekends at Revonoc. There were faster ways of making the trip there, but I always took the way I had known as a child—the old Merritt Parkway, the Henry Hudson, the West Side Highway, and then on under the river through the Lincoln Tunnel to New Jersey. I loved the view you got of the George Washington Bridge at dusk when it came alive with the tiny lights of cars, that great fragile web thrown across to the Palisades in a way that always made me think of Walt Whitman's noiseless, patient spider launching forth filament, filament, filament out of himself in the hope that it would catch somewhere, O my soul, on the far side. I loved the looming hulls and silent stacks of the liners moored at the piers along the West Side Highway and then rolling like a Tinkertoy down the ramp into the tunnel. When I was a small boy, my father told me once that we were traveling under the river and if I kept my eyes open I might see fish swimming by, and that mild whimsy has so stuck in my mind all these years that every trip I've ever made through that tunnel since has given him back to me again for a moment or two, my poor young father who died before I got around to knowing who he was. Whenever at night I dream about tunnels, I'm sure it has nothing to do with what Freud would say but that it's my father I'm dreaming about, and I suppose Freud would have something to say about that too. You can't be too careful what you tell a child because you never know what he'll take hold of and spend the rest of his life remembering you by.

I went to Revonoc for the weekends because I needed to see Bebb, needed to have someone I could talk to about Sharon—especially after Anita Steen's broadside —and about the life I was leading without her, to use the word life loosely, and about the life she was leading without me or that was leading her. It wasn't that I needed Bebb to give me advice so much as I needed him simply to give me his attention—to reassure me, simply by listening to my story, that it wasn't just a story, wasn't just something I had dreamed up, but something that was actually happening to me, something that had had a beginning and was having a middle and that someday, I hoped, would have like everything else an end. The irony of the thing, as I might have explained it to Stephen Kulak, was that Bebb hardly noticed my need. My need and his not noticing. Two things.

It was Gertrude Conover who explained Bebb to me. Bebb himself was off somewhere, and she was giving me tea in her upstairs sitting room. She was stretched out on a chaise longue with her feet up and a Siamese cat named Fred in her lap. She said, "Leo is round. He has always been round. The things that man has done with his life—all his lives—and the things his life has done to him, they have made him round as a ball. They have made him the shape of a boulder, the shape of an apple."

What I wanted to say to her was that Sharon was

hitting the Jack Daniels, that Anita Steen and I weren't the only things in pants that had rung her bell since I'd moved out, that all through my supper with Bill I had had to sit on my hands to keep from pumping him about her, listening instead as he sat there over his congealing hot roast beef sandwich looking at me through his mother's eyes, more green than brown, and chattering on about what he wanted for Christmas as if it was the most natural thing in the world that we weren't all living under the same roof any more. But Gertrude Conover either didn't notice what I wanted to say any more than Bebb did or else she was approaching it, as she walked, sideways. She said, "You know those toys they have for children, those boxes with the lids cut out in diamond shapes, star shapes, cross shapes and so on so that the child has to pick out the right shape block to get it into the box through the right shape hole? That is the law of karma in a nutshell. The shape you make of your life this time round has everything in the world to do with the shape of your life the next time round. If it is an angry, jagged shape, the only life it will fit into next time will be an angry, jagged life—a wolf, perhaps, or somebody like that awful New Hampshire journalist who made poor Muskie cry."

I said, "Bip is a ball?"

She said, "He even looks like a ball. You can see it for yourself, Antonio. You don't have to be a theosophist. He is tight and solid and round. He rolls like a ball. He bounces like a ball. He is hard to get hold of like a ball because a ball has no corners or edges to get hold of it by. In all his lives his karma attracts him to round, ball-like people like round Nancy Oglethorpe. Everything she's got is round. And to round places. You were with him at Stonehenge. Why do you think he was so much in his element at Stonehenge? You saw the way he looked there—as if he'd come home. My dear, Stonehenge is a circle. And now Alexander Hall. Don't think it's an accident that Leo Bebb found his way to Alexander Hall. Besides there are no accidents. That's karma for you. In a nutshell."

Alexander Hall, that roundest and most Bebbsian of all University buildings, that great mound of rough-hewn pink brownstone with its round Romanesque arches, its fat, round turrets with their conical roofs, the bulging sides of its circular, glassed-in arcade that you have to pass through to enter the rotundity it encircles, that omphalos of varnished oak and Homeric mosaic where public lectures, concerts, Roman Catholic masses, and other such miscellaneous University activities take place. Alexander Hall was where, by accident or otherwise, Bebb and Nancy Oglethorpe came to preside over their Love Feasts for a while. Gertrude Conover helped arrange it through her Nassau Hall connections, thus making herself the agent of karmic potencies.

The article in *The Daily Princetonian* was what started the ball rolling, to use an expression that Gertrude Conover would have said was no accident. It hit the front page, and there were pictures. Bebb standing beneath the stone lions of Revonoc. Waiters, musicians, guests hurrying down the front steps on their way to invite in the uninvited. Nancy Oglethorpe making her apologia under the chandelier. The reporter played his story straight for the sake of laughs, but there were no laughs of the kind the reporter had played it for because right from the start Bebb was taken up like Tiffany glass or Art Nouveau, not as something to laugh at but as a base from which to laugh instead at the kind of people who would find him laughable. If Bebb had appeared in beard and beads playing Jesus rock on an electric guitar, the chances are Princeton wouldn't have given him the time of day, but he came in his gents' furnishings suit and Happy Hooligan hat talking about the blood of the Lamb as if it was delivered to his door by the quart every morning, and Princeton lapped it up with an enthusiasm that I think caught even Bebb by surprise.

Bebb gave much of the credit to Nancy Oglethorpe. He said, "Antonio, that woman is a powerhouse. I don't care spit how she used to tom-cat around out there at the grad school, she come clean about all that the first feast we ever had. Though your sins be as scarlet, they shall be white as snow, Antonio, that's how clean she come, and she's been giving her all to Jesus ever since. Why she's better than Brownie ever knew how to be, and she's no kind of pussyfoot like Brownie is either. The trouble with Brownie is that life threw such a scare into him from the word go, he never lived it, just stuffed it inside his drawers and sat on it. That Nancy Oglethorpe, she's lived. She knows what she's talking about when she talks. And she knows what I'm talking about too."

Knew what Bebb was talking about and with her organizational skills and convert's zeal saw to it that what he was talking about was given maximum coverage and distribution by peeling those original Thanksgiving banqueters, whose names and addresses she managed to get down in shorthand before they left, to a hard core which she deployed through the town and campus like Vigilantes armed with flyers announcing each subsequent Love Feast as it came along and suggesting the menu. *Put your hand in the hand of the man who fed five thousand. Eat your troubles away at the Supper of the Lamb. Ho, everyone that thirsteth, come!* And they came, more and more as the weeks went by until finally Revonoc wasn't big enough to hold them, thirsting for God (if anybody) knew what and fulfilling the dream Bebb had gone to sleep on all those years of gypsying around the world with Gertrude Conover and fulfilling too, I suppose, some round, Babylonian dream of Nancy Oglethorpe's. She too came into her own in that round of feasting, found herself for the first time not dictated to but dictating, not typing but typed at last as some kind of camp Magdalen forgiven much because she loved much, loved among other things being all dressed up in beehive and fruit salad with somewhere to go for once where she wasn't the one who got paid but who paid for a change and, as Bebb was her partner, paid out in good measure, pressed down and shaken together and running over. Bebb was the master of the feasts and Nancy Oglethorpe the caterer who saw to it that there was more than enough of everything to go around including herself.

Who came? In an interview in the *Prince* Nancy Oglethorpe was quoted as saying, "Being as how I took psychology at Hunter College and it has been a life-long interest of mine ever since that time, I am more psychologically oriented than Bible oriented vis-à-vis the so-called Love Feast movement here in town, and though we end up meaning the same thing I would use a different type language than Leo Bebb to describe what's going on. Mr. Bebb says the individuals we are relating to are lost sheep, and I say more they are like myself lonely and insecure persons with the kind of self-destruct hang-ups you got to expect anywhere this day and age but especially in a cultural scene like Princeton which attracts a basically introverted and egg-head type of individual. Who comes? You name it, at Love Feasts we got it."

What did they find when they got there? The detractors of the movement—because of course detractors were inevitable and when they came, they came not without ammunition—the sour mouths, nitpickers and malcontents said that at any given Love Feast you could find whatever you were looking for, meaning the worst, needless to say: winos finding winos, acid-heads acid-heads, fairies fairies, victims victimizers, and so on, everybody confessing his sins and then cozying up afterwards to the ones who had a taste for the same kind of sinning he did. The supporters of the movement no less than the detractors agreed that the genius of the Love Feasts was that much of what you always found there was each other, was other people exposing themselves as you yourself were exposed. Whether the exposure was decent or indecent was left to the eye of the beholder to decide, was left finally to the eye of God himself just as I suppose it was left to the eye of God to decide about the whys and wherefores of Bebb's exposing whatever it was he had been charged with exposing all those long years before out in back of a seafood restaurant in Miami Beach to a bunch of children playing niggerbaby with a tennis ball. Was he coming clean or was he coming dirty? Was it to those kids he was laying himself bare or to himself or to Jesus or to all three at once? I doubt if Bebb himself knew though I never came right out and asked him. I doubt if anybody but God knew about Bebb or the Love Feasts either.

Anyway, what they found at those Love Feasts was

each other and food. Drink. The original turkey and claret punch gave way to simpler fare. While Revonoc was still the scene of operations, they experimented with various possibilities. They tried Kool Aid, milk, and a combination of ginger ale and Welch's grapejuice. They tried Slim Jims, Sultanas, Fritos. It was Bebb the teetotaler who said he didn't care much what there was to eat but thought what there was to drink should have some kick to it. He said it over Nancy Oglethorpe's objection that if word got around alcohol was being used, it might attract the wrong kind of people, to which Bebb said, "Sister Nancy, it's the wrong kind of people Jesus wants. Why, that's the whole thing about Jesus. And he wants the right kind of people too. I was raised a Baptist, and a Baptist takes to spirits like Satan takes to holy water, but I can't help that. It's spirits helps oil the hinges between the wrong people and the right people, and it's spirits Jesus served the night they come to take him, not soda pop, though there's Baptists would tell you different." So what they ended up with was a kind of punch that was partly for Jesus' sake and partly too, I think, for Lucille's sake because like the Tropicanas that Lucille had drowned her sorrows in and finally herself, there was a lot of orange juice in it, only then, in place of the gin and in far less majestic proportions, a dry, white wine. It even tasted like Tropicanas if you didn't think too hard about it. "Here's to Jesus," Bebb would say, raising his paper cup high to start things off, and then with their Tropicanas in hand, everybody would turn to his neighbor and say, "Here's to you." That was the way the Love Feasts opened. They closed, as on Thanksgiving, with the kiss of peace.

And what went on between? The big difference between the movies of my childhood and the movies of today is that the old ones seemed to have so many more people in them. It wasn't just Cecil B. DeMille with his casts of thousands either. *Marie Antoinette* with Norma Shearer and Tyrone Power, *Captains Courageous*, the Marx brothers, *Ninotchka*, in the big-scale ones and the small-scale ones both there were not only all the people you could see on the screen but I always had the feeling that off-screen too—behind every closed door and around the bend of every corridor and outside on the street—there were always at least as many people again all in full costume just waiting around in case a door happened to blow open or the director decided to aim his camera in another direction. I suppose extras came cheaper in those days, or maybe it just seemed there were more people in the old movies because in my own world then there were so comparatively few—just Miriam and me and whatever nurse happened to be looking after us at the time—but in any case they always gave me a sense of there being inexhaustibly more than enough of everything to go round including people. In movies then, as in my life then, I had the sense that the fun of it was never going to run out. And so with the Love Feasts. In between the toast to Jesus at the beginning and all the kissing and squeezing at the end, there were not only all the people who were actually present but all the people who might be corralled in off the streets—because at each Love Feast Bebb sent out a deputation for that purpose—and all the people also that the ones who were corralled in might in turn corral in themselves, and so on, world without end. Whatever you found at Bebb's Love Feasts, you could be sure it would be more than you had bargained for.

And you could be sure, of course, that there would be

Bebb himself, that *round* man, that snowball gathering substance somehow as he gathered momentum, growing rounder and fuller as the weeks went by until you felt that the time would come when his tight skin, his tight face and raincoat, must surely split. No wonder he failed to notice the obscure needs I brought with me from Sutton. Once in a while, he tried. If I mentioned Sharon's name, he would sometimes glance my way over his shoulder as a miler might at the shout of a familiar voice from the bleachers—"You got to keep the wires open between you and her, Antonio, and between you and Jesus," profundities like that—but then on back to the relentless dash and downhill barrelling again. He had his hands full, more than his hands.

The Love Feasts were feasts, which meant anybody could propose a toast, propose anything. There was an instructor from the History Department, for instance, a man named Roebuck, with a handlebar moustache and combat boots. He came regularly. When he spoke, you could see his teeth through his moustache. There was something antiphonal about the propositions and counterpropositions that he and Bebb exchanged.

"Every place I look I don't see Jesus," I remember Roebuck's saying once. "Where is he?"

"Wherever two or three are gathered together in his name, that's where he is," Bebb said.

"Can't see him," Roebuck said.

"He sees you," Bebb said.

"We have this twelve year old, this sick one. His hands don't work," Roebuck said. "He wears a little helmet with a piece sticking out from the forehead with a Magic Marker attached to it. That's how he writes his name."

"Jesus said suffer the little children to come unto me

and hinder them not," Bebb said. "You bring him on in here next time."

"You will make him all better," Roebuck said.

Bebb said, "Lord, I believe, help thou mine unbelief."

Roebuck said, "You will give him the use of his hands and fingers. You will make it so he can walk like a human being instead of a bundle of broken sticks."

Bebb said, "There's nobody knows the grief in your heart save only one. It's like your grief is his grief."

Roebuck said, "Since Thomas Aquinas, the fattest of all the saints, there have been five classic proofs advanced for the existence of God. There's the ontological proof, the teleological proof, the proof from consensus, and so forth. Do you have a favorite?"

Bebb said, "I never got past grade school. I wasn't much bigger than your boy when I took my first job so I couldn't prove the six-times table. Jesus, he believed God existed. That's the best proof I got."

"Of course there's one place I haven't looked for God yet," Roebuck said, "or Jesus either."

"Where's that you haven't looked for him?" Bebb said.

Roebuck stood there in Alexander Hall with the bottoms of his trousers bloused out over his combat boots. "Up my bleeding ass," he said.

Or Bebb on power: "The American Free Enterprise system couldn't never so much as been if it wasn't for Jesus. The Christmas trade alone is a for instance. Right here in Princeton, New Jersey, more gifts are being bought and wrapped up this very minute in the name of Jesus than in any other name in the Yellow Pages or the whole telephone directory. That's power for you."

Or Bebb on confession: "It's not like Jesus doesn't

know all the things you ever done that are wrong without you telling him about them. But until you lay your cards on the table and level with him, they're the great gulf fixed between you. It's only when you tell it to Jesus like it is that they become the Golden Gate Bridge."

Or Bebb on travel: "All the roads in the world are one road when you come right down to it because your dirt tracks, your superhighways, your Park Avenues, the place they all end up at is the same place, and that's the funeral parlor. We all got that to look forward to before we're through, and we all got rough places and smooth places both till we get there, so in the meantime let's stick close to each other while we follow the road to Jesus. This cup I'm hoisting now, it's one for the road."

Bebb with his cup raised to eye level, his viaticum—he only wet his lips with it. Bebb with his spooked eyelid making its secret signal. As once among lions, Bebb among the gleanings of Holder Hall, Cottage Club, Ivy, the ghettoes of John Street, Quarry Street, Witherspoon, the faculty room in Nassau Hall where once the Continental Congress sat. They came to those Love Feasts to see Bebb just as I came to see Bebb, driving south to see him from Sutton on out past the Palisades loop-the-loop across the twilit Hudson, beneath the prows of the great ships and down through the tunnel that was the tunnel to my father and to the mystery of myself. Or was Roebuck right that the only mystery was that there was no mystery? I carried with me to Bebb all the needs his Love Feasts didn't leave him time enough or heart enough to notice, what with all of Princeton to save. Unless the truth of it was that he did notice them and aimed his cornpone homilies at them—carried Sharon in his belly as I carried her in mine, the vision of her hitting the Jack Daniels with Anita Steen standing by to count the dead soldiers as they were carried out feet first, my son Bill trying to get it through to her that for Christmas it was a long-handled machine you could find buried treasure with that he wanted most, as which of us doesn't, I suppose. If there was nothing more than Bebb to find at the Love Feasts, at least there was nothing less. And there was also, of course, Nancy Oglethorpe.

Like Superman, her true identity remained hidden from the majority of mankind. She went right on with her career as itinerant stenographer, and nobody would have looked twice to see her misfiring up the hill to the grad school in her black Chevvy with her electric type-writer on the back seat, her Corrasable Bond and sharp yellow pencils. Even if somebody had looked twice, the most he might have seen on the second go was a Nancy Oglethorpe who no longer offered the variety of services she had of old but who entered those ravaged scholars' rooms armed now with the breastplate of righteousness and the helmet of salvation to fend off temptation. Like unassuming Clark Kent, who only when he stripped down to his acrobat's tights and waist-length cape re-vealed the superstrength that enabled him to fly through the air like a bird and batter down steel walls with his bare fist, it was only at the Love Feasts that Nancy Oglethorpe was seen for what she truly was.

She presided over the distribution of the Tropicanas. She organized the rescue squad that followed Scriptural precedent by combing the streets for the uncombed. She handled press releases to the *Daily Princetonian* and, as word spread, to the *Trenton Times* and *Newark Evening News*. She did the mimeographing and sent out the notices and when the practice started of collecting love offerings at each feast, managed the banking and book-keeping of that too. But her real power was as Bebb's *eminence grise*, the Dale Arden to his Buck Rogers.

Bebb was crazy about her from the start. Partly, I suppose, it was because hers was the first heart he gave himself credit for opening since the old Holy Love days and partly because she was the first to suggest that the original Love Feast should be perpetuated. I think too that Bebb was impressed by her beehive, her French heels, her poison green coat and found it all far closer to his idea of *haute couture* than Gertrude Conover's muted woolens, far closer to what he thought might catch the wandering eye of the Pepsi generation. Or maybe Gertrude Conover was right and what attracted Bebb to her most was that like him, like Stonehenge and Alexander Hall, she was round, only round with a round-ness that, unlike Bebb's, you could get hold of, a down-filled, yielding roundness. She was also, as she put it, psychologically oriented, that oriental odalisque, and from Hunter College days she brought certain En-counter Group techniques and ploys which in time Bebb came to adapt to his own ends.

She said, "It's got to be more give and take, Leo, not just you giving and them taking all the time. Nobody can relate to a father figure indefinitely. Eveybody wants a piece of the action," so there came to be feasts where instead of preaching to them, Bebb would simply stand up on the platform and throw words out to them. The words he threw out were old sawdust trail words like *salvation* and *sin* and *faith*, and his congregation would come back at him with whatever words first entered their heads, sometimes a word at a time, some-times a whole barrage of words at once.

Jesus Bebb would wing at them like a big league pitcher, and *Christ* they would bat back at him, *Christ* and *cross* and *crutch, cripple* and *couple* and *two, one, win, wine, waste.* Heaven he'd send sizzling down toward some plate, then duck to avoid being clobbered by *sky, pie, day, night, light, dark, dreaming, Daddy.*

I heard peace get him *sleep,* get him *sack* and *sex, languor* and *anger* and *fight, truce, truth, together, tomorrow* and *sorrow;* love get him *found, food, fool, full, feel, heal, holy* and *Hell.* Sometimes the words sailed up between them like birthday balloons.

Sometimes it was more like Francis Scott Key's bombs bursting in air, the red glare of rockets like *armageddon, marmalade, Mama Cass, piece of ass, peace of mind, matter, shatter, shit, shalom, home, sweet, sweat, blood, tears, beer, fear,* and the only proof through the night that the flag was still there would be the star- and sweat-spangled face of Bebb himself standing up there on the platform where Eleanor Roosevelt and John Mason Brown had stood before him. Many a time that winter by the twilight's last gleaming I watched him up there with his face buttoned tight against the storm he had unleashed. And sometimes I watched him up there having failed to unleash anything, calling out old names that he had lived with all his life and getting nothing back at all. *Beelzebub, Cherubim, Goshen*—like astronauts on a space walk they would hang suspended in the echoing silence of Alexander Hall.

I remember riding back with him one snowy night in Gertrude Conover's Lincoln on the way to take Nancy Oglethorpe home and hearing him say to her, "Sometimes it's like Pentecost, Miss Nancy, and sometimes it's like what you find scratched up on a outhouse wall."

"It's for real," Nancy Oglethorpe said. "It hits you where you live."

Bebb said, "Sometimes I think it's no substitute for old-time Gospel preaching." He was leaning forward over the wheel to peer through the whirling flakes. "It is not telling the good news to the poor."

"Pardon me for living," Nancy Oglethorpe said through the fur collar of her poison green coat.

It was Nancy Oglethorpe also who introduced a new method of confession into the Love Feast liturgy. Originally confessions had been made the way Nancy Oglethorpe had made hers at the first Love Feast—one person would stand up when he felt like it and say his piece. I remember a seminarian with all his hair shaved off and a loose-fitting grey sweat-shirt saying that he stole on the average of a dozen books a week from the U. Store. I remember a nurse from the hospital telling how the sight of the dying filled her with secret loathing, and a varsity tennis player with a golden beard telling how he had corrupted a twelve year old girl on the shores of Lake Carnegie. I remember a janitor with the face of a Supreme Court justice describing how in Normandy in 1944 he had for no reason he could explain shot a child out of a tree like a squirrel.

After each confession Bebb would come lay his hands on the person's head and tell them Jesus had forgiven them the way he had forgiven the good thief on the cross who said, "Jesus, remember me," and Jesus had said, "Today thou shalt be with me in Paradise." There wasn't one of us, Bebb said, that Jesus wouldn't remember when the chips were down. Then another one of the Feasters would raise his Tropicana and say, "Here's looking at you," and the one who had confessed would raise his, and the two of them would look at each other across their paper cups, and I suppose that meant that even if Jesus was still dragging his feet, at least they could look at each other. It was a step in the right direction.

Nancy Oglethorpe said, "I'm asking you, how many got what it takes to stand up and do it like that? Six or seven maybe? Ten out of a hundred? You need guts to come clean in public like that, and if you had that kind of guts, you probably wouldn't have sinned in the first place. It's a vicious-type circle." So again she persuaded Bebb to do it so that everybody could get into the act, and the way she taught him was this.

When Bebb gave the word, everybody was supposed to pick out a person to confess to so that there was a lot of milling around and changing places, and for a while it looked like a bargain basement with everybody trying to find the one it would cost him least to spill the beans to—townie dropouts and varsity jocks, Aquarian potheads, coed madonnas with ironed hair, butterfly-crotched peace-freaks who put flowers in the barrels of ROTC rifles. When everybody was finally coupled, the Oglethorpian rite was simple. Your partner held his hands up side by side, palms out. You made believe his hands were a mirror. You looked into that mirror and described out loud what was wrong with your face. Then your partner described in turn what was wrong with his face as he looked into the mirror of your hands. When you were both finished, for absolution you fed each other the sacramental elements. If crumbs got into your beard or Tropicanas slopped down over your love-beads, Nancy Oglethorpe said so much the better. It helped break the ice. An ice-type breaker.

The only time I gave it a try myself was soon after my conversation about Sharon with Anita Steen. It was the first Sunday the moveable feast had moved into Alexander Hall. There was a bigger crowd than at Revonoc—maybe a hundred and fifty by then—but because of the new setting with its lingering aura of people like John Kenneth Galbraith and Edward Weeks up there on the platform, things were a lot more subdued than usual. People didn't do much singing and jostling and hugging before the show got rolling but just sat down in the curved wooden pews with their paper plates and paper cups in their laps and more or less quietly waited.

I was sitting with Gertrude Conover, and when Bebb gave us the word to choose our partners, it was like dancing school at the Plaza when old Miss Bloss would tell us the same thing, and I knew I ought to choose Gertrude Conover because I'd brought her, but I didn't want to. I didn't feel like telling her what I saw in her hands that was wrong with my face—through theosophical channels she probably knew it already—and maybe even more than that, I didn't feel like having her tell me what she saw that was wrong with her face. In a way she was the closest thing I had just then to a rock to cling to, and I didn't want to find out that she was a secret drinker, say, or was making out with the gardener. In memory of Miss Bloss I was just about to do my duty by her anyway when to my great relief a red-haired woman I recognized as a waitress from Lahière's came and did it instead. The relief was short-lived, however, because the next thing I knew, I felt a hand on my shoulder and turned to find Nancy Oglethorpe standing in the aisle asking me in effect if she could have the next dance.

The way she held her hands, her face was concealed

103

behind them so at least I didn't have her eyes upon me as I stood there cringing at the thought of anatomizing myself in her overpowering presence. The trouble was that it wasn't my face I saw in her hands, but only her hands themselves, those white, pat-a-cake palms with their fleshy mounts of Venus and her destiny chain-stitched all over them in pink. All around us in that great varnished rotunda the sound of the other Love Feasters shriving each other was like what you hear in a theater when the house lights go up and everybody starts reclaiming for himself a part of the silence.

Looking into her hands, I did the best I could. I said, "They say husbands and wives get to look like each other after a while so part of what I see in my face is my wife's face. The hitch is my wife and I have split up so the part of my face that's got her in it has split up too, cracked like a plate you might say. It won't work any more anyway. When I took our little boy out for supper, just the two of us, I couldn't make it work worth a damn. My face is turning into a deadpan. It's turning into a dead-pan because there's this part of it that's dead. Maybe it's what always happens when you get to be in your forties. Maybe it's what I even want to have happen. I'm afraid that's all I can see in my face right now, Nancy, but it'll have to do, You're next. Amen."

I raised my hands quickly then to have them there to hide behind before Nancy Oglethorpe had a chance to lower hers. I just made it. Out of the corner of my eye I could see Gertrude Conover and the Lahière's waitress going at it. Gertrude Conover had her hands up with one ear pressed to them and a dim, astral smile on her face as though she was listening to familiar footsteps through a wall.

Looking at herself in the mirror of my sweaty palms, Nancy Oglethorpe was saying. "My name's Obenzinger. I took Oglethorpe as my professional name, but every time I see my face I know I'm Obenzinger. My face has got Obenzinger written all over it. Whoever's going to enter into a permanent one-to-one relationship with a person that's got a face like mine except another Obenzinger? I hate my face for being like it is. I hate myself for hating it."

She stopped talking then, and I felt I couldn't just stand there behind my hands in silence. I thought of saying I'd never guessed her secret—had taken her for a classmate of Jackie Kennedy's, a member of Piping Rock, a Daughter of the American Revolution. I even thought of making a little joke about how some people's problems are psychosomatic and other people's problems are psychosemitic and it wasn't anything she ought to feel too bad about. But as things turned out, I was spared having to say anything.

Over the tops of her fingertips I could see her beehive bending so near me that if my hands hadn't been between us, we would have been eyeball to eyeball. I didn't know what she was up to. Some darker confession that she had to come this close to whisper? Some unspeakable encounter-group ploy like suddenly spreading my hands apart by the thumbs and taking my nose between her teeth? Instead what she did was this. Taking my hands by the wrists, she planted a moist, pneumatic kiss dead in the center of one of them. I can feel it there still.

Was it my need she kissed or her own? I don't know, but the next moment there we were like a bride and groom feeding each other the first piece of wedding cake. I took a sip of Tropicana from her Lily cup. She broke off a piece of my Ritz cracker with her tiny teeth and swallowed it, unchewed, like the true host.

Maybe the cynics were right, I thought, and all that Bebb's feasts were was a chance to look the field over. Maybe the Tropicanas and Ritz crackers were only the hors d'oeuvres, and the meat and potatoes came when you met in the sack afterwards. It's possible that Nancy Oglethorpe wasn't absolving me with her kiss at all but only trying to establish at last a permanent one-to-one relationship with somebody who wasn't an Obenzinger. But it's possible too that the lines can't be drawn as sharply as that, and as I drove back to Sutton that evening, drove north past the Cloisters and the piers of the great bridge, it occurred to me that one way or the other maybe her kiss was as close to the kiss of peace as any I was likely to find anywhere else just then. Things being what they were.

CHAPTER SEVEN

THE WEEK after I got back from Princeton was the last one before vacation, and I spent the afternoon of the final day of classes helping straighten up the gym after the Christmas book fair. In the overheated world of Sutton High it is always mid-August and under the bright overhead lights of the gym in their wire cages it is always high noon so that during the hours I spent packing the unsold books back into cartons and lending a hand with the trestle tables, I lost all track of what the weather was up to outside. It was only when I stepped out into the parking lot around five that I discovered that about four inches of snow had fallen, and it was still coming down hard.

The damp linen smell and coarse-woven silence of the snow. The fan-shapes of light from the gym windows and the sight of my car almost unrecognizable as it crouched there lonely and white. To teach school is to catch from the children you teach not only their colds but a little of their childhood too, and I stood there at the gym door with a panic in my stomach no less sweet and wild than Stephen Kulak's, say, at the thought that school was out and vacation had begun, at the unexpected sight of the snow. In the fullness of time, the Scriptural phrase goes, and for a moment or two it was as if, filled to bursting, time had split apart at last, and there at the heart of it was the mystery laid bare. It was time to go home, or the heart of time *was* home, and I had been there all along without knowing it just the way all that hot, bright afternoon of dismantling the book fair I had been part of a snowfall without knowing it. Then Ralph Milliken, the Principal, thrust his way out through the door at my back in his clinking galoshes and velour cap with ear-flaps saying, "Plan to be home for Christmas?" as he pushed on past me, and with my briefcase heavy in one hand and my portable typewriter heavy in the other, I realized that home was Mrs. Gunther's and vacation was watching Dean Martin ham it up as Santa Claus on Metzger's TV. For the time being anyway, I couldn't face either and drove downtown instead.

Most of the stores were open late for Christmas, and the lights were on in the Sharanita Shop. From the other side of the street I could see the shelves laden with vitamins and the revolving stand of paperbacks. There were open barrels of things like brown rice and sunflower seeds, nuts and dried fruit lined up in apothecary jars. Only Sharon, if she was there, I couldn't see. With no clear intention of going in but just to touch base at the sight of her, I crossed the street and, standing off to one side, looked in through the plate glass at where she usually sat behind the cash register. The chair was empty, but over the back of it was a sweater I recognized. It was a camel's hair cardigan she had bought at Sevenoaks the day we drove down in Gertrude Conover's rented Daimler to see Hever Castle because it was where the Boleyns came from and of all Henry's wives, Anne Boleyn was my wife's favorite. The sweater had pearl buttons down the front and was too long for her, and I remember telling her it made her look like a Nanny. In the ashtray her cigarette was smoking, and over a doorknob hung a canvas bag that must have gone back to Armadillo days. It had *The Sunshine State* and a palm tree stenciled on it. Even your worst enemy's belongings, left defenseless and alone that way, can be more eloquent than the Gettysburg Address, and it was that cardigan that made me open the door and step into the empty shop. The smoldering cigarette was two thirds ash, and I stubbed it out.

I studied the paperbacks for a while. There was *Drink Your Troubles Away: the Health Cocktail Habit* by somebody named John Lust and *The Miracle of Vitamin C* with a reproduction of Michelangelo's God creating Adam on the cover. There was *The Hidden Menace of Hyperglycemia* and *Overfed but Undernourished.* I had just put back *Magnesium, the Nutrient that Could Change Your Life* and picked out a copy of *Vigor for Men Over Thirty* when I heard a thump and rumbling in the plumbing, and in a moment or two a door into the back of the shop opened, and Sharon came out. She was wearing a wrap-around crazy-quilt skirt over the black leotards she wore to yoga class. If she was surprised to find me there, she gave no sign of it. Just a moment's hesitation at the door as she pulled the skirt around at the waist to make it as straight as her face.

"Hey," she said.

I said, "Merry Christmas."

We didn't shake hands or anything, just faced each other there over the health foods and life-enriching vitamins, and I knew it was a mistake to have come, maybe even to have been born. I thought of the barbecue at Herman Redpath's ranch where in a dress the color of moonlight she had come toward me once between a marimba band and a portable outhouse with Bebb whispering in my ear, "Behold new Jerusalem coming down out of heaven like a bride adorned for her husband," and in an effort to say something, anything, worthy of the occasion, I had asked her to marry me. I wondered if any such thought crossed her mind as she went and took her usual seat behind the cash register so that it was from above I saw her, like a teacher proctoring an exam—her cheekbones, the glimmer and dividing of her hair.

"I was fixing to give you a call one of these days," she said, lighting what I took to be one of Anita Steen's king-size Winstons. "Bip's got me worried half sick."

"Bip's fine," I said. "He's the belle of Princeton. There's nothing to worry about."

She said, "Did he tell you the new one he's pulling on the IRS this year?"

I said, "He doesn't tell me the time of day any more. He's too busy with the Pepsi generation."

"You're lucky," she said. "He's been on the IRS shit-list for years, and this time he's really stuck his neck out. He was so tickled he called me up special just to read it out over the phone."

I said, "Read what out?"

"His tax form," she said. "He's filled out his tax form this year like he wasn't filling it out for himself but he was filling it out for Jesus. Right down the line, that's how he's done it. Like where it says put down your first name, he's put down the first name Jesus, and where it says last name, he's put down, 'I am the first and the last, says the Lord.' "

She said, "The place where it says wages, he's put down 'The wages of sin is death.' He's filled out that whole thing with words out of Scripture like it was Jesus filling it out, 'Render unto Caesar' and all that stuff. He says all his income, it's going out for Jesus, so why not send it in like it was Jesus's income. He was pleased as punch when he read it over the phone.

"This time they're going to get him," she said. "They're going to jail him sure. The best he can hope for is they'll pack him off to the funny farm."

"He's been in worse spots," I said.

She said, "I remember the time they jailed him before, the time they had him up for what they said he pulled on those kids in Miami. I was just a kid myself. I was playing in the yard with a cat name of Mercy that Brownie gave me. I remember Luce come out in a wrapper half stoned and told me. She told me they were fixing to lock my daddy up five years for doing something that hadn't hurt a soul and was just his nature, and right then when she told me, I was sick all over that poor cat Mercy."

She said, "Way back when Luce first started hitting the Tropicanas, the most either of us ever had was each other, Bip and me. Even if he's from outer space like Luce said, he was always real good to me. I never heard him say a mean or spiteful thing, and he never took a strap to me all those years though there was plenty of times he should of. He took me on trips with him soon as I was big enough to take, and he told me his troubles, some of them, same as I told him mine. He made a fuss over me like he was trying to make it up to me because I wasn't his own flesh and blood. Sometimes I used to think I really was his own flesh and blood though he told me different—not Luce's, but his—and there's still times I'm not sure. There's lots nobody knows about Bip. It didn't seem like I was ever going to get over them locking him up in jail five years."

I said, "I guess it wasn't the easiest thing in the world, being Bip's daughter."

She said, "I never thought about it like that."

I said, "Don't think about it." I could hear a car trying to get unstuck out in the snow somewhere, the panicky sound of tires spinning. "Your life isn't something to think about too much. You just live it the best way you can."

She said, "When you start thinking about it, you're sunk." As she raised her head, some vague fragrance reached me that could have been perfume or Bourbon or something fruity she'd had for lunch. She said, "It's like Mickey Mouse, the way he can walk off the edge of a cliff and go walking right on in thin air without thinking a thing about it. Soon as he looks down and starts thinking about it, that's when he starts falling."

"Mickey Mouse always comes through in the end," I said.

She said, "When I come through in the end, I'll let you know."

She said, "How about you, Bopper? Is everything OK?"

"I'm OK," I said.

She said, "You go out and have yourself some fun, hear? There oughtn't to be any time you can't find some way at least to have some fun in it."

"How about you?" I said. "Are you having any fun?"

She said, "Not one hell of a lot if you want to know," and then the bell over the door tinkled, and a black girl came in with snowflakes in her hair.

She said she was looking for Mu tea, and while Sharon was hunting around for it, I stood there by the brown rice and sunflower seeds wondering what I had come looking for myself. Somebody to go to bed with again as lovers do and friends do, both—a lover to make the most of darkness with, a friend just to let the dark be dark with until it covers you up like snow? Somebody to say no when I said yes and never when I said now, to give a shape and edge to the emptiness of things even if it was a cutting edge? Maybe all I was looking for was just somebody to grow old along with me like Rabbi Ben Ezra so I wouldn't end up traveling around the world like Gertrude Conover to make myself believe I had a home to come home to that I was homesick for. I thought about walking out of the gym into another world and about what Bebb put down for Number of Dependents when he was filling out his form 1040 for Jesus. I suppose what Bebb put down was Everybody. For myself I would have to put down Nobody.

Several more customers came in while Sharon was making change for the black girl with snowflakes in her hair, so I picked up a brown bottle with a pink label on it and took it up to her to pay for it before the others got ahead of me.

"The miracle of Vitamin C," I said, and I thought of Michelangelo's God on the paperback cover reaching down out of his cloud to touch Adam who is stretching out his hand in such a languid way to receive the gift of life that you wonder if he really wants it. Maybe he had an inkling of all the strings attached.

Sharon wouldn't take my money.

She said, "It's a Christmas present," then leaned over the cash register and breathed into my ear, "Shove one of these up three times a day and you'll feel like new." This time there was no doubt it was Bourbon.

I'm coming home, I thought of saying, thought of leaning forward and burying my face in her sleep-smelling hair as the customers waited their turn. The trouble was my symptoms were the reverse of Charlie Blaine's. Charlie Blaine complained that after each move he made, he could feel some shadowy presence inside him making the move all over again, a death inside him echoing his life. For me, it was the shadow that came first, a dim impulse to reach out, to touch, that I had nothing inside me substantial enough to carry out because I had the idea it was my death that was real, my life the echo.

In Alexander Hall Nancy Oglethorpe had fed me from her Lily cup and in the Sharanita Shop Sharon had made me a present of Vitamin C, but neither of them was powerful enough to bring the roses to my cheeks. I said, "Maybe it's magnesium I need, the nutrient that could change your life," but by that time a man in a ski parka had stacked his purchases on the counter, and Sharon was starting to add them up for him, tapping them one by one with the eraser of her pencil, so I drifted back out into the night again like snow and wandered around town the better part of an hour with a frozen carrot for a nose and two thumbprints where my eyes should have been.

114

CHAPTER EIGHT

IT WAS BROWNIE who unexpectedly saved Christmas for me—Laverne M. Brown, that is, Bebb's former assistant and factotum in whose hands Bebb had left the new Church of Holy Love that Herman Redpath had built for him at his ranch outside Houston. When I first met Sharon, she told me that the reason Brownie always smelled so strongly of after-shave was that he drank it, but she admitted she'd never caught him at it, and I don't think she really believed the charge herself. Brownie smelled of after-shave because he doused himself with it, that's all, and he doused himself with it because he was by nature given to always trying to make fragrant and comforting anything that might otherwise smell of mortality. As a biblical exegete, for instance,

there was no barbarity of Scripture that he wasn't prepared to interpret in terms that wouldn't have been out
of place in the works of Louisa May Alcott. In that
passage in Galatians where Saint Paul wrote that there
were certain troublemakers who he wished would go out
and castrate themselves, Brownie explained once that far
from giving vent to vindictive anger, Saint Paul was
speaking with their best interests at heart. "Think of all
the trouble it would save certain poor souls, dear," I
remember his saying, "not to have anything down there
for the Devil to pull them around with any more."

His calling people *dear* was another case in point. He
called everybody dear no matter who they were, and
after the first shock of hearing him do it, you realized it
was just another example of the same thing. It may be
true that a rose by any other name would smell as sweet,
but by calling everything a rose indiscriminately, he
could sell you the idea that even skunk cabbage had a
sweetness all of its own. And then there was of course
his smile. Brownie's smile was the creation in part
of the low hung set of china teeth he wore, and like
those teeth it was fixed so firmly in place that it kept right
on smiling even when on the inside Brownie himself can't
have felt much like it. I have seen him smile when there
were tears rolling down from behind his glasses, those
glasses with the heavy tortoise-shell rims on top of the
lenses only which gave him a look of perpetual despera-
tion. Brownie's smile was the smile of the man in the old
joke who says that the only time the arrow in his back
hurts him is when he laughs.

Brownie phoned me at Mrs. Gunther's the morning
after my meeting with Sharon at the shop and invited
me to spend Christmas with him at the Red Path

Ranch. He said, "I have heard from Mr. Bebb these are troubled times for you, dear, and I want you to know that the latch string is always out."

"Brownie," I said, "you don't know the half of it," and standing there under the stairs in my bathrobe and slippers with Mrs. Gunther's mortuary curios gathering dust all around me and my tap water Maxim keeping warm on the radiator in my room, I told him I would catch the first plane I could get. Tony had already left to spend the vacation upstate with his father and Billie Kling, and Metzger, after all, had both Mrs. Gunther and his TV, so it wasn't as if I was abandoning anybody.

The last time I had seen the ranch was some four years earlier soon after Lucille had died there with her life slipping out of her wrists as she rocked back and forth in her chair in the dark and listened to the sounds of poor Brownie, all unaware, reading Scripture. The residential compound of tile-roofed mission houses, Herman Redpath's swimming pool, Holy Love built to look like the Alamo with its carillon that sent *Lead Kindly Light* and *When I Survey the Wondrous Cross* trembling out over the scrubby flatlands as far as the greenhouse and John Turtle's Tom Thumb golf course—it all seemed much the same to me. Going on a hundred and eleven, Maudie Redpath was still in circulation looking as though it was only her peekaboo blouse that held her together. Ever since doing that birthday dance by which she had so nearly succeeded in changing herself into a blackbird that they say she managed to travel five or six feet off the ground as far as the swimming pool, she had been none too steady on her feet, but she still got where

117

she wanted to go in Johnson Badger's electric golf cart. Bea Trionka had lost seventy-five pounds, she said, but she still looked as much as ever like a pan-fried Pope John the Twenty-third. Harry Hocktaw, that moon-faced tabby cat, met me at the airport in huaraches and a Harry Truman sport shirt looking no older than he had on the afternoon I had heard him trying either to hold death off or give him a royal welcome by rattling a dried gourd full of seeds in an erratic and absent-minded way while Herman Redpath slowly melted away like chocolate in a room full of kinsmen including all the black-haired papooses he boasted of having begotten on one or another of the ladies present. And John Turtle was there, the Joking Cousin himself. He was the one who was on hand to greet me at Brownie's house when I arrived from the airport—Brownie was down at Holy Love signing mail-order diplomas, he explained, with his gold-framed teeth flashing—and he was the one with whom I spent the most memorable part of my first and only Texan Christmas Eve.

The function of a Joking Cousin is hard to put your finger on, and none of the books about Indians that I have tried looking it up in has ever been much help. In general a Joking Cousin is somewhere between the Lone Ranger and the Marx Brothers. His job is to be on hand at all the most holy occasions in the life of a tribe, like deaths and marriages and major real estate transactions, and to ham them up in as many appalling and unholy ways as he can think of. When they had Herman Redpath laid out in his satin box at Holy Love, for instance, it was the Joking Cousin who went over and took a leak on him. Bebb told me once that he thought what the Joking Cousin was up to was trying to keep the evil

spirits from realizing how holy the occasions were because that way they wouldn't horn in and take things
over. Maybe it was the Great Spirit himself the Joking
Cousin was trying to hoodwink with his shenanigans, the
Great Spirit as Margaret Dumont.

In any case, John Turtle was there with the rest of
them that Christmas Eve. Brownie was living in the
house that had once been Bebb's and Lucille's and invited all the Indians in for supper. Lizard Shoptall was
there with his jazz combo so there could be dancing. The
Johnson Badgers were there with their troublesome
nephew Buck who had once gotten himself stuck in an
Electrolux. Maudie Redpath was there wearing a gar-
denia behind an ear that looked like a smoked oyster.
Bea Trionka came with her three daughters and their
husbands and children, and there was a wide representa-
tion of Poles and Hocktaws. Harry Hocktaw and his sons
set off some fireworks out on the terrace, and through
the picture window we watched skyrockets, pinwheels,
and clouds of different colored smoke light up the sultry
Texan night while Lizard Shoptall and his boys belted
out some of the racier carols like *I Saw Mommy Kissing
Santa Claus* and *All I Want for Christmas is My Two
Front Teeth*. There was a tree, of course, decorated
entirely with things to eat like strings of popcorn and
cranberries, kumquats and marshmallows and braids of
red licorice. For the cocktail hour Brownie had put
together a temperance eggnog which looked and tasted
like Wildroot Hair Oil, but when some of the Indians
brought along whiskey, Brownie raised no objection. He
spent most of the time before supper out in the kitchen
getting things ready, and I joined him there after a while
not because all the noise in the living room was too noisy

but because there kept being moments when it made the silence inside myself seem too silent. He had on a frilly apron that must have been left over from Lucille's day and his sleeves rolled up so that his pale, hairy arms were bare to the elbow. There were dark sweat stains under his arms, and every time he bent over to stir something or peer into the oven, his china smile looked so precarious I was afraid it might turn up somewhere in the supper later like a favor in a Jack Horner pie.

He said, "It's a little hard to remember what day this is, isn't it, dear? It's hard to think of the Savior's birth except in northern climes where there's a fire crackling on the hearth and the snow is coming down."

I said, "Even up north it's not always that easy, Brownie."

Brownie said, "How's Sharon, dear? How's the baby?"

I said they were great.

"Some ways," Brownie said, "Christmas is a sad time for all of us. The snows of yesteryear, dear."

When suppertime came, Brownie gave a blessing with a lot of peace on earth in it and tidings of great joy and glory to God in the highest, and everybody started popping snappers at each other and blowing out long paper buzzers with feathers on the ends.

To eat, there was chile and tortillas and tamales and a huge trough of green salad full of honeydew balls and slices of onion and beefsteak tomatoes. There were lots of other things too, Indian things with names I had never heard of, some of them corn on the cob yellow and sweet, some of them bitter and dark. But the main thing was one of Roland Birdbear's piglets. Lily Trionka brought it in on a platter and set it down in front of Brownie. It had its small, fat legs tucked in under it with

120

the trotters cut off, and its chin rested on a pillow of parsley and aluminum wrap. Its eye-sockets were empty and puckered up, and in the silly little grin of its mouth there was a silver dollar. Its rubbery snout was scorched on the underside, and it looked so much the size and shape of a baby that when Brownie started in to carve it, I looked the other way. There was plenty to look at.

When Roosevelt Pole arrived dressed up like Santa Claus with a clothes mop beard and his paunch swelling out over a pair of skintight red bathing trunks and the fuzz on it parted down the middle, the sack he carried over his shoulder turned out to be full of dry ice and cans of beer so cold it made your throat ache. For the children he had sarsaparilla and frozen bananas dipped in chocolate and grated peanuts, and some of the children put pieces of dry ice in their sarsaparilla so that billows of milk-white vapor slid out over the table like ground mist. Old Maudie Redpath got so carried away she threatened to try dancing herself into a blackbird again, but Harry Hocktaw, who had been the one to pull her out of the swimming pool the last time she'd tried it, talked her into singing a song instead. She said it was a song that was supposed to restore your potency in case you had lost it and consisted of one series after another of very high, rapid notes that sounded like a bosun's whistle with Harry Hocktaw filling in the silence between series by shaking his dried gourd full of seeds.

John Turtle took over while the dishes were being cleared off. He had brought along his guitar, and against a background of chords that had a tendency to flatten out and slide like the mist from the dry ice he sang a number of carols, some of them straight and some of them not straight. He sang *O come all ye faithful* and *God rest you Mary Musclebound.* He sang *The first Noel* and *It came upon a Greyhound bus.* "Silent knife, holy knife, all is man on top his wife," he sang with the veins on his neck standing out. Everybody who wasn't doing something else joined in on *I'm dreaming of a white Christmas,* and then he did a solo of "We three strings of Turtle's guitar. Ho ho ho, and har har har." Brownie asked for *O little town of Bethlehem,* and when John Turtle finished that he went off into "Away in a manger, so hot and so sad, the little lord Jesus raise up all he had," and Brownie whispered to me, "You have to remember they're just children, dear. They don't mean a bit of harm."

Then Brownie said, "How's Sharon?" not remembering that he'd already asked me that, and this time I decided I'd tell him something different. He looked so pillaged and distracted sitting there over the wreckage of the meal with most of the Indians on their feet and milling around by this time that I figured he probably wouldn't hear me anyway. I said, "Brownie, do you believe in reincarnation?"

He said, "That's not a Christian belief, dear."

I said, "Does that mean it's wrong?"

"It means I don't have to believe it," Brownie said. "I've got enough to believe as it is."

"If it's true, it explains a lot of things," I said.

"Like what?" Brownie said.

I said, "Well for one thing it explains why some people are born young and some people are born old. I think Sharon was born old. I think she's lived more lives than most people. That's why life has got to add up to more for her to make it worth her while. She's been around too many times to just settle for the same old shit. She gets restless." There was something about Brownie that made you want to use words like shit even though you hated yourself while you were using them.

He said, "You know the old prayer. 'Keep me ever restless until I find my rest in thee.' "

"She isn't restless for rest," I said.

"Rest doesn't mean a nap, dear," Brownie said. "It means peace."

I said, "What is peace, Brownie?" I knew I sounded like Pilate as I said it, very cool and Ivy League, but my tone was mostly the product of my vocal chords just as Brownie's smile was mostly the product of his teeth because on the inside I didn't feel cool at all and asked the question, as for all I know Pilate did too, in hopes that maybe he had an answer.

He was scraping dirty plates as I passed them up to him, and he paused with one of them in his hand, looking down at it as though maybe what he was looking for lay buried in the scraps.

He said, "Whatever peace is, we know it best from the empty place in our hearts where it's supposed to be. Until we find it, dear, we're all strangers and pilgrims on the earth."

"I hope you find it, Brownie," I said.

Brownie reached over and pressed my hand. He said, "I think of you as one of my dearest friends." But for all the kindness of his words, I felt the part of his heart they came from was not so much the part he loved his friends with as it was the empty part.

Later on that evening, by the time my son Bill would have pinned up his stocking and gone to sleep with the

Charlie McCarthy that Tony had given him, I put through a long distance call to Sutton, and while it was ringing once, twice, three times, and as clearly as I could see the bare hall where I stood, I could see Sharon come out of the bathroom in the terry cloth beachrobe she wore for a wrapper and walk across to the table by my side of the bed where the phone was. I could see the way she sat down on the bed, tucking one bare foot up into her lap, and the way her hair fell as she leaned over to pick up the phone. Just as her fingers touched the receiver, I hung up.

Some of the Indians had gone home or passed out by then, but there were still plenty of them in the living room watching TV, dozing, playing cards and so on, and out in the kitchen the big clean-up was still going strong. Brownie and the Trionkas were doing the lion's share, and the air was so steamed up from many runs of the dishwasher that the black hair of the Trionkas hung down their fat necks in damp ringlets and you could see the outline of Brownie's underwear where he had soaked through his shirt. John Turtle had taken his shirt off and was sitting naked to the waist at the kitchen table where the slops for Roland Birdbear's pigs were piled high in front of him. His hairless, brown chest was ribbed like a washboard, and he was drinking a can of beer. He called out to me in the hall to come take a load off my feet, and I went into the kitchen and took the chair opposite him. There was a long-legged yellow dog cleaning himself under the tail over in one corner, and John Turtle said, "If I could lick old rusty like that, I'd even give up Tom Thumb golf."

"You got a dirty mouth," Lily Trionka said to him over her shoulder.

"You got big tits," John Turtle said and from the pile in front of him winged a piece of pig at the dog who swallowed it like a pill and then flattened his chin out on his paws.

John Turtle smiled at me in a penetrating way and scratched himself in one cavernous armpit. He said, "Joy to the world, cousin. Time for puff-puff now."

Out of his pants pocket he pulled a small pipe. It was made of clay like the kind they sell on Saint Patrick's Day, only around the bowl the white of it had turned yellow from use. He also pulled out a small leather bag with draw strings and filled the pipe out of it with something that looked blacker than any tobacco I was used to, more like tea. He tamped it down hard with his thumb and then added a little more.

He struck a long kitchen match and waiting for the sulphur to burn off lowered it with care to the bowl of his pipe. The mixture he was using was so dry that when he sucked the flame down into it, there was a little bubble of fire mixed in with the first cloud of smoke. It made him sneeze, a loud, wet sneeze that caught the light in a transcendental way as it sprayed out over the slops. Then he took a long drag and with his eyes shut held it in for a while before letting it flare slowly from his lips and nostrils. The second drag he held in an equal amount of time but then with his cheeks puffed out like the South Wind on an old map blew it toward me in a blue stream. "Like that smell?" he said.

I said, "It smells like somebody set fire to a wig."

He said, "OK, Wig. Now you go puff-puff," and held the pipe out to me across the table.

God knows it was the last thing in the world I felt like, but remembering about peace-pipes and Indians and not wanting to give a Joking Cousin offense, I took it from him and held the wet bit to my lips.

"Two puff-puffs," John Turtle said. "One for earth and one for sky." He sat there picking his nose and looking at me in an amused and curious way.

The first puff I took burned my tongue and brought tears to my eyes, and as I exhaled it, the inside of my head felt mentholated and foolish and the ends of my fingers went numb.

"Don't forget earth," I heard John Turtle say as if from some distance, and at the second puff a cloud of nausea swelled up from my stomach and my face turned cold. First I thought I was going to be sick, and then I thought I was going to die. Then I thought I was sick and dead both.

Along the side of big roads you sometimes find a billboard painted on something like a Venetian blind so that when the slats are tilted one way, there is one picture, and then, when by some inner gadgetry the slats are tilted the other way, there gradually appears another picture, and that is how it happened there in Brownie's kitchen. First I was looking at one thing, then I was looking at another.

John Turtle and I were walking along together across a broad, moth-eaten looking plain that reminded me of some of the back country around Armadillo, Florida. The sun was directly overhead and the sky had a bleached-out look from the heat of it. There were some spindly palm trees off in the direction we were moving, and a few white cattle-egrets picking around among the cowflops. John Turtle was kicking up the dust with his

126

bare feet as we walked and at the same time singing a song that he matched roughly to the rhythm of his stride.

He sang,

Tell me the story about them feet, Joking Cousin,
What's the story about them feet?
Right foot, he's walk a hundred mile and left foot only sixty,
But they sweet on each other just like sugar all the same.

How about them two hands, Joking Cousin?
How's about them hands?
Well, the one's for fooling around with and the other's for wiping your ass
But when they starts in clapping, makes folks want to dance.

What's up with that old pecker, Joking Cousin?
What song he got to sing?
Old pecker, there's just one of him and he don't got much to say,
But he always smiling anyhow with his little pink eye.

I said, "There's something following us, Joking Cousin." I didn't want to look behind either for fear I'd see it or for fear I wouldn't see it, but I wanted John Turtle to look behind. He didn't. He was holding his left shoulder with his right hand and his right shoulder with his left hand, and he shimmied from side to side as he walked.

"Listen," I said. "Do you hear anything?"

We both of us stopped, and John Turtle let go one shoulder and cupped his ear with his hand.

He said, "I hear something all right." He crouched

down to a squat and I thought maybe he was going to flatten his ear to the ground like a scout. Instead he fumbled around in the dust with his long brown fingers and poked out a pebble the size of a nut. He put the pebble in his mouth and rolled it around so I could hear the clicking of it against his teeth.

I said, "How come you did that?"

"That stone was thirsty something cruel," he said.

I turned and looked over my shoulder. The view behind us was just like the view ahead of us—miles of empty plain, an egret or two. The quiet of it was like the quiet in between the verses of the Joking Cousin song.

"What you see, cousin?" John Turtle said. He said it thickly with the pebble still in his mouth bulging out one cheek. He was still squatting in the dust, and he had a feather stuck in his greasy black hair.

I said, "I don't know as I see anything." I remembered somebody telling me once that the way to see things far off is to look above where you think they are because you can see more out of the corner of your eye that way than you can looking at them head-on. I tried letting my gaze travel slowly from left to right just a little above the horizon, and once I thought I saw a small, dark shape moving along close to the ground maybe a mile or so away, but when I lowered my eyes to look at it directly, it wasn't there.

John Turtle took the pebble out of his mouth and held it in his fingers. It glistened like a pearl with his spit on it. He put it back on the ground, covered it over, and messed the dust up all around it so you couldn't tell where it was any more.

We walked quite a long way in silence then, and it was such a restful, warm day and the walking was so easy along that dusty scrub that for long stretches at a time I quite enjoyed myself. But every once in a while it would be like when you've lost yourself in a good movie, and then all of a sudden you remember something sad and hard you've got to do afterwards so that for a few moments you and your self are back eyeball to eyeball again and your stomach turns over inside you. Every once in a while as John Turtle and I walked along, I remembered in the midst of all the pleasantness of it that something hard and sad was bearing down on me from behind, and every time I remembered it, my stomach turned over inside me. I didn't mention this feeling to John Turtle, but maybe he sensed it because he started reeling off a lot of old jokes.

He told me the one about what the Indian said to the mermaid and another one about what the big dog said to the little dog and a few others which I've forgotten, and at one point we both of us got to laughing so hard that we leaned on each other with our arms wrapped around each other's shoulders, and the smell of his sweat was so much like chicken broth and the smell of his breath so much like honeydew that I buried my face against his slippery, warm neck and I thought that if whatever the small, dark shape was that was following us showed up just then, the chances are I wouldn't even notice it.

Then John Turtle said, "You know what the little piggy went to market say?" and I told him I didn't.

John Turtle said, "He say Wee wee wee all the way home," and at that point I wasn't laughing any more and not not noticing things and my stomach didn't turn over so much as it turned inside out because I suddenly knew what that small dark shape was I had seen out of the corner of my eye. It was the pig Brownie had served us for supper.

I could see the way it had looked when Lily Trionka

brought it in on the platter with the silver dollar in its mouth, exactly how it had looked without one detail spared me. I could see its little puckered up eye sockets and its cut-off feet. I could see the turned up corners of its mouth. I could see the scorched, rubbery snout. I hadn't been able to get much of it down—the meat had a sweetish taste to it and was so tender that it tended to fall apart in your mouth—but I had had my share right along with the rest of them, and I knew it was after me now with a vengeance. As clearly as I could see John Turtle, I could see it scuttling along through the white birds and moving as fast as it could on what was left of its hoofless stumps. I could see its gay, appalling little smile.

"Isn't there some place to hide?" I said to John Turtle as if my life depended on it because I was absolutely certain that it did.

He said, "Which place you want anyhow?" and "That one," I said. "I want that one over there."

Not more than a few hundred yards ahead of us there was a high fence made of heavy wire mesh such as you find in zoos, and there was a set of gates in the middle of it standing wide open. Leaving John Turtle in my dust, I sprinted through them.

There was a stream across my path, and I ran down into it sending great fans of water dazzling up into the air as I splashed my way to the far bank and clambered out on all fours. I tore off down the path on the other side not daring even to think about looking back and followed it on through a groove of palmetto and yucca and straight ahead till a big outcropping of tan rock barred my way and I had to loop around it. It was on the other side of those rocks that I came out into a place I knew I'd seen before.

It was a mangy, zoo-colored place, roughly circular in shape, and the yellowish earth of it was packed down velvety hard. Around the fringes of it there were some scraggly palms and a few other trees I couldn't identify that had trunks that looked like cement and greenish brown leaves as big as picnic plates. From the trees, the ground sloped slightly down toward the center, and in the center there was a wide pool with some patches of high grass growing here and there around the edge. It reminded me of pictures I've seen of African water holes, and then I remembered what the place was and when I had been there before.

It was a kind of outdoor menagerie and tourist trap called Lion Country where you paid your money at the gate and then were free to cruise around wherever you felt like it watching the uncaged animals through your car windows. The last time I'd been there was way back when I first met Sharon, and Bebb had driven us out for the afternoon from Armadillo because he said it was the unwindingest place he knew and he needed to unwind. It had never crossed my mind that I'd have occasion to see it again, and standing there looking at it now I thought to myself, well, there it is, and in a lazy, semi-tropical kind of way the place seemed to be saying the same thing to me. Well, there you are. Then I saw the lions.

It was like seeing old friends. A pair of them was sauntering along the far s¹.ore of the pond with their narrow hips and heavy, sunflower heads. A lioness with half-closed eyes was suckling some cubs under one of the cement trees. An old male with its tail out straight like a pump handle was taking a crap. Another was crouching by the pool to drink, and ripples drifted slowly out over the water from his lapping tongue.

Out toward the middle of the pool something was moving toward me that I thought at first might be a water lily cut adrift or the snout of an alligator, but as it drew nearer I could see it was somebody swimming. All I could see was just the head and every once in a while one of the hands when it broke the surface of the water as the swimmer sculled slowly backwards. When the figure was still some five feet from shore, it stood up, and I saw that it was a woman. When the woman turned around, bending over sideways first to shake some water out of one ear, I saw that it was my mother-in-law, Lucille Yancey Bebb. She had on a two-piece bathing suit that hung loose about her flat chest and skinny thighs, and on her head, with the flap over one ear turned back, she wore a bathing cap covered all over with rubber petals. She had on her dark glasses, and when she made it to dry ground, she paused for a moment to take them off and wipe her eyes underneath. Then she put them back on and padded her way up the hard-packed yellow earth toward me.

I have learned from sad experience that when you run into the dead in your dreams, it is just as well not to try engaging them in conversation. They almost never seem as glad to see you as you are to see them, and if you go up with your arms outstretched and years' worth of gossip on your lips, more often than not they won't even try to look interested. So I just stood my ground while Lucille approached, dripping water at every step, and when she finally reached me, I didn't say a word, and she didn't say a word either. She just let her jaw drop slightly in what I knew from experience was a smile and reached out to take me by the hand. In silence she led me up to one of the largest of the palm trees and showed me I was to sit down. Then she peeled off her petaled bathing cap and sat down near me. I can still remember the peace of that moment with the trunk of the palm tree between my shoulder blades and no need to run any more, with crazy John Turtle lost somewhere in the outer fringes of Lion Country and the lions themselves going about business as usual as though there wasn't a human being within a thousand miles.

I don't know how long we sat there, Lucille and I, until out of the corner of my eye I caught sight of some movement and turned my head to find my sister Miriam standing not far away. Her hair was tied back with what looked like a piece of florist's lilac-colored ribbon, and because the long, burnoose-like robe she was wearing reached the ground, I was afraid for a moment that maybe underneath they still had her in that awful A-shaped cast she'd died in and that she couldn't move. But when she saw I had noticed her, she came over to me and this time it was more than I could do not to say anything so I said her name. She said, "*Ciao, mio caro,*" in a rather hushed way and sat down on the other side of me from Lucille.

Everything was quiet. The lion at the pool's edge finished drinking, and the surface flattened out. The lioness who had been suckling her cubs was also through. She had one of them between her front paws and was washing him with long, upward sweeps of her tongue. A low-hanging, brown palm leaf gave a papery rattle above my head, but otherwise there was no sound to speak of. After a while, I saw two figures approaching from behind the outcropping of sand-colored stone. I had no trouble recognizing who they were. The taller one in back was John Turtle. The shorter one in front was Herman Redpath. They were both naked, and Herman Redpath was carrying a shoulder-high staff with a bunch of feathers fastened at the top.

Herman Redpath wasn't all dried up and wizened the way I had known him, with the skin of his face pulled so tight he couldn't get his lips closed over his teeth right. Instead he was shiny and supple like a piece of well-oiled leather and I would have said he looked years younger except that years younger would mean he still had old age ahead of him, whereas the impression he gave me was that he had it somehow behind him as if it was a nut that had split open and the Herman Redpath I was looking at was the meat inside. He walked up to where I was sitting between Lucille and my sister and then stopped. John Turtle squatted down on his heels a short distance behind.

Herman Redpath raised his feathered staff and planted the end of it squarely in the center of one of my shins.

First on that shin and then on the other he drew with his staff a series of little dots like the markings on dice from the knee down to the ankle. "Those are wolf tracks," he said. "They're so you won't ever get wore out."

Then on the insteps of my two bare feet he drew a small cluster of x shapes from the ankle down to the toes. "Those are dragonflies," he said. "They're so you won't ever run into more trouble than you can handle."

He paused for a moment then, that sawed-off little Sioux, that oil-rich Ojibway, and looked at me as if maybe now it was my turn to do something, but not knowing what he expected, I didn't do anything, and he continued. With his staff he tipped my feet up so they were resting on their heels, and on each of the bare soles he drew an upside-down v. "Those are mountains," he said. "They're so as you can walk from hill to hill without ever bogging down in the valleys."

While all this was going on, I couldn't help noticing that, squatting on the ground behind him, John Turtle had started in playing with himself in a kind of desultory way, but just as he showed signs of having more to handle than what he'd started out with, he picked up a dried gourd like Harry Hocktaw's from the ground beside him and started playing with that instead. Chicka-chicka, chicka-chicka went the seeds inside.

Herman Redpath turned his staff the other way round and aimed it roughly at my heart. With the feathered end this time he drew a large circle on my chest starting from the pit of my throat, around the outside of one nipple, down almost as far as the navel, and then up around the other nipple to the throat again. "That is the teepee circle," he said. "It's so you won't never want for a place to come in out of the rain."

Chick-chicka, chicka-chick-chick went John Turtle's rattle in a slower, more elusive rhythm. Like priests turning to face the altar, he and Herman Redpath had both turned around to look at the water hole as I was. Herman Redpath reached up and took hold of a small whistle I had noticed hanging around his neck on a leather bootlace. He raised it to his lips and gave two sharp tweets.

And there it was—the pig, the same pig Lily Trionka had carried in on a platter. It appeared on the other side of the pool, hesitated for a moment, and then came trotting around the shoreline skirting the patches of high grass. Its stumpy legs and dainty hooves were a blur, they moved so fast. Its rump waggled from side to side with its tail curled up like a Greek alpha. Its oversized ears were cocked forward, veined and rose-colored with the sun shining through them. Its snout was close to the ground. Its eyes were demurely lowered and its long lashes the color of flax. When it reached where I was sitting, it settled down on its hindquarters and raised its head a little. I reached out with one hand and touched the end of its snout. It felt cool and wet and gritty, like Lava soap. Then it opened its mouth and dropped into my hand the silver dollar.

On the dollar there was something written, and—how do I say it? What was written on it wasn't Antonio Parr or Tono or Bopper or Sir or any of the other names I've been called by various people at various times in my life, and yet it was my name. It was a name so secret that I wouldn't tell it even if I remembered it, and I don't remember it. But if anybody were ever to show up and call me by it, I'd recognize it in a second, and the chances are that if the person who called me by it gave me the signal, I'd follow him to the ends of the earth.

I came to at the kitchen table with my cheek cradled in a slippery green wedge of honeydew rind. Brownie's smile hung low above me like a new moon. He said, "He should never have made you try puff-puff, dear. You've been sick all over your nice Christmas suit."

CHAPTER NINE

SOON AFTER I got back to Sutton, there was a thaw. The temperature rose into the fifties, and off and on for two days it rained until the only snow left was in a few front yards where you could see the remains of what had once been snowmen. The earth looked as bare and vulnerable as I felt—sodden, olive drab grass, dog-droppings, mud. They kept Tony at school late helping lay down wooden duck-walks to the students' parking lot and the science lab. Mrs. Gunther's cellar flooded. Then it got cold again, and ice froze on Metzger's TV aerial so that his reception went from bad to worse and he lost UHF almost entirely. He said, "UHF was my Ho Chih Minh trail, and now all that comes through is ghosts. If CBS goes, I've had it. CBS is my goddam umbilical cord."

137

There was a note waiting for me from Sharon when I got back. It said, "Bill and I are taking off for a while to rest up after Christmas. Anita says she'll keep an eye on the furnace and the mail. Bip's been trying to get in touch with you. I guess things are closing in on him. Keep an eye on him for me." She signed it, "Mickey Mouse."

Tony seemed morose. His vacation with his father and Billie Kling had been a flop. He said, "You know Dad. This time it was his eyes. They gave him a test for glaucoma and told him he was in great shape only the pressure in one eye was a hair higher than the other so he's sure he's going blind. Every half hour he'd ask me if I noticed the light was getting dim, and then he'd make me let him feel my eyeballs to see if they felt any harder than his did. I mean Jesus, Tono, what kind of vacation is that having somebody feeling your eyeballs the whole time? Besides the skiing was lousy, and I was too broke to go anyplace else so most of what I did was eat. Like I've gained about ten pounds if you want to know the truth."

I think it was his weight that depressed him more than anything else. Every evening before he went to bed he worked out with his barbells, and mornings he'd do jogging in place until Metzger complained. What bothered Metzger, I think, was that if he started having a coronary, nobody would hear him give his three thumps on the wall above the thumping of my nephew's bare feet. So Tony took to jogging outside instead, four times around the block before breakfast every day in his grey sweatsuit with a towel around his neck, fair weather and foul. He had turned twenty in November and felt the pressure of the years. "Once you hit twenty," he said, "even a jock like me doesn't stay in condition unless he works at it," and I remember his inward-looking frown as he said it. It was partly the frown of a man who knows that staying in condition is uphill all the way and partly, I thought, the frown of a man who, after three years of Phys. Ed., shop, and maintenance work at Sutton High, isn't sure just what he's staying in condition for.

I knew I ought to talk to him about it—his prospects at Sutton in particular, his future in general—and I suspect he would have been grateful if I had, what with nobody else much to talk to, least of all his father. At the faintest sign that somebody wanted to talk about something that might make waves, Charlie Blaine would either go upstairs for one of his longer naps or get Billie Kling to taxi him down for an electrocardiogram. I should have talked to my namesake more about things that mattered, but I was gun-shy, I suppose, afraid always that he would tell me more than I wanted to know. It was a way he had. When I told him Sharon had gone away for a while, for instance, he said, "I told her she ought to fly, but she said the only way they'd ever get her on a plane was if they let her drag her feet, so she took the bus. I told her it was a crazy way to do it, but she got me to take her to the bus station anyway."

He and Sharon had been seeing each other, in other words. There was no reason why they shouldn't have. He'd never given me any reason to believe that they weren't. But I'd never stopped to think about the possibility before, and I didn't want to stop to think about it now. But Tony kept charging forward. "They're in Armadillo," he said. "She said she felt like seeing her old buddies again. You can't blame her, Tono. It's no life for her up here by herself."

I thought of the phone calls I had interrupted him at under the stairs and of how Anita Steen had told me I wasn't the only thing in pants that had rung the doorbell since she had been there alone, and now whether I wanted him to or not, he was putting two and two together. We were sitting in my classroom where I'd stayed late to correct papers, and it was raining outside. Tony was leaning up against the blackboard. He had rung the bell, and Sharon had heard it. He had come in, and she had come down. He had said something, and she had laughed maybe or not laughed, had gotten him a beer, turned on Johnny Carson, told him to take his cruddy feet off the coffee table—God only knew what they had done. As for me, I didn't want to know. All I knew was that once two people have made love, a door is opened between them that not even years of noblest resolve can ever entirely close again because the flesh has a pitifully weak sense of time and honor both, and old wounds throb like new again at the approach of rain. That day in the dentist chair, for instance, my hand had found its way to Laura Fleischman's hand so easily for the simple reason that it had been there before and knew the way even though I myself had forgotten it. And Tony and Sharon had also known the way, and whether they had followed it again in my absence and where it had led them if they had, I had no wish to find out.

"Where's she staying in Armadillo?" I asked because it was a question that took her out of the house and away from the sound of his ringing and put her about fifteen hundred miles south. She was staying at the Salamander Motel, he told me. She'd left him the phone number if I wanted it.

"She's been there before," I said—I hoped enigmatically. It was my attempt to end our exchange with a story I chose not to tell him rather than with one I chose not to have him tell me. It ended nothing.

He said, "She gave a going-away party the day before she left, and I drove down from Dad's for it. It was New Year's Eve. Anita was there, natch, and some of her yoga class and a few health food freaks thrown in for good measure—nobody I knew especially. She and Anita played the guitar and there was dancing and booze and vitamins. I don't know when old Bill got to sleep. He sat up at the top of the stairs with his legs through the rail, having a ball watching. Everybody had a ball," he said. "The only rough part was when Sharon got sick."

"Feel free to make a long story short," I said.

"Not booze sick," he said. "Sick sick. She was off booze into some kind of health juice. She said maybe that was the trouble with her. She said you can stand only so much that's good for you, and then you start needing something that's bad for you, and if you don't get it, then you start being bad for yourself. She looked awful, whatever it was. It was after everybody had gone home. She was upstairs trying to get rid of it only she couldn't. She said it was because what she was trying to get rid of was herself. She scared hell out of me."

He took a piece of chalk and drew a line on the blackboard with such a sudden, fierce stroke that the chalk snapped and fell to the floor. "That scared," he said—that heavy, swift diagonal stuttering off at the lower end where the chalk had broken. He said, "You gone, Bip gone. All her friends gone that she didn't know all that much better than I did so they wouldn't have done her much good even if they'd stuck around. I was all she had. I told Mrs. Gunther to leave the door unhooked, but I couldn't just walk out and leave her. Christ.

"I spent the night," he said.

I remember the rain at the windows. They were the old-fashioned kind that open at the top with a long pole, and I took the pole and closed them because it was starting to rain in a little. There was another kind of quiet in the room then.

"You want a lift home?" I said.

He was standing with his shoulders against the blackboard, the line he had drawn going through him like an arrow. He said, "She just needed somebody to hang onto, that's all. The next morning I put them on the bus for Florida. I wanted to tell you, Tono."

I found myself thinking vaguely of Stephen Kulak, the pudgy ninth grader I'd once explained irony to in that same classroom where now the rain was drumming softly at the window. Irony as two things, Stephen Kulak. My nephew's wanting to tell me and my not wanting him to.

Tony had his ankles crossed like Nijinsky as he looked at me through the dark and operatic eyes of my twin sister.

I said, "You're a good man, Charlie Brown."

He said, "I'm a dumb, overweight jock."

"I didn't say that," I said. "You said that."

He said, "I'm sorry as hell, Tono."

"Just give me an ounce of civet, good apothecary," I said, "to sweeten my imagination."

She didn't come back that week, Sharon. I called the house from time to time, but there was no answer, and from various places of concealment across the street I could see on various occasions that it was Anita Steen, not Sharon, who was minding things at the Sharanita

Shop, that withered little Fauntleroy sitting behind the cash register in a cloud of what I assumed must be the kind of cigarette smoke that puts apples in your cheeks and helps stave off the hidden menace of hyperglycemia. Sharon didn't come back that winter at all. She wrote me that she had decided to stay on in Armadillo. She said she could think things out better down there and the people at the Salamander Motel had given her and Bill special rates. Anita had told her that she would look after the shop while she was away.

Sharon didn't come back. Tony didn't tell me any more stories I'd just as soon have passed up. The weather didn't change for better or worse but continued to ice up by night and turn to mud by day. It was a winter when nothing particular happened one way or another out where you could see it but only inside, I suppose, where luckily or unluckily you couldn't see it unless you were Gertrude Conover with an eye for karmic stirrings, an ear for whispered cues from the prompter's box. And that was fine by me. I needed to have nothing happen for a while, and that was why, although I knew Bebb was trying to get hold of me, I made no effort to get hold of him. A number of times that winter he called at Mrs. Gunther's while I was in, but each time I got Metzger to tell him I wasn't. Metzger didn't even ask me why, and I didn't spend much time asking myself why either, let alone feeling guilty about it. Whatever Bebb wanted, I didn't have it in me to give. Whatever Bebb had to give, there wasn't enough of me just then to want it with.

And then one day in early spring he turned up—at a time when I least expected him, Stephen Kulak, which was also the time when I had most reason to expect him because part of the *roundness* of Bebb was always, like the ball in a pinball machine, to pursue his goal no less relentlessly for all the bumpers, buzzers, baffles and blinking lights put in his way.

I came back from school late one afternoon to find him in my room. He was lying on my bed in his shirt-sleeves with his tie loosened and his shoes off. He had hung his jacket neatly over the back of the desk chair with his hat perched on top of it and his shiny, black shoes lined up on the floor where his feet would have been if he had been sitting there, so that at first glance it was as if there were two Bebbs, the natty one at the desk and the mussed one on the bed. It was as if, waiting there in my room with nobody around to bother about, he had taken a break from being himself. The effect was startling. It was like coming upon Oliver Hardy resting between takes in a T-shirt and jockey shorts.

He said, "It's a day of trouble and of treading down, Antonio. That's why Gertrude Conover gave me the loan of her Lincoln so I could drive up. The fat's in the fire, and I need a sharp young go-getter like you to help me figure it because I'm not as young as I once was. There's been goings on in Princeton, New Jersey, you should have been there with your Bell and Howell to get pictures of. If you've got a few minutes, I'll run them off for you."

The first scene he ran off took place in the office of the Internal Revenue Service in Trenton, New Jersey.

Bebb said, "There was a bunch of us got letters ordering us to show up at the same time, and I was the first one to get there and the last one to get seen. Antonio, I cooled my heels the best part of three hours while one by one everybody else got called in ahead of me. There was a pane of crinkled glass like a men's

144

room, and I watched the whole pack of them through it getting their business done in there and coming out again. I looked at every wore-out magazine and dog-eared newspaper there was till finally all I had left to look at was the plain fact I was being put in my place. By the time they finally got round to calling my name it was the middle of the afternoon and I hadn't even had my dinner yet. Inside there was a agent sitting at a big desk name of Connor. He wasn't much taller than a parking meter and he had eyes rolling around in his head like marbles and a breath on him you could have got money for in a package store. He made me stand there must have been five minutes while he diddled around with some papers he had, and then he looked up at me and said, 'Do I have the honor of addressing the King of the Jews?' That miserable little pen-pusher, I gave him as good as he gave me. I said, 'My kingdom is not of this world,' and he come back at me quick as a water moccasin. He said, 'Well, maybe your kingdom isn't, but your form 1040 sure as hell is.' He had a secretary in there with a mouth painted on her didn't have any more to do with where her real mouth was than the map of China and she set in to snickering. I told them I was a U.S. citizen, one, and a ordained minister of the Gospel, two, and if they thought I was going to stand there and let them use me like that, they were mistaken."

I said, "Sharon told me about your 1040, Bip. I'm afraid you asked for it."

"I asked for a hearing," he said. "I didn't ask to be held up to shame and ridicule."

He said, "Antonio, it's no secret I've been having trouble with the IRS for going on forty years, and you want to know why? It's not on account of I've cheated on my income. I've got an income. I never once let on I didn't. My finances are an open book. The love offerings, the Gospel Faith tuition fees, the nickels and dimes coming in every Sunday year in year out plus all the weddings and funerals I'd as soon have done for nothing except what a man doesn't pay for he doesn't value. And the great generosity of Herman Redpath, Antonio. I'm including the hundred thousand too. Why, averaged out I've had more income out of serving the Lord than most anybody I know in this type of work, and being pretty much a one man operation save for Brownie, I never had much overhead either."

He said, "Antonio, I got an income but I also got an outgo, and I'm going to tell you where my outgo goes to. First off, I'll tell you where it doesn't go to. It doesn't go to Leo Bebb. Leo Bebb hasn't got any stocking full of fifty dollar bills stuffed up the chimney. He hasn't got any blue-chip securities or life insurance, and he hasn't got any pension plan either. Blue Cross? The only cross I've got is the cross of shame and glory. No sir, except for the clothes on my back and the incidental expenses of living, everything I've got goes to the church. This side of starving to death, my income and my outgo are dollar for dollar the same as each other because everything I got coming in goes out to Jesus. Right down to the last dime, it all goes out to feeding his lambs just like he told us."

I said, "The trouble with that, Bip, is you don't have a church any more," and he said, "Antonio, I am a church."

It was one of his classic utterances, of course, one of the golden sayings or *fioretti* of Leo Bebb like the first time I ever met him when, after we'd finished our business, I walked him to the Lexington Avenue subway in the rain, and just as he'd gone about half way down those urine-smelling stairs he turned with his hand on the rail and said, "All things are lawful to me." Or like the time of Herman Redpath's death when I asked him what he believed, and he said, "Antonio, I believe everything," and when I told him he made it sound almost easy, he said, "It's hard as hell."

I am a church, he said, this new pronouncement, and I thought how in a way he looked like a church—some sprawling, bald-domed Hagia Sophia or chunky, sun-bleached seamen's Bethel—as he lay there on my bed with the room smelling of his feet.

He said, "I did the best I could to explain it all out to that pitiful little Pontius Pilate how come I filed in the name of Jesus like I did and the point I was trying to put across doing it that way. He was just about as interested as he was whether I put on clean drawers that morning. They're going to investigate me, that's the long and the short of it. Connor and that Jezebel with lips painted on her wouldn't fool a blind man, they're going to go through every record I got clean back to the creation. They're going to have me up for malfeasance and contempt and willful attempt to defraud the U.S. Government.

"Antonio," he said. "They're going to nail me up."

That was the first scene Bebb ran off for me. The second took place at Princeton, in the Nassau Hall office of some assistant dean. The assistant dean himself was there with a beard and one of the denominational chaplains with a turtleneck and a pectoral cross. Unlike the experience at the tax office, here Bebb was treated very well. The chaplain offered him a cigarette which he refused. The assistant dean showed him a clapper that had been stolen from the Nassau Hall bell in oughty something. The assistant dean inquired after Gertrude Conover, whom he knew socially. The chaplain told a little joke about a Black Muslim and a southern Baptist meeting at Saint Peter's gate.

I wondered as Bebb described it if he had recognized in that office the terrible advantage he had—the advantage of Armadillo over academe, the bush leagues over the Ivy league. I could see them so clearly, the dean and the chaplain—not crew cut and gray flanneled as in my day but the dean with his beard, the chaplain with his turtleneck, trying no less to be all things to all men as with Bebb they undoubtedly fell all over themselves trying to be Bebbs. I could see them searching for prepositions to end their sentences with—*this is where we're at, Mr. Bebb*—scratching themselves where it didn't itch, wishing they'd boned up ahead of time on Uncle Billy's Whizzbang and the language of the sawdust trail. Bebb being Bebb wouldn't try to be anything else because he couldn't if he wanted to, just sat there in Nassau Hall as he would have sat on the can while they dithered around him.

Bebb said, "They came down to it finally, what they'd called me in there to say. You could see they didn't want to. They'd been put up to it. It was that plain.

"They have closed the doors of Alexander Hall to me, Antonio. They have closed them and bolted them tight."

There was the mess for one thing, they told him. Love Feasts no less than fish fries left litter—crumbs and wrappers, paper cups and Tropicana stains. Even after the supper of the Lamb somebody had to pick up the pieces. The dean laughed at the sheer triviality of the thing, his feet propped up on an open desk drawer, but there had been flak from the janitorial staff, and good janitors were harder to find than good deans. Or good shepherds, the chaplain said. Besides which there was the eternal question of precedent, the dean said, striking while the iron was at least lukewarm. It was one thing to make Alexander Hall available to a group like Bebb's for what had it been now—six weeks, two months?—but to perpetuate the thing beyond that was not only to give it official University endorsement which was something the trustees might be as hesitant to offer as Bebb to accept—*It's the kiss of death around here these days*—but also to open the door to you name it. Gay Lib, Leary's boys, Jehovah's Witnesses, Transcendental Meditators—if the University wrote Bebb a blank check, on what basis could they justify writing anything less for the Honorable Elijah Mohammed?

"Antonio," Bebb said with his head sunk back on my pillow, gazing out at Metzger's aerial against the grey sky, "there's plenty I could have said, only I didn't say it. Nancy Oglethorpe, she's got a clean-up squad goes over that place after every feast so there's not a janitor in the business could find fault with it. And talk about your sodomite societies and your Hindu jamborees, they're no more like—Antonio, Love Feast isn't some kind of Lodge or Clam Bake. I'm not asking the Nassau Hall crowd to do any more for me than that chaplain's asking them to do for him. I'm there to preach the good news to the poor, I'm there to give a cup of cold water to the least of these my brethren, these fine young brethren they've got there at Princeton University that are the salt of the earth except that they're tempted every whichway by things like drugs and sex and knocking the American way of life."

Bebb didn't say that at this point in the interview the dean lit his pipe, but even at that remove in time and space I could smell it—could smell that whole world of deans and pipes and stolen clappers that I had known myself in the early fifties. God knows times have changed and maybe people don't come as young as they used to, but even so I can't help believing—because with part of me anyway it's of course what I want to believe—that for everything I knew then there is still at least a reasonable facsimile going now: the tipsy labyrinth of a football weekend and the jolt of bouncing your first check to discover that life goes on anyway; courses in things like *Love and Death in Nineteenth Century Fiction* or *The History of History,* with titles so enchanted that not even taking them could ever quite break the spell. I wanted to believe that it was because the young still accepted all the ancient verities as basically unassailable that they could afford to assail every last one of them with the abandon of apes. I wanted to believe that they too believed, just as I had once believed, in the endless procrastination of old age and death, the lifetime guarantee of boyhood friendships and the inevitable victory of the martini over the Manhattan, Mozart over Mendelssohn, marriage over masturbation. In any case, as Bebb evoked that whole never-never land by his account of his brush with it at Nassau Hall, what moved me was not the thought of how it had menaced Bebb but of how Bebb had menaced it and what a fragile thing it was.

Bebb said, "The chaplain told me how way back in

the twenties sometime there was a group like Love Feasts got started on campus where everybody collected together and confessed things in public that were better left private. Sex things, Antonio. He didn't come right out and say sex things, but it was what he meant mostly. He said how it got out of hand and a lot of loose talk and loose living come out of it, and it gave the place a bad smell. I told him that wasn't the kind of show we were running at Alexander Hall and what was coming out of it wasn't loose living, it was souls saved for Jesus. Well, the dean, he put his oar in again. He said all they had to go on was what they'd heard tell from people who had been there. So I asked him what people, and that stopped him. He said he didn't want to get into personalities. He said there was no point naming names. And I'm going to come clean with you, Antonio. He was right. There was no point naming names because I knew what the name was without anybody had to name it. Roebuck, Antonio. From the first time I laid eyes on him, I knew Roebuck was out to get me.

"I went to see him," Bebb said. "That same day after I finished with the Nassau Hall boys, I went straight to that little hole-in-the-wall Roebuck's got him for an office over to McCosh Hall and put it right to him. He was there all by his self in those Army boots of his and a saucer full of cigarette butts. I said, 'Roebuck, you never made a secret of how you felt about me, and I never held it against you. Every man's got a right to come to Jesus in his own way, and if my way's not your way, there's no hard feelings. But you've kept on coming to the Love Feasts anyhow, and no matter what spiteful things you said, I never meant you anything but good. But all the time I was meaning you good, you meant me evil,

Roebuck, and now you've gone and turned this place against me. Roebuck, Roebuck,' I said, 'why persecutest thou me?' Then he took me by surprise, Antonio. I'll give him credit for that.

"He said, 'I believe we've met somewhere else, Mr. Bebb.' I didn't know what he meant, and I told him so. 'Let me refresh your memory,' he said. He doesn't look you in the eye when he talks to you. He looks at you up around where your hairline is, if you've got a hairline. He makes you feel like you've got another pair of eyes up there you never thought to use before."

Those two Bebbs. The one sitting at my desk straight as a chair-back in a Tyrolean hat and a pair of Thom McCann shoes not saying a word, buttoned up tight. The other one spread out on my bed like the stuffing of the first one.

Bebb said, "That man knows his history, Antonio. It's his special subject, and he knows it inside and out. He reeled off a whole list of times and places where he said we'd met before. He told about the days they had children eight, ten years old and up working in mines like pack mules maybe twelve hours at a stretch till their pitiful little bodies were nothing but skin and bones and they couldn't hardly see in the daylight while people like me went on looking the other direction and preaching thy kingdom come. He told about the days they tore the living flesh off people with red-hot tongs and broke their legs with hammers because they didn't believe like they should about doctrine. He went on how those old-time crusaders used religion for an excuse to rape women and raise hell and how back in slavery times there was ministers of the Gospel owned slaves just like everybody else and proved out of scripture it was the way things

152

was meant to be. I don't suppose there was a single miserable thing anybody ever did in the name of Jesus that Roebuck didn't spell out chapter and verse before he was done. He enjoyed it. You could tell from the way he worked his face what a good time he was having.

"He said each one of those times and places I was there, Antonio, and that's where we met before. He said I wasn't the type that beat the slaves and raped the women and tortured the heretics because I didn't have the balls for it. No, I was the type just closed my eyes to it and helped other people close their eyes to it by telling them a lot of fairy tales about Heaven. This trick eyelid of mine that goes shut on me sometimes without me even knowing about it, Roebuck said you didn't have to be a expert psychologist to explain that. He said that eyelid was a dead giveaway how the only way a man like me can go on believing in Almighty God is by pulling that eyelid down like a window blind between me and all the shit in the world that proves there isn't any Almighty God and never was or will be.

"You take a word like shit, Antonio. A preacher isn't even supposed to know there is those kind of words, and Roebuck, he thought he'd throw me a curve just using it. I said, 'Roebuck, you think I don't know about shit? What you've been telling me about isn't even a millionth part of all the shit there is because you've stuck to just the religious shit, and that's only one kind of all there is because piled up right alongside it there's a million other kinds. You take your big business, your politicians, your high-class colleges like Princeton. You take your haves and your have-nots both, your whorehouses and your W.C.T.U.'s. You take not just your redneck nigger-haters but your N double A's and your civil rights parades, not just your hard-hat flagwavers but your peaceniks and C.O.'s and love-ins. You take anything people have ever done in this world, and the best you can say about any of it is that it's maybe one part honest and well-meant and the other nine parts shit. If I close my eyelid down on all the shit there is in the world, I've still got to face up to all the shit there is in me, because I'm full of it too, Roebuck. I'm not denying it. And you're full of it. It's the shit in us is part of what makes us brothers, you and me.' I used that word shit to him till it begun to sound like I invented it.

"He caught me by surprise. I caught him by surprise. A preacher talking about things like—Antonio, shit is what preachers have been talking about since Moses except the word they're more like to use is sin. Only Roebuck didn't know that. It shut him up for a minute. Then he said, 'If the world's mostly shit, Bebb, where's God?' Just like that—where's God? As if I could say, 'Look, there he is, Roebuck, He's squeezed into one of those books you got on your shelves. He's out there a zillion miles northeast of the Milky Way. He's catching forty winks over in Alexander Hall till the next Love Feast gets off the ground.' That Roebuck was like a bird floating in the sky asking where's air, only I didn't say that then because I didn't think of it till later.

"I said, 'I'll tell you about shit, Roebuck. Take it from an expert. There's two main things about it. One thing is it's stink and corruption and waste. The other thing is if you don't pile it up too thick in any one place, it makes the seeds grow.' I said, 'Roebuck, God's where there's seeds growing. God's where there's something no bigger than the head of a pin starting to inch up out of the stink and dark of shit towards the light of day.' I said,

'Roebuck, God so loved the world he sent his only begotten son down here into the shit with the rest of us so something green could happen, something small and green and hopeful.'

"Roebuck said, 'I don't even know what you're talking about, Bebb,' but I could see he knew more than he was letting on just like all of us do, Antonio. A man that believes in the Almighty knows worse than he's letting on and a man that doesn't believe in the Almighty like Roebuck knows better, but we all of us know more. I said, 'Maybe you don't know what I'm talking about, Roebuck, but I know what you're talking about. All this about God and ancient history and so on, down deep what you're talking about is that boy you got home can't use his hands and feet. That's the main shit the world tossed in your direction, isn't it, Roebuck?'

"He said, 'Bebb, he can't even take his pecker out when he needs to make a leak. All his life he's going to have to have somebody around to take it out for him or just let go in his pants. Maybe someday he'll learn to hold a pencil in his asshole like that girl that draws Christmas cards. That's the only green and hopeful thing he's got.'

"Antonio, there's a whole mess of scriptures that has to do with things like Roebuck's boy, the pointless, dirty things that make you wonder if life's anything more than a popcorn fart. My ways are not thy ways, saith the Lord. Fear not. I could have rattled off a dozen of them without batting an eye only I didn't have the heart to, and it wouldn't have made a dent on Roebuck if I had. There wasn't a solitary thing I knew to say that I felt like saying, and it seemed as though Roebuck had run out of ammunition too. We both of us just sat there staring at each other. Then I saw something I didn't notice up till then. It was one of those little signs they have on desks with your name on it. Virgil M. Roebuck it said. All I knew up till then was just Roebuck, and then seeing that sign I thought to myself how this wasn't any old Roebuck. This was the Roebuck they'd settled on calling Virgil. This was the special Roebuck they'd pinned that special name Virgil onto and raised up to amount to something special, and here he was, not one of your big time professors that get their pictures in the papers but just Virgil Roebuck that smokes two, three packs a day if he smokes one and has this boy he's got to take his pecker out for him every time he needs to take a leak.

"Antonio, I busted in there mad as a hornet, but you can't stay mad when you start thinking things like that. Once you commence noticing the lines a man's got round his eyes and mouth and think about the hopeful way his folks gave a special name to him when he was first born into this world, you might as well give up.

"I said, 'Virgil, the night is dark, and we are far from home.' How come it was the words of that old hymn popped into my mind just then to say? I don't know, but it did. I said, 'The night is dark, Virgil Roebuck, and home's a long ways off for both of us.'

"He didn't say a word for a while. He just sat there at the desk in his Army boots and his cigarette between his teeth the way he does. Then he cupped his hand up over one eyebrow and tossed me one of those two-for-a-nickel highball salutes they used to do. He's out for my scalp, Antonio. I'm sure as I'm sitting here he's the one talked them into kicking me out of Alexander Hall. But he saluted me, Antonio, and it wasn't just to mock at me either. That salute was him saying maybe we're in two different battles. Maybe we're on two different sides. But when you come right down to it, the war we're in is the same war. Antonio, we're far from home, all of us are. Who's going to judge which of us has got the farthest way to go through all the shit and the dark?"

Bebb swung his legs over the edge of the bed and sat up to describe the last scene to me. His shirt had come untucked in back from the way he'd been lying and his trouser legs were hiked up baring his hairless, white calves. He leaned forward with his elbows on his knees, and I had the impulse to plump him into shape like a pillow and stuff him back into his tight-fitting jacket where he belonged.

He said, "It never rains but it pours. As if it wasn't enough to have the IRS and Nassau Hall both on my neck, I got a letter last week from the insurance company that handled things back when Open Heart burned down. Of course the people we rented from was the ones that had the insurance, but being as I was the tenant when it burnt, I had to fill in some forms and explain how I'd been using the barn for a church and so on. Everything was open and above board, and the people got money for a new barn without a hitch. Only now, four years later, the company's opened the whole business up again.

"Somebody's been telling tales out of school, Antonio. Back when the fire happened, it never come out Clarence Golden was living in that barn. I never made a feature of it because to tell the truth there didn't seem any cause to. I never set his name down in those forms because Fats Golden, he's had his share of hard knocks in this world and then some, and I didn't want to lay any more on him. It wasn't as if he was doing anything he shouldn't have, just camping out there because he didn't have anywheres else to lay his head. Inasmuch as ye have done it unto one of the least of these my brethren, ye have done it unto me, Antonio. That's why I told him he could bunk down out there while we were overseas. I didn't see any point stirring up the insurance company over a thing like that. Well, they've been stirred up.

"They wrote me somebody's gone and sent them an anonymous letter. Somebody's written a letter they didn't have the crust to sign their name to telling how the summer Open Heart burned down, there was a friend of mine living in it that once a long ways back did time. I expect you know Clarence Golden did time once, Antonio. He never was one to make a secret of it. So they're reopening the case on the grounds the fire that burned down Open Heart wasn't necessarily an accident. They didn't come straight out and accuse anybody, but they said they've got their lawyers working on it. They want me to come answer some questions.

"My nose is clean, Antonio. I wasn't there when that fire happened, and even if it was set on purpose, I didn't stand to make a dime out of it. I lost a lot of property including the pulpit and the undertaker chairs and the hymn books and that big preaching Bible I wouldn't have taken any kind of money for. It wasn't me that collected on the insurance, it was the people that owned the place, and there's not a lawyer in Christendom could prove any different. But there's two things that keep me awake nights, and I'll tell you the worst one first.

"A man has enemies. In my line of work, it goes with the territory and you got to expect it—you even got to be thankful for it. Blessed are ye when men shall revile you and persecute you and shall say all manner of evil against you falsely for my sake. It's a honor to have the same kind of enemies Jesus had. Like that banty rooster tax collector, that Connor who's trying to force me to render unto Caesar what isn't Caesar's because it's Jesus's and I've told him so to his face. Or Roebuck. Roebuck's just the latest, souped up model of the fool that saith in his heart there is no God and is out to nail anybody that says different because deep down he's scared of the competition. Roebuck's scared. Why do you think he wears those boots of his like there was a war on? But whoever wrote that anonymous letter and didn't sign his name to it, that's another kind of enemy. I don't know who it is, Antonio. I don't know why he's out to get me. He could be a stranger. He could be somebody I've done some deep and hurtful thing to without even knowing it. He could be anybody, and there isn't hardly a person I know or ever did know I haven't tried fitting his face onto just for size. Even in dreams. He's a enemy without a face that follows me even into the dreams where a man goes to find rest and guidance for the days ahead.

"The second thing is Clarence Golden. There's some ways Clarence Golden's the—*five years*, Antonio. Him and me, we were together five years day in day out till there wasn't hardly any closer two people can come this side of matrimony. I'm not saying there aren't times he's an awful pain in the tail. You never know when he's going to turn up or what way he's going to find to devil you about something. Like the way he covered the walls of Open Heart with pictures straight out of my life, private things, Antonio, I could no more have left up there for the world to see if that fire hadn't happened than I could have stood up and preached the Kingdom buck naked. But he's my old friend, and I don't want any harm to come to him, and now he's in worse trouble than I am, and it's on my account he's in it. When those insurance lawyers start looking into things, they're going to look into Clarence Golden."

Bebb had been staring down at his feet all this time, but at this point he looked up at me, and for one moment his trick eyelid fluttered.

He said, "Antonio, Clarence Golden is a firebug. What those lawyers are bound to dig up about him is the thing he did time for way back was arson."

Thus the woes of Leo Bebb. He stood up, ready by then to move out, go somewhere, and I stood up too, ready, God knows, to have him go. He threw his arms up over his head in a monumental stretch, groaning and making faces, tossing his fat shoulders around to loosen them up, and I found myself echoing his gesture so that we stood there facing each other for a moment both with our arms in the air.

Our woes met, Bebb's spoken and mine unspoken because how was I to speak to him of Sharon and Tony holding on to each other for dear life? It was like a high sea at the beach when the waves rolling in and the waves rolling out collide with a teeth-rattling slap and sky-high explosion of foam—Bebb's speech and my silence meeting head-on with such a jolt that it had us both on our feet like fans at a touchdown.

Conner. Roebuck. The writer of the anonymous letter. The possibility that they would all somehow get together to overthrow Bebb if in some subterranean way they hadn't gotten together already, weren't in fact all three the same person in three clever disguises. Bebb wasn't there for either my advice or my condolences, however, and whatever fumbling combination of the two I started to serve him up he literally turned his back on as he vigorously set about putting himself back together again—tucking in his shirt, tightening up his tie, putting back on his jacket and shiny black shoes, until there was only one Bebb again, as buttoned up and battened down as ever.

He was also apparently not there to inquire into the state of things between Sharon and me. At the diner later, where he insisted on paying for my supper, he made at least a stab at raising the subject but waited until I had my mouth full of cheeseburger to do it and by the time I'd swallowed enough to choke out something about how there wasn't really much new, he was off into plans for a student demonstration against Nassau Hall for exiling him from the campus. I don't know why Bebb was there. All I knew was that not even the rock of ages can cleave for thee very well when it's round as a pumpkin and rolling downhill at seventy-five miles per hour.

CHAPTER TEN

"LAURA?" I said. "This is Antonio Parr." Not Antonio. It was too soon for that. Not Mr. Parr. It was too late for that. I was using the phone underneath the stairs. The kitchen door was open, and I could see Mrs. Gunther opening a can of Puss 'n Boots. She had the radio on with the dial set somewhere between the six o'clock news and the bagpipe version of *Amazing Grace*. Upstairs Tony was taking a shower. Metzger was alone in his room reading the evening paper out loud. The cat Mrs. Gunther was fixing supper for was stretched out on the glass top of a display case full of hat pins and souvenir spoons with one paw hanging over the edge.

"Oh my goodness," Laura Fleischman said. "I thought I recognized your voice."

I knew where everybody in the house was at that moment, and looking back on it, I picture where everybody else was at that moment too.

Sharon is at the gas station across the road from the Salamander Motel. There is a sandwich machine out front, and she is standing in front of it in a halter and shorts while Bill reaches up to drop the money in. The sun is blinding on the white stucco gas station wall and on the white road.

Spring has come to Gouverneur Road, and Bebb and Gertrude Conover are coming home from a drive with Gertrude Conover at the wheel. She sits with her chin pointed down toward one shoulder and seems to be gazing as much out of the side window as through the windshield so that even while driving she looks like a passenger. As they turn into the driveway of Revonoc, Bebb reaches out through the window like a Chinese emperor and breaks off a sprig of forsythia.

Nancy Oglethorpe is typing out a dissertation on The Civil Service Reforms of Chester A. Arthur, and as she leans forward to make an erasure, her breasts crush against the keys and trigger the tabulator which slams the carriage back to the farthest margin and rings the bell.

Charlie Blaine is walking slowly from the garage back to the kitchen porch. He steps on a crocus without knowing it and skins his bare arm against the side of the house. His eyes are closed because he is checking out what it is going to be like to be blind.

Darius Bildabian has stayed overtime at his office to make some denture repairs. With an upper plate in one hand and a lower plate in the other, he holds them out at arms' length through the curtained door of the waiting room where his twelve year old son Mardik is waiting for him and clacks them up and down to make them say, "What's up, Doc?"

Roebuck, a red bandanna handkerchief tied around his forehead like a pirate, is playing squash with a colleague from the Philosophy Department, and after a long day at the shop, Anita Steen is soaking in a hot tub with a bourbon on the floor beside her and a copy of Rod McKuen in one dry claw.

I say, "Does that invitation for a homecooked meal still hold?"

"You mean tonight?" Laura Fleischman says. In the background I can hear a noise like a car going over railroad tracks. "Let me turn the washer off."

At the unmistakable sound of Mrs. Gunther's setting the plastic dish down on the linoleum, the cat drops lightly to the floor and starts toward the kitchen hugging the wall with her tail in the air. A thump overhead makes me wonder for a moment if Metzger is signaling for help at last, but craning out as far as the telephone cord will let me, I catch a glimpse of Tony's bare rump as he stalks heavy-footed to his bedroom and think to myself that it is not given to every man to behold with such Olympian detachment the nakedness of his wife's lover.

"Look," Laura Fleischman said, "I just checked the ice box, and I mean if you don't mind taking pot luck, I can whip up something if you want to come over. Mother had to go to Toledo because her sister's dying, so there's just me."

"And we will take upon us the mystery of things," I said for lack of anything else. "As if we were God's spies."

The mystery of things. To year after year of Sutton

High seniors I have explained that what the old king seems to mean is that only God and his spies see that it is the things themselves that are the mystery—all the people there are, in all the places there are, doing all the things they are doing at any given moment of time. While I stood there under the stairs making my call, at the same moment Mrs. Fleischman's sister was dying in Toledo and upstairs Tony Blaine was studying his young flesh in his dresser mirror for signs of advancing middle age. All the people in the world are always doing something, somewhere, and for all I know the dead are too—Lucille floating like a water lily in the lion's pool and Herman Redpath with his whistle around his neck. In a classroom smelling of steam heat, chalk dust, flatulence, pencils, hair spray, breath—themselves all part of the mystery—I tried over the years to explain that to see things the way Lear says God sees them is not so much to see through them to some mystery beyond or within as just to see them as they are. As mysteries go, that is staggering enough for anybody. I clipped my fingernails. I put on a clean shirt. I took two of the vitamin C pills Sharon had given me. I picked up a fifth of Dewar's on the way. Ripeness is all.

I had never been in Laura Fleischman's house before, the chief mystery of which was that for a house that had seen all twenty-odd years of her comings and goings, it seemed to have left as little mark on her as she on it. The nubbly wall-to-wall carpet of swimming pool blue, the Barcalounger in homespun vinyl, the cataract stare of the TV which wore like an old lady's hat a foil-wrapped pot of African violets on a crocheted doily and the what-not shelf of Reader's Digest condensed books with a tinted photograph of the late Mr. Fleischman on

165

top—to have an eye for the kind of things that mark the boundaries between classes in a classless society is curse enough let alone to blunder into marking them sharper still as I knew I had the moment I produced my fifth of Dewar's and set it down on Mrs. Fleischman's sewing table. A drink before dinner—I had grown up in a world where that eloquent little semicolon between the clauses of a day was as inevitable as day itself. Even alone at Mrs. Gunther's I had my evening drink as at Revonoc Gertrude Conover did and elsewhere all the blue-haired ladies and the old Tigers and Elis they were married to. More than the clothes we wear or the language we speak, it is the final shibboleth that will give us away when the African violets and tinted photographs of the world rise against us at last, and all I can say is that the poise with which Laura Fleischman stepped out into the kitchen for glasses and ice was in its way no less memorable than the relaxed banalities of the astronauts as they first stepped out on the alien surface of the moon.

Unlike the day when she had caught me by surprise at Bildabian's office, this time we had both come prepared with conversation enough to see us through and to spare, but if forewarned is forearmed, it is also foredoomed, or at least foredoomed to stick to your conversational guns until the last round you have come grimly supplied with has been fired.

Her job with Bildabian, and her plans for the future; her sick aunt. The old days at Sutton High, the prospects in track that spring, the wet weather. Salvo after salvo, we shot them all off, each from his own emplacement, until I despaired more and more of the moment's ever coming when like opposing troops on Christmas eve we could crawl out and meet like brothers in the no man's land between. I sat on the couch with my feet on the coffee table. Laura sat across from me on a leatherette ottoman with her bare arms and shoulders tanned by some burst of sunlight that must have happened that week while I was looking in the other direction. Facing us was the Barcalounger of Mrs. Fleischman and the tinted likeness of Mr. Fleischman from the shelf with the condensed books.

She was thinking of leaving Bildabian, she said, because there were things about the job she didn't like, then maybe moving in with a friend in New York and trying to find a new job there. I said I thought Sutton stacked up pretty well in racing but didn't stand a chance in the javelin or shot put. I said there had been a lot of changes at school since her day, but there were most of the same old faces on the faculty. I had two scotches to her one, but each swallow left me only soberer than before to the point where my despair was so great by the time she got up to go check on supper that I asked if there was a john I could use less because I needed to use it than because, like getting up and walking around the card table, I thought the move might change our luck. It was upstairs, she said. The second door I came to.

I opened the first door I came to instead and found myself in her room. *Blue night* was what my son Bill called twilight in those days, and blue night lay light as snow on the ruffled tester of the four-poster bed and the white nurse's uniform on a hanger hooked over the closet door. A muslin curtain floated out on the damp air, and on the wall near me hung a photograph of her graduating class, the girls in their long white dresses, with a slip of Palm Sunday palm tucked in behind the frame. The bed was opened with her nightdress laid out over the foot. There was a desk in the corner and on the desk a copy of her class yearbook. I had brought my glass of Dewar's with me, and setting it down on the desk, I turned on the lamp and took the yearbook up in my hands. Downstairs I could hear the sound of the ice box being opened and shut, the click of china, and I thought of how the labor of our conversation-making must have left her as tired and sad as it had left me, and of how once we had eaten our supper and I had stayed out my time and gone home, this was the room that she would come home to. I pictured her reaching up into the night-dress she had laid out for herself like her own nurse, pictured her reading herself to sleep in that cool bed. Like a child on his way to the principal's office, I thought how in a few hours I would also be, if not safe in my own bed because maybe there is no place on earth less safe, at least reprieved in it for a while as I looked back through closed eyes on the failure of our evening together.

I opened the year-book at the page that was marked, and on that page there was a picture of myself frowning into the sun in my baggy sweat suit complete with clip-board and stopwatch. Marking the page there were two things—a red plastic muddler from the Grand Central bar where we had once met by accident and a note I had apparently written from France, some five years before.

It said, *Dear Laura,*

> *Congratulations two weeks late on your 18th birthday. 18 is a good age to be as ages go, and I hope you will hang on to it as long as you can. I read your letter at an inn where they say Sir Francis Drake got word that the Armada had been sighted*

*off Land's End, and a theosophist who was traveling
with us said our room was obviously haunted. Can
you tell me a room that isn't? I am writing this from
a hotel in Paris where the armada of traffic under
our window all night makes such a racket that it's
like sleeping in the Lincoln Tunnel. The only ghost
that's with me at the moment is yours. I can see you
sitting at the back of the classroom in your usual
seat trying like a waiter not to catch my eye for fear
you'll be the one I call on if you do. I should be
haunted by ghosts like that more often. I'm sorry to
hear about you and Carl West, but I'm glad you're
taking it philosophically if not theosophically.
Never mind, someday all in green your love will
come riding, and in the meantime thanks for your
letter and think kindly once in a while of your old
English teacher and friend, Antonio Parr.*

That cumbersomely avuncular note enshrined there
like a piece of the true cross—I replaced it with the
muddler between the pages where it belonged and had
turned to go back downstairs when I found Laura Fleischman standing at the door.

"So now you know," I said. "I'm one of God's spies."

"I told you we all had a crush on you," she said.
"Every paper you ever wrote a comment on I kept put
away somewhere. You must think I'm an awful fool."

I said, "The fool that wrote that letter was an awful
fool. I don't even remember writing it, if that's any
excuse."

"I remember getting it," she said. "I bet I read it fifty
times the day it came."

I said, "Maybe it starts to grow on you after a while."

"Anyway," she said, "supper's ready. I was afraid you'd given up hope," and I said, "Everything but," and switched off the lamp on the desk so that the room turned into blue night again.

She said, "I feel so stupid sometimes when I'm with a person like you, talking a blue streak about a lot of stuff I'm not even all that interested in myself. Maybe it's my job that's made me such a chatterbox. When you've got your hand in somebody's mouth, the only one that's left to do the talking is you."

We were both standing together in the doorway now, and as she turned around to go, I put my hands on her shoulders and turned her back again, and that was how we finally met face to face in no man's land.

The Chinese Emperor places the spray of forsythia in a glass of stale water threaded with bubbles while full of tubes and needles the sister of Mrs. Fleischman dreams of walking along a beach at low tide. Sharon slides a five dollar bill through the window, and a pair of tickets leap up at her like tongues, a pink for her, a green for Bill. Billie Kling places the thumb and forefinger of one hand on the eyeballs of Charlie Blaine, and in the voice of somebody making a transatlantic phone call tells him he has nothing to fear but fear itself. Alexander Hall is dark and empty, and under one of the pews a single potato chip lies like an autumn leaf. The mystery of things.

"And what more shall I say," wrote Saint Paul in a passage that I heard Bebb hold forth on more than once. "For the time would fail me to tell of Gideon and Barak, of Samson and Jephtha, of David also and Samuel and the prophets. These all died in faith, not having received the promises but having seen them afar off, confessing that they were strangers and pilgrims on the earth." I put my hands on the shoulders of Laura Fleischman, and in that room with the curtains afloat and the blue night deepening, one thing led to another thing until at the end of all the things that happened, I received the promise, received from that twenty-two year old girl what would have stopped David himself dead in his tracks and made all the prophets drop their shaggy jaws.

The girls in their long dresses waited with their backs to the wall. The white tester trembled above us like a coif. The headlights of cars drifted slowly across the ceiling. To the consternation of Samson, there came a point where I was afraid my rod and my staff would fail me and I would have to be content like the rest of them with having only seen that promising land I could not enter. It nearly came to that, I don't know why—less the scotch, I think, than my sense of history—but in the end it didn't. I was spared that lesser, fleshly failure for the sake of a ghostlier and greater, which is to say that I made my entrance straight and tall only to find that even then I was still afar off, a stranger and a pilgrim to that fragrant earth.

I remember lifting her hair, weightless, in my hand and finding that it weighed about what blue night does or rain. I remember remembering that to make love is to make nonsense of opposites like soft and hard, chill and warm, swift and slow; it is no longer either-or but both-and, each a pair of ways to speak a single truth. Desire and despair.

I remember that after a while we slept for a little with only a fringe of light from the hall to cover us, and when I woke, she was asleep beside me like a pool of shadows except where the light made her islands in a pool, and I was all gooseflesh in the cool air, trying to withdraw to some deep place inside my skin, or to the warm places where our skin touched, to keep from shivering her awake. She was asleep with one arm unfolded across me, and I thought of all those months I had watched her at the back of my classroom, that girl who from the highest flight of her beauty could go nowhere, I thought then, but away from it, away from me, but who lay there asleep now at my side while downstairs our uneaten supper lay in ruins, the sherbet melting into the fruit salad. I dreaded the moment she would open her eyes and I would have to say something, pick up somehow and go home when I had no home to go home to and knew she was not my home either any more than I was hers as she was bound to know too as soon as she opened her eyes, if she didn't know it already. Only she didn't open her eyes. She spoke with them closed so that for all I knew she'd been awake the whole time too.

She said, "We used to have a bet to see which of us would be the first to kiss you, and Lois Kinney almost won. You were leaning over to correct her paper once, and she said she came so close to it she almost died, only at the last moment she chickened out. You probably didn't even know."

She said, "You don't have to worry this was my first time or anything like that because my first time was with Carl West. I didn't want to, but he wanted to so much I let him. That time you and I met at the station, I knew the moment you touched my hand that I would with you too, if you asked me to. Afterwards I used to think about it going to sleep at night, thousands of times. I'd think where we'd have gone together and how it all would have happened. I knew it was bound to happen someday just the way I always dreamed it would."

With her eyes still closed and her words more breath than sound in the hollow at the base of my throat, she said, "I just want you to know I wanted it to happen, and I'm glad it happened the way it did, and I don't want you to worry about anything because it was the way I wanted it."

I tried to say something, but I was stuttering with cold by then, Stephen Kulak, and it was like every joke you'll ever live to hear about the green bridegroom on his wedding night because I rolled over on my side to face her closed eyes then and ran my hand down between her shoulder blades and the length of her spine to her cold little tail for all the world as though no one had ever explained to me that there was any more to it than that, and when to my slapstick dismay I found myself rising again to the very occasion I had every cause to shrink from, time again would fail me to tell of the sadness and loneliness of my pilgrimage. To make love with so nearly a stranger usually fans the spark of an old lecher's heart, but to make love when he is himself the stranger is to turn the heart to stone. This time we both fell asleep, and when I woke again, it was daylight, and Laura Fleischman was gone.

When I went downstairs, I found her in the kitchen making breakfast. She had on her nurse's uniform with her hair brushed back into the silver barette, and I was unshaven with my teeth unbrushed, my hair in my eyes. I said, "The man who came to dinner," and she said, "I had to throw the dinner out. It wasn't much anyway."

She said, "I was just about to come up and wake you. I knew you wouldn't want to be late for school," and I wondered if that was really what she had been about to do and how she would have gone about doing it and how things might have turned out differently for us both if she had. In her place, I would probably have sneaked out the back door with as little noise as possible.

She was standing at the counter in her white dress, her white stockings and shoes, pouring milk into a pitcher like a girl in a Vermeer, and I said, "What time are you supposed to be at Bildabian's?"

"I'm supposed to be there like about ten minutes ago," she said with her back to me still, "but I always arrive a little late so the appointment girl's sure to be there first. I don't like being there alone with him."

"Is he after you?" I said.

She said, "That's why I'm quitting," and as she turned toward me with the pitcher in her hand—frowning at the thought of Bildabian's toothy advances, I suppose, of quitting her job and moving to New York—for a moment it was no longer she in one place and I in another place and the emptiness between us a place that wasn't home for either of us, but both of us were together in the same place, and it was a place I was afraid I might be homesick for for the rest of my life if I had to leave it now. As she came toward me frowning that way with her eyes lowered, I was for a moment her teacher again and she was my student, and within the protection of that old relationship I felt secure enough to face the possibility that for better or worse I could never leave her again at all. But only for a moment, because as she sat down at the table and looked up at me finally as if it wasn't the easiest thing she'd ever done in her life but not the hardest either, she was not my student any more but a girl I hardly knew in a world where there was no protection, and the only way I dared to play it was to play it safe.

I said, "Listen, I'm not Bildabian, but I'm not Prince Valiant either. I'm a nice place to visit, but you wouldn't want to live there. I had a dream at Christmas time that all these years I haven't even known my right name, and even after they told me what it was, I couldn't remember it."

She said, "There's nothing you have to be sorry about. You don't have to say anything you don't want."

I sometimes think that all the major dramas of my life have taken place in kitchens, and maybe that's because in kitchens there's always something else to fall back on if the going gets tough, like cooking or eating or doing the dishes. And maybe that's the real drama after all— just keeping yourself alive day after day and cleaning up afterwards. I remember watching Laura Fleischman pour milk out of the pitcher into her dry cereal with the rustle of autumn leaves. I remember sunlight on her bare arm as she reached out for the sugar, and I remember the bitter taste of my coffee. We were keeping alive.

I said, "Do me a favor, will you, and be happy for God's sake? I mean right now I could list all the happy people I know on the back of a six cent stamp, and I'm not even sure about them because it takes one to know one."

She looked at her watch and said, "Bildabian's not going to be happy. I've got to take off." So it ended up that I was the one to see her to the door instead of the other way round, and there in the hall, with Mrs. Fleischman's Barcalounger facing us from the living room, what I kissed goodbye was more than just a girl who smelled of breakfast and Ivory soap.

I read an article in the *Times* once on the stages that the old go through on their way toward death, and somewhere along the line they apparently go through one called *decathexis,* which the *Times* defined as "an emotional detachment from life." Ordinarily this stage comes on gradually and toward the end of the line, but for me it came rather abruptly and no nearer my end than I was as I stood just inside the Fleischman's screen door.

Having entered such a place as Gideon and the others only dreamed of, I discovered that even there I was a stranger and a pilgrim with years to go ahead of me still and my heart no longer in it. As I kissed Laura Fleischman goodbye there in the hall, my heart wasn't even in the goodbye let alone in the kiss. There was nothing I had to let go that I hadn't let go already, and though I suppose that if the loss hadn't mattered at all, I wouldn't have noticed it, all I can say is that it didn't much matter to me that it mattered. With hardly a pang I watched her swing out of the driveway and drive off in the direction of town. Decathexis.

After she'd gone, I went upstairs to get my jacket and tie, and while I was at it, I made the bed too, made crisp hospital corners and smoothed the white spread flat with the palm of my hand. A feather came out of one of the pillows as I plumped it, and before I left, I opened the year book on her desk and laid it between the proper pages. Then I closed the book and went on back to Mrs. Gunther's to wash up and shave.

CHAPTER ELEVEN

AT BEBB'S INSISTENCE I went down to Princeton the following Saturday to be on hand for the historic march on Nassau Hall protesting his eviction from campus, and for a man who had so recently become emotionally detached from things, I went with surprising enthusiasm. To let go of your life does not mean that your life necessarily lets go of you. I've heard it said that in great office buildings even after the boss has gone home and the doors have been locked behind him, the self-service elevators continue to work off the uncompleted calls of the day, those empty cars moving relentlessly from floor to floor for hours afterwards. Sharon and Laura Fleischman, my nephew Tony and my son Bill, not to mention my students and colleagues at Sutton High—they all continued to work at me if only in my head, and it was more to elude them for a while than to witness how things were going to turn out for Bebb in Princeton that I set out again on the well beaten track past the great bridge, Grant's Tomb, the West Side piers, and down under the river through my father's tunnel.

It was the first really lovely day of spring we'd had and nowhere lovelier than at Princeton when I arrived. The magnolias were out at Revonoc. The swimming pool was full. A negro with cotton in his nostrils was mowing the lawn, and the house was full of the fragrance of newly cut grass. Gertrude Conover met me in the hall and greeted me with such an unusual air of distraction that I wondered if she had sent her astral body off on an errand somewhere. She said that Bebb had already gone on to Alexander Hall where the marchers were assembling, and if I wanted to be on time, I'd better hurry.

She said, "I don't need to tell you this isn't the first of his incarnations I've known, and in every single one of them he's gotten himself mixed up in something like this. His aura gets bright as a hundred watt bulb, and the rest of us are drawn to it as moths to a flame. That time in Egypt when he was a priest of Ptah, for instance. Don't think for a minute that I was the only one to get burned. Even the Pharaoh is still paying the price, a man who had every reason to expect that by this time he would have made a nice little advance toward cosmic consciousness. And look at him now."

I said, "Where is the Pharaoh now?"

"His name is Callaway, and he is mowing the grass," she said. "His second wife has left him with seven children to support, all of them under ten. They have a cold-water flat on John Street."

"How much does he know about his previous incarnation?" I said, and it was moments before she seemed to hear my question as she stood there on the black and white tiles like a threatened queen.

Finally she said, "All that poor man knows is that he's been having nosebleeds ever since Leo moved in. He thinks it's some kind of allergy. Imagine it—a man who once held the power of life and death over thousands right in the palm of his hand."

"Here," she said. "Leo is going to want this for the march. Do you mind taking it to him?" It was Bebb's maroon preaching robe which lay draped over the bannister, and by the time she'd picked it up and handed it to me, I think she'd forgotten why.

Bebb was delighted to get it. I found him—that hundred watt bulb and scourge of Pharaohs—standing in the midst of some hundred or so followers who were milling around in front of the glassed-in Romanesque entrance to Alexander Hall. His bald head was pearled with sweat in the spring sun. He had on the kind of dark glasses that you can see through only from the inside. He was in his shirtsleeves and pale with excitement as he threw his arms around me and hugged me to him. It was the first and last time he ever hugged me to him. He said, "Antonio, this is the day that the Lord hath made. Let's you and I rejoice and be glad in it," and when I'd helped him into his robe and he stood there larger than life in the red of martyrdom with mirrors for eyes, he could have been the god Ptah himself.

In describing the great march and everything it precipitated for Bebb and all of us, I lean heavily on a special issue of the *Daily Princetonian* which was

brought out the next day under the banner headline
BEBB EMBATTLED: THE FALL OF THE HALL. For all his
excessively alliterative and telegraphic journalese, the
undergraduate reporter did his homework thoroughly
and supplied a wealth of detail including the *ipsissima
verba* of various eyewitnesses which help convey the
overall sweep of the thing better than I could, who was
caught up in my own particular backwash. Backwash is
the word. Two cups of coffee have always had the effect
on me of two quarts of beer, and having foolishly not
taken time to relieve myself after leaving Sutton that
morning, I was so preoccupied with my own inner dis-
tress that everything I saw was colored by it. I suppose a
man's view of history is always colored by something,
and if I saw the gaudy events of the day primarily in
terms of the occasion they might or might not offer for
satisfying my homely need, the undergraduate reporter
seems to have seen them in terms of conspiracy.
Whereas what I saw behind every tree was a potential
haven for myself, what he saw was new evidence that
Bebb had planned everything out with extraordinary
foresight and cunning. I don't think this view is correct.
I think many of the things that happened happened by
chance. But who knows? Maybe right from the first day I
ever laid eyes on him, Bebb was more cunning than I
ever gave him credit for. Or maybe Gertrude Conover's
theosophic dictum is right and there is no such thing as
chance anyway.

Be that as it may, the *Prince* begins with a verbatim
transcript of Bebb's address to his followers before the
march began as Nancy Oglethorpe captured it on her
tape recorder, holding the small black microphone up
at him like an enema tube. They had all gathered on

the blacktop between Alexander and the Presbyterian Church carrying their home-made placards and bed-sheets lettered with slogans like *Love is a Feast* and *Tell Your Troubles to Jesus, Ban the Bomb not Bebb* and *Nassau Hall Go Home*. There was a Campus Cop named McCartney on duty in his little kiosk right in the midst of them, but he gave no sign of being particularly disturbed by what was going on all around him, and there seemed to be no reason why he should have been. In their jeans and bell-bottoms, their shorts and bare feet, they looked no more menacing than the usual bunch you might find queued up at the movies any night of the week. There wasn't so much as a water pistol in sight, and such shenanigans as there were could hardly have been more pastoral and innocent. Some flower children presented Officer McCartney with a daisy chain, and a black track star scaled one of the squat turrets to scatter a bag or two of paper rosepetals, and that was about the length of it. Officer McCartney apparently phoned in a routine report just to play it safe, but the Proctors' Office didn't even bother to investigate. "In Nassau Hall business went on as usual," as the *Prince* put it. "President's secretary typing out honorary degree citations. In University Chapel choir rehearses *Also hat Gott die Welt Geliebt* for Sunday service. Dean Borden is home sprucing up for alumni dinner in Allentown, Pa. Rainbow colored Frisbies tossed among sun worshipers in nearby Holder court."

It was somewhere around eleven when Bebb finally mounted a green wooden bench and delivered his marching orders. He took his text not from Scripture for once but from the annals of the American Revolution. He said, "It's going on two hundred years since General

George Washington struck a great blow for liberty right here in Princeton, New Jersey, and today we're going to follow in his footsteps and strike us another one. You and me, we're going to march on Nassau Hall and ask for the liberty to keep on having our Love Feasts here in Alexander Hall where we've been having them right along. That's the whole show in a nutshell. I've got a petition in my hand signed with near on to three hundred John Hancocks, and I'm fixing to put it personally right into the hand of the President himself. Folks, we're not asking for the moon. All we're pushing for is the liberty to keep on saving souls on this historic campus just like they're supposed to be saving them over there to the University Chapel."

Bebb launched forth then into a rather rambling account of the Battle of Princeton and the events leading up to it. He told how Washington had first struck at Trenton while the Heinies were still hungover from Christmas, and how he had taken it as easy as taking crackers off a shelf. He told how then the British in their fancy red jackets and tight pants had hotfooted it down from Princeton to win it back the next morning and how Washington had outfoxed them by marching around their lines under cover of darkness and striking at Princeton the next day while it was virtually undefended.

According to Virgil Roebuck, who was interviewed by the *Prince* later, it was in this section of the speech that Bebb had tipped his hand as to the foxiness he had in mind himself. "You got to hand it to that mother," Roebuck was quoted as saying. "He as good as gave the whole show away when he told about the Princeton campaign, but who the hell learns anything from history?" I'm not sure about that. As things turned out, it is undeniably true that Bebb employed some of the same tactics as his famous predecessor, but it is hard for me to believe that he was playing cat and mouse in his oration. If he was tipping his hand, I don't think he knew that he was. If he was making any comparisons, I don't think it was a comparison of tactics with tactics but of himself with Washington—both of them down on their luck, beleaguered, up against terrible odds. I remember the emotion in his voice as he stood there with the sweat running down and describing how Washington crossed the Delaware "with cakes of ice the size of refrigerators on every side," how he resisted all temptation to "throw in the jock and head back for Virginia where the future First Lady of the land was waiting to welcome him with open arms."

Then "Boys," he said. "Boys, we got the Father of our Country on our side and we got our Father who art in Heaven on our side too, and that's a hard combination to beat. Let's move off to Nassau Hall for Jesus." So Jesus, God, General Washington, and maybe the Sphinx too if he remembered Gertrude Conover's theory that the Sphinx was only the General in an earlier avatar—I believe it was they, rather than any elaborate strategem, that filled Bebb's heart as he led his followers forward, with me and my distended bladder keeping up as best we could.

From Alexander Hall to Nassau Hall is no distance at all if you take the direct route, but in order I suppose to give the thing maximum exposure, Bebb followed a very indirect one. We headed toward Witherspoon first, and from Witherspoon off toward the Blair arch where with our shoe leather clattering like applause down the enormous flight of stone steps we descended into the lower campus. The marchers must have numbered well over one hundred and fifty by then, and needless to say they attracted a good deal of attention as they snaked slowly along with their hymns and placards. Faces appeared in dormitory windows, and bodies choked the entryways. Sunbathers abandoned their transistors and six-packs to fall in behind. Passers-by stopped dead in their tracks, and some of them fell in behind too. Bright as a Kentucky redbird against the grey Gothic stone, Bebb strode along at the head of the long procession like a visiting head of state, but he kept breaking ranks to shake hands and exchange pleasantries with the onlookers, then hoisting his skirts to catch up again at his fat man's lightfoot trot. The column was stretched out at such length that sometimes a hymn would rise up from one segment of it and something like *Going Back* or *Crash through that Line of Blue* from another. Nancy Oglethorpe and her aides kept fanning out to distribute flyers that showed a mug shot of Bebb with the astonished stare of a man shot out of a cannon—above him WANTED, below him FOR BRINGING THE GOSPEL TO GOMORRAH. All of this in the loveliest spring imaginable with only a few clouds gathering on the horizon, a kind of children's crusade with Bebb as Peter the Hermit or an overstuffed Pied Piper.

Ambushed by Atheists was the subhead under which the *Prince* reporter described the single untoward incident that marred the otherwise leisurely, picnic air of it all, the only foreshadowing of trouble to come, and the way it happened was this. The marchers wound their way around past the lower battlements of the gym, then up the sloping road that leads back to the heart of the campus again where it turns sharp right past those twin Greek temples, Whig and Clio, and on toward the

184

library and the Chapel. The rear of Nassau Hall loomed up on our left like the Promised Land, massive and ivy-covered, and we could have approached it from there, but Bebb's idea was to make his grand entrance at the front instead so we continued on past it until we reached Murray Dodge, and it was there that the incident took place.

An undergraduate group that called itself Atheists for Democratic Action had set up a roadblock. There must have been fifteen or twenty of them all told. Some of them were holding up a huge placard that showed a caricature of Bebb as a fat convict in prison stripes with a halo over his head and the legend *Back Behind Bars with Bebb*. Others had stretched an American flag out across the road where the parade had to pass with an atheist at each corner to hold it down and several others armed with cameras to record the desecration in case Bebb chose to lead the faithful over it. The procession came to a halt. There was a certain amount of catcalling back and forth. The atheists set off some firecrackers when Nancy Oglethorpe tried to approach them with a handful of flyers. Bebb walked forward with his right hand extended to offer peace. The rear portions of the procession had crowded forward to see what was going on, several of them got their hands on the flag, and the next thing I knew, a scuffle had broken out.

It never turned into a free-for-all luckily—the action was pretty much limited to where the flag was—but both Bebb and Nancy Oglethorpe were caught up in it. Neither of them actually gave battle as far as I could tell, but I could see their heads bobbing around in a sea of heaving shoulders and flying elbows. I remember Bebb's flushed and desperate face, his robe pulled half off one

185

shoulder, and I wondered if like Washington he was tempted to give the whole business up and go home to the open arms of Gertrude Conover and the peaceful terrace of Revonoc. But "I am a church" he had said that dreary time in my bedroom at Mrs. Gunther's, and I suppose that meant to him that you took things as they came whether they were the ravening lions of martyrdom or this sweaty Mardi Gras of ponytailed Princetonians most of whom didn't give a hoot in hell whether the church stood or fell flat on its face. Anyway it didn't last long. The Atheists for Democratic Action were vastly outnumbered. The Love Feasters captured the flag, and the next time I saw it, Nancy Oglethorpe had it draped around her shoulders like a beach towel. With her beehive in tatters and her face streaked like a Comanche's with her melting pancake, she started the march going again. It was at this point that, unable to contain myself any longer, I ducked into Murray Dodge to find a can, and by the time I came out again, hysterical with relief, the mob had disappeared around the far end of Nassau Hall to take up their vigil out front.

There must have been close to three hundred of them by then gathered out under the regal elms. The atheists had joined them and so had brunchers from the Student Center and scholars from the Firestone stacks. Shoppers had drifted in off Nassau Street and so had a flock of Lawrenceville seniors on a tour of Revolutionary War sites. Some townie girls had commandeered a sprinkler and were horsing around with it by the Dean's house, but most of them had crowded around the steps of the main entrance, a few sitting astride the bronze lions that stood guard there. Bebb had already entered the building with a few of his principal lieutenants to present their

186

petition to the President, and Nancy Oglethorpe, still swathed in the Stars and Stripes, was trying her best to lead a pray-in outside while the rest of us waited for Bebb to reemerge and announce the outcome.

If anything substantiates Roebuck's theory that like Washington in 1777 Bebb had his whole stratagem planned out well in advance, it was the events of the next half hour or so, and since like everybody else I spent that time waiting under the tall elms, I must rely entirely on the researches of the *Prince* for what took place behind the scenes.

The first thing that took place was that the Proctors' Office received an anonymous phone call to the effect that if Bebb was thwarted in the attempt to deliver his petition to the President in person, or if the petition was turned down flat, his followers were planning to enter Nassau Hall by force if necessary and stage a sit-in in all the major administrative offices. Whether this actually was the plan or, if not, whether Bebb wanted the authorities to think that it was and thus to that end contrived the anonymous phone call himself, remains among the hidden things of history, but in any case, whoever baited the hook, the Proctors' Office lost no time in snapping at it. Within minutes all the proctors and Campus Cops that could be contacted were ordered to take up battle stations at Nassau Hall including, significantly, Officer McCartney, who left his post at the kiosk by Alexander Hall and proceeded to join the rest of his colleagues on the double.

While this maneuver was going on, inside Nassau Hall Bebb and his deputation made their way to the President's office where they were received by a secretary who said that the President was in an important conference and asked them to take seats and wait for him. This step is one that Bebb obviously couldn't have planned, and thus it seems to me to knock at least a small hole in Roebuck's theory. The next step, however, is something else again. Instead of waiting in the President's outer office with the rest of them, Bebb asked the way to the washroom and left.

Alerted by the proctors to expect a possible sit-in, most of the office staff had closed and locked their doors, and for that reason the *Prince* was unable to locate anybody who actually saw what Bebb did next. That he went to the washroom is attested to by the discovery there later of a sheaf of flyers left on the edge of a washbasin, but how he proceeded from there is anybody's guess. It hardly matters. Somehow—either by one of the side doors or possibly, I like to think, through a ground floor window—he managed to leave the building undetected, and while everybody including by then the entire security force of Princeton University was waiting for him to appear on the front steps of Nassau Hall, he hightailed it instead to Alexander Hall where Officer McCartney's kiosk stood empty except, reported the *Prince*, for a well-thumbed copy of *Penthouse* and a half-eaten swiss-on-rye. If Bebb's followers had founded a new religion in his name, I suppose they would have started their calendar with the Year One as the year of this historic flight, this hegira that Bebb made unseen by human eyes from the one great hall to the other.

Officer McCartney was not there to greet him, but others were. Gertrude Conover was there for one. She had arrived in her low-slung Continental driven by her black gardener Callaway. En route to the U Store with a malfunctioning typewriter, an undergraduate named

Max Bridenbaugh happened to be there also, and Bridenbaugh was the *Prince*'s source for all this.

A handful of Love Feasters who had not been along on the grand march had gained entrance to Alexander, and as soon as Gertrude Conover's Continental drew up, they ran out to help Callaway unload. According to Bridenbaugh the back seat was piled high with gallon jugs full of Tropicana, bags of potato chips, paper plates, paper cups, and a huge silver punchbowl bearing the Conover arms. All of this was rushed into the building, and Bebb and Gertrude Conover and the handful of Love Feasters followed, locking the glass doors behind them.

Holding his blood-stained handkerchief to his nose, Callaway revved up the Continental, parked it near the entrance to Holder, and left the campus on the run. Max Bridenbaugh shoved his broken typewriter into the abandoned kiosk just in time to prevent its being trampled to pieces by the hordes that almost immediately started streaming in from Nassau Hall, myself among them. Bridenbaugh, whose opinion as chairman of the Ivy bicker committee was given considerable weight by the *Prince*, stated that the whole operation was carried out in a way that suggested split second timing and a degree of co-ordination that bordered on the supernatural.

There was something aquarium-like about the scene that followed with those few pale faces floating dim and ghostly on the inside of the glassed-in rotunda and everybody else on the outside. The proctors had formed a cordon around the doors, exhorting the crowd to disperse and threatening disciplinary action if it didn't. There were more older faces mixed in with the others now. Except for Virgil Roebuck, who had arrived with his son in a wheel chair that looked several sizes too big for him, I didn't recognize many of them, but the *Prince* identified such notables as Stanislaus Fuchs, the Nobel laureate in physics, and James Ingram, that year's poet-in-residence. Somebody told me that the enormous man in the white beard and pith helmet was Dean Emeritus Nelson Higby Ackroyd.

The *Love is a Feast* and *Ban the Bomb not Bebb* posters were as much in evidence as ever and the hymns kept coming, but holy hell had all but swallowed up what little was left of a holy cause when word flashed around that Dean Borden had arrived, and the crowd divided like the Red Sea to let him through. It was one of the great encounters surely—on one side of the glass Dean Broadus Borden, Philadelphia-born former Rhodes Scholar and holder of honorary degrees from Harvard and Lafayette dressed for his Allentown dinner in pearl grey dacron and regimental stripes, and on the other side of the glass Leo Bebb, sweat-stained and grim with his trick eyelid doing its trick like a broken window shade. They made a brief attempt to communicate through the dusty panes like a Head Curator and a blowfish, but when this failed, Bebb gave the word and one door was unbarred just wide enough for the Dean to squeeze through sideways, scraping his glasses off in the process.

In a few minutes the door opened and the Dean came out again with one lens missing, the other cracked, and Bebb came with him. Like Eisenhower at a fund rally, the Dean held his arms up high above his head, the mob fell silent, and into that silence he dropped the terms that he and Bebb had agreed upon. The marchers were to be permitted to enter Alexander in an orderly fashion to conduct their feast, and in return Bebb guaranteed that afterwards they would disband peaceably and abide by whatever decision the President reached on their further use of University property. The Dean then turned to give Bebb a symbolic handshake, and as though in token of divine endorsement, there was a clap of thunder, and the rain started coming down in sheets as the two lords, spiritual and temporal, retreated into the Hall with the nimbleness of vaudeville hoofers to avoid being crushed to death by the advancing horde.

There was a rumor that the Tropicanas that were served inside were spiked with something stronger than the customary white wine, and an unidentified freshman was quoted as saying, "Man, like that stuff was a real *bomb*," but in her own interview with the *Prince*, Gertrude Conover denied this. She said, "It is a scientific fact that matter can be converted into energy. It is a spiritual fact that energy can be converted into matter. It was the karmic energy of Jesus Christ at the Cana wedding that turned the water into wine, and I believe that it was the karmic energy of Leo Bebb that had a similar effect on the Tropicana punch." When they asked her to comment on the rumor that an empty case of Mr. Boston gin was discovered among the wreckage later, she said simply, "I have already given you my comment." As for how the last Love Feast unfolded, the *Prince* account proceeds as follows.

Picture Alexander Hall crammed to capacity. Picture J. A. Holzer mosaics of Homer and his Heroes looking down on seething bouillabaise of believers and unbelievers, faculty and undergrads, cops and catechumens.

Picture rainforest atmosphere, soggy and steaming. Bodies soaked to skin. Flesh glistening pink through sopping garments as downpour continues outside. Some strip to bare essentials. Shirts and blouses scuttled. Air heavy with scents of spring, sweat, wet clothes, wet hair, orange juice and karmic gin.

Parrot squawks and primal screams rend jungle miasma as mob jostles for seats in pews. Balcony packed with Back Behind Bars with Bebb *poster draped down over railing.*

Cops and proctors form cordon with shoulders to stage apron. On stage Dean Borden broods with head in hands. Miss Oglethorpe mans massive punchbowl while aides prepare paper cups and platters of potato chips. Atheists for Democratic Action chant God is Dead *to block-that-kick cadence from balcony while Westminster Choir belts out* When the Saints.

Varsity halfback helps History Department's Virgil Roebuck hoist son in wheelchair to position of safety on stage. Bebb lends a hand. Light in auditorium Götterdämmerung dim as rain rattles windows. Enthroned in central panel, Homer goggles down blind as faith as Bebb mounts lectern and calls for order.

Bebb's voice bursts through overcharged PA *system like atomic blast: "Come unto me all ye . . ." (triggers feedback* YE-E-E-E-E *of such lethal pitch three hundred pairs of hands shoot up in chain reaction to three hundred pairs of ears as system cuts out). "Who labor and are heavy laden . . ." (sifts out unamplified and floats down soft as radioactive ash over stunned survivors). "And I will give you rest," intones Evangelist Bebb in hushed Gospelese. You could have heard a pone drop.*

Bebb raises paper cup to propose toast: "Here's to Jesus." Bends elbow. "Here's to you." Bends elbow again. Places potato chip on tongue and swallows sacramentally. Crowd quiet. Oglethorpe committee starts distributing holy elements.

Chaotic clamor rekindled as karmic concoction passed around. Dean Borden booed when he refuses. Booing billows as proctors follow Dean's lead. Turtlenecked chaplain almost chickens out too but then chug-a-lugs. Crowd roars approval. A.D.A. recommences God is Dead chant as Bebbites battle back with God is Good to same beat. Transubstantiated Tropicanas guzzled by gallons. Bebb Buddha-like at lectern. Campus Cops brace for action.

Human pyramid formed in back pews. Stripped to jockey shorts black feaster shinnies up to tear down Back Behind Bars banner. Slugfest breaks out on balcony and starts to spread when Bebb at mike raises arms and blasts out, "Little children, let us love one another" as cue for Kiss of Peace.

Pandemonium! Agape vies with Eros as Gott-und-Ginvertrunken cultists rise in pews embracing with dionysiac abandon. Aisles aswarm with sweating, rainsoaked bodies. Barechested boys and bra-less coeds tangle. Beardless frosh hug hairy-legged lettermen. Even atheists amorously aroused as inhibitions wilt in steamy atmosphere of Turkish bath or Methodist massage parlor. No holds barred in multiple clinches. Ejaculations, pious and otherwise, pierce humid air of Bebbsian bacchanal.

Topless teenybopper seen riding piggyback on grizzled custodian. Miss Oglethorpe heaved from hand to hand like huge blanc mange. Prone on stage turtlenecked chaplain titters in tongues as barefoot nymphet treads his shoulders free of knots. Tab Hunter and Jane Fonda lookalikes finger each other like blindmen reading braille while overstimulated undergraduate upends punchbowl into pith helmet of Emeritus Dean and serves it round as lovingcup.

Comments seminarian, "The question isn't was it an orgy or was it a sacrament? It was a sacramental orgy, that's what it was. All I can say, if God is dead, it was one hell of a wake."

"When Bebb started dancing," states another, "I knew the age of miracles hadn't passed."

Two hundred pounds of cornfed evangelist are bouncing like giant beachball. Pearshaped blur of white flesh spins like top. Like cotton candy in cotton candy machine spiritual leader seems to whip up substance from surrounding celebrants and waxes bigger as he whirls. Circle clears around him.

As spinning slows, sweat-spangled moon-face comes in focus. Bebb opens mouth as wide as crater to shoot forth moon-mad Pig Latin incantation: INNYNAY MADGEEZERS RYZENWOCK. Points plump finger toward rim of circle. Stage silent.

INNYNAY. Points at what? Whom?

MADGEEZERS. Points at aluminum and leather rig with glittering wire-spoked wheels like spotlit circus unicycles. Invalid son of History's Roebuck throned there.

RYZENWOCK. Broken boy bends forward in chair. Shaft of moonlight shoots from Bebb's finger. Boy fights one foot free of footrest. Thrusts with back to push to front of seat, all sinews straining. Second foot follows as Bebb repeats command in mothertongue.

"In the name," Bebb bids,

"Of Jesus,

"Rise and walk!"

Boy has risen, stands stiff. Takes step, toe trailing. Takes step, toe just clearing floor. Third stiff step lands him half the way to Bebb at circle's center.

Robed now in sacrament-stained Revonoc tablecloth,

Bebb spreads great wings wide in welcome, baring whale-belly pale barrel-chest and God knows what-all. Moby Dick? Boy's knee start to buckle but braces them and falters forward.

Hall mesmerized by miracle. Romanesque rotunda rocked with whoops and whistles. Halleluiahs. Then:

BLAM! BIFF! POW!

Borough Police bursts through doors at rear. Tear gas threatened. Everybody ordered out. Mass exodus starts as Campus Cops join Keystone contingent in keeping exits clear. Stage emptied in seconds. Love Feasters leapfrog pewbacks. Atheists stream down balcony stairs. Proselytes pour out on rain-slick blacktop and disband.

Damage to Hall estimated at $1500.00 and massive clean-up underway as Prince goes to press. Love Feast leaders booked on charges of disturbing the peace and up for suspension by Nassau Hall. President turns thumbs down on petition. Miss Oglethorpe in Princeton Hospital with fractured collarbone incurred in flight from stage. Mrs. Conover called to police headquarters to answer questions. Evangelist Bebb sought for inciting to violence and rumored also to be wanted for Income Tax evasion and insurance fraud.

Bebb's present whereabouts unknown. Last seen shielding Roebuck boy in arms as all around them stage surges like chorusline of Hair. Missing Conover Continental found abandoned at railway parking lot suggests guru may have made mad getaway on P.J. & B.

Interviewed at Revonoc, lanky, olive-skinned son-in-law Antonio Parr admits to mystification. When asked his estimation of Bebb, High School English prof Parr quotes Browning:

195

We that had loved him so, followed him, honored him,
Lived in his mild and magnificent eye,
Learned his great language, caught his clear accents,
Made him our pattern to live and to die."

So much for the *Prince*. I stayed on at Revonoc for what was left of that shattered weekend because Gertrude Conover asked me to. She took to her bed as soon as she returned from the interrogation at Borough Hall, and I did not see her again before I left, but she wanted me on hand to take care of the telephone and handle the press. Beyond that, her theory was that by remaining under the same roof, our auras would combine with that of the Pharaoh in his current incarnation and provide a kind of beacon light by which Bebb could find his way wherever he was going.

As she mounted the stairs to her bedroom, her blue curls hanging limp from the day's exertions, she paused with her hand on the bannister to explain this to me. Then she said, "Events he did not anticipate have shaken him loose from his karmic field. For the time being the gravitational pull of his destiny has no more effect on him than a magnet on an egg. If we stand by him now, you and I and Callaway, it is just possible that this time Leo Bebb may break free once and for all and rise to cosmic liberation like a balloon."

CHAPTER TWELVE

BIP, I said. PRINCETON. TROUBLE. GONE . . . shouting all the key words so that it was like hearing them for the first time myself, getting my own bad news. I might as well have saved the cost of the call for all Sharon could hear over the terrible connection, she at the Salamander Motel, I at my usual post under Mrs. Gunther's stairs. But she got the gist of it well enough, her voice crackling back at me like the sound track of an old movie: *Jesus. That Bip. Hand.* You had to hand it to him?

Home. It was like one of Bebb's free association sermons. *Bill. Bus.* There was a thunderstorm blowing across from the gulf, she said. I could almost hear the palmettos and cabbage palms rattling, the lions with

197

their backs to the rain by the riffled pool as the lightning clove our talk in two. She would come. I would meet her. Then *I miss you*, I said. MISS YOU.

Afraid she'd be struck, she hung up as I was saying it, the blips and pizzicati of connections being disconnected becoming the small Bronx cheer of the dial tone so that again my message ended up being for me. I missed her.

I did what I could to get the house ready for my wife and son. Junk mail lay in drifts under the slot, and I waded through the importunities of congressmen and missionaries, catalogues full of nose hair clippers, early American fondue forks and personalized pencils. Ice had gotten in under the flashing during the winter, and there was a damp stain on the dining room wall as though a firing squad had finished off the Czar and his family there. A pot of petrified Cream of Wheat stood in the kitchen sink. Nobody had bothered to take out the Christmas tree, and I found it in the living room, a ragged brown scarecrow in a pool of needles.

I opened some windows and picked up the mail. I plugged in the refrigerator and filled the trays. I ran water into the Cream of Wheat and left it to soak. Before I was through, there wasn't a room I didn't enter, not a door I didn't push open half expecting to find something mouldering in a corner behind it. When I opened the door of the little attic room where Bebb had lived, I wondered if what I would find would be Bebb himself hiding out in a pool of dead flies, as sere and pillaged as the Christmas tree. The room was empty. In Sharon's and my room, the bed was unmade, last slept in, I suppose, the New Year's Eve when she had gotten sick and Tony had stayed to comfort her.

More even than to keep the weather out, the purpose of a house is to keep emptiness out, I thought—to box ourselves off from a sky that is too spacious, a horizon too far-flung, to carpenter for ourselves a space we can handle and feel at home in. But something had gone wrong. Instead of boxing emptiness out, those abandoned rooms had somehow boxed it in, emptiness not as an absence but as a presence: our house so filled with emptiness that it was hard to imagine there ever being room again for anything else.

Later that day I drove to Stamford to meet them, and I can see them still as they got out of the bus, Sharon carrying a string bag of grapefruit she'd bought on the trip and Bill in a straw hat with an alligator on it. Spotting them before they spotted me, I saw for a moment how they looked when they didn't have me around to look at, how they must have looked all those weeks without me in Armadillo or would have looked if I'd been lying in my grave instead of standing there by a cigarette machine watching them without their knowing it. Sharon had her hands under Bill's arms to lift him down from the bus steps, and it must have tickled him the way he was cracking up as she swung him down to the street. That was how they looked, and having seen it, I found myself not wanting to see any more, shifting my position so that the cigarette machine stood between us. Maybe it was a clue to the standoffishness of the dead when you run into them in dreams. It's not because they don't love you any more that they keep their distance but because they have their business to get on with and you have yours and under the circumstances maybe that's just as well for you both.

When I kissed Sharon, she kept hold of me with her cheek pressed against mine just long enough to make me wonder why, but it turned out to be only because her gold hoop earring had gotten snagged on my jacket, and having that to fuss about was as good a way to get through the moment as any. Bill gave me a wet smacker on the chin and handed me something done up in a Kleenex and a rubber band. It was a sand dollar.

"Hey, Antonio," Sharon said.

There was no lack of conversation on the drive home. It was as if they had simply been away on a vacation and wanted to catch me up on how things had been with them. From the back seat Bill told about a cat named Shell who went into the closet when you were away and made messes in your shoes. He told about a beach where he'd worked his treasure finder to locate an oarlock and a pirate's tobacco can and about a man named Mr. Chuck Warner who had hair in his ears and chewed up live shiners for chum. Sharon said she'd gotten her old job back part time at the souvenir stand where they sold shrunken heads and carved coconut husks and rugs with sunsets and palm trees on them. She said that a boy she used to know named Jitter Baskin had turned the building where Holy Love used to be into a seafood restaurant and that the house where she had lived with Bebb and Lucille was vacant now and up for sale. She had gotten the key from the real estate agent and taken Bill through it one day—Lucille's TV room out back, the pull-chain john with the varnished brown seat, the gingerbread verandah where Herman Redpath had stood to have his picture taken the day Bebb had ordained him and all hell broke loose.

As they chattered on I tried to imagine what it had been

like for them; I tried to get the feel of finding a cat-mess in your shoe or entering again that Charles Addams manse where I had first seen Sharon coming down the front steps in white sailor pants and a raspberry shirt as Bebb had leaned on the horn to hurry her. I tried to hear between the lines as they spoke, to search their words for some clue I could find my way back to them with; and all the while I was doing it, my son from the seat behind me was exploring me with his hands. He was reaching around and tracing the line of my jaw, my lips, running his fingers against the grain of my beard, and it occurred to me that in his own way he was trying to do the same thing. It was as if he was searching my face for something buried there, for secret treasure he maybe even half knew was a clue to the secret of himself as every time I drove through the tunnel where my poor father had told me once to keep a lookout for fish I half knew it was my own secret I was tunneling toward.

I thought of all the things I could tell them, when my turn came, about how life had been for me while they were gone. I could tell about puff-puff, how there by the lion's pool where I had seen Herman Redpath again and Lucille and Miriam, Brownie's suckling pig had rooted me out, that *porcus Dei*, dropping into my lap a name that lay deep beneath all my other names, my true and hidden name which I had never since been able either quite to remember or quite to forget. I could tell about Laura Fleischman and how in the blue night I had been granted my heart's desire only to discover that something less than my heart was in it. More than anything I could explain about decathexis—how the habit, I suppose, of keeping too sharp an eye on your own life can precipitate you prematurely into that geriatric state where life itself becomes a kind of spectator sport in which there is nothing much left either to win or to lose that greatly matters.

Bill with his treasure-seeking hands on my face—if anybody was to find there some scrap worth salvaging of the life I'd let go, surely he was the one, my child. He owed me that, or I him. I could have told him that too. Instead, I caught one of his fingers between my teeth the next time it came near enough and held him by it for a moment, his alligator hat knocked cockeyed against the back of my head. Then I let him go.

"That didn't hurt," he said, sinking back into his seat, and I said, "That's what you think."

What I actually did tell them about when my turn came was mostly Bebb's adventures—the march on Nassau Hall, the final Love Feast, Bebb's mild and magnificent eye as Roebuck's boy had staggered those few steps toward him across the stage. It became a kind of comic strip the way I found myself editing it for Bill's consumption, and I left until some other time the job of filling in for Sharon the little clouds that come puffing out of people's heads with the light bulbs, question marks, and undressed ladies in them.

After we'd eaten the sandwiches I'd gotten in and put Bill to bed, Sharon stood in the hall for the first time in four months looking up those empty stairs. She said, "I wish I had a dollar for every time I've dreamed about this place. It's the same dream every time. I'm back here again just like now. Everything looks normal as hell. I check it all out. Then the same thing always happens. I open some door or turn a corner, and all of a sudden I'm looking at a part of the house I never saw before. I think what a queer thing it is that all the years we lived here there was this whole bunch of rooms we never used because we didn't even know they were there."

Then "Today it's like coming home for a funeral," she said, "only nobody's died."

I said, "Speak for yourself."

She stood there with one hand on the banister and with the other reached over her shoulder to unhook her blouse at the top.

She said, "Listen, I know there's a whole mess of things we've got to hash over, but it seems like we were six months on that Greyhound, and my tail's dragging. If it's OK by you, I vote we sack out. We can start out even in the morning."

The business of bags, supper, bedding down Bill had given us a common ground to meet on, but without warning she pulled it out from under us now. She stood with one foot on the bottom stair, her unhooked blouse showing where her tan ended, and I stood under that same hall light where once Tony had hung up his jock-strap with a pot of African violets in it. It was no longer the last few months we had to contend with suddenly but the next few minutes.

What could we do to help Bebb? Was our marriage washed up permanently? If so, how about Bill upstairs asleep in his alligator hat? They sounded like subjects for doctoral dissertations compared with the one she'd dropped naked and quivering between us. Sack out *where* became the only question with flesh on its bones —she upstairs in our unmade bed and I back at Mrs. Gunther's or, if I stayed, in Tony's or Chris's room or up in Bebb's attic with the dead flies? It was left to me to answer somehow, and she did nothing to make it easy, watching me in silence with those somber eyes.

203

"It's OK by me," I said. "Mind if I stick around and play a few hands of solitaire?" Then, without warning again, her smile.

The secret of most faces is the look they have in repose, turned inward on where the secret is, but with Sharon it was always that minstrel show flash of white teeth that let the cat out of the bag, made anyone she flashed it on a party to the secret of who she was.

"Be my guest," she said. "Just do me a favor first, hear? Get that tree out of the sitting room. It gives me the creeps.

"And piss on the side of the bowl," she said.

So she went upstairs with her brown back showing down to where it wasn't brown any more and her long hair streaked by the Armadillo sun and her tail dragging, and I went into the living room to deal with the tree. Every time you touched it, a million more needles fell to sweep up, and I had to unscrew the stand and roll back the carpet, but I got it done eventually and dragged the tree out back to the compost heap.

There was a sharp-edged white moon overhead and stars thick and quiet as dust, the *silence éternelle* that scared hell out of Pascal but to me has always seemed a somehow plumed and floating hush over the scariness of things. Near the compost was that great A-shaped wooden contrivance of knobs and dowels and slotted laths that I had put together during the first years of our marriage and with Tony's help had set up in the back yard. It hung on a rusty chain from its tripod the worse for wear and weathered silver, broken here and there by the weight of snow, the kids who sometimes came and fooled with it. I gave it a little shove with my foot and watched it as with a gallows creak it turned ponderously

204

in the moonlight, the slow passing behind one another of its parts giving it the look of movement within movement. I thought of the Hayden Planetarium where Miriam and I had been taken as children and of that crouching, two-headed machine that projected the stars onto the domed roof as now it seemed to me this old toy of mine was projecting them in all their colossal pointlessness and beauty. I stopped it with my foot to make the stars stand still. The light was on in our bedroom.

Everything stands still, the old riddle goes, and motion is in the eye of the beholder if it's anywhere at all. A comic strip, an arrow in flight, a life—like a movie, they are all a succession of stills, a parade of unmoving moments that only seem to move. No matter what happens next, everything that has happened is for keeps. No matter how long Orphan Annie goes on, each frame along the way remains intact. My monument on its chain, for instance. The Christmas tree on the compost heap. I stand beside them to this day wherever else I've found to stand since. There is a cloud coming out of my head as I stare up at our lighted window, and Sharon is in that cloud. She is looking the way she did the first time we made love together in the Salamander Motel the winter before we were married. She has just come out of the shower, and the towel she had wrapped around her like a sari lies at her feet where it fell when I reached up and touched the tucked-in place at her shoulder. Light comes in through the slats of the Venetian blind. She is wearing only water. In that frame too I stand to this day, and so does she.

She was asleep by the time I got upstairs, the light turned off, and talk about your comic strips—Daisy Mae lying there on her side as warm and loose as silk beneath the moon-drenched sheet while with slapstick caution Li'l Abner climbs in beside her all gooseflesh and stiff as a poker. Frame after frame he lies there not daring so much as to gulp.

In bed at night, shadows have a way of turning into substance, thoughts into things you can catch your toe on so that you feel the bed shake as you literally fall asleep when that time comes. My day was drifting back at me as I waited for sleep there—the tour of our empty house, the bus, Bill's hands on my face—and the sadness of it got all confused with a dryness in my throat, desire confused with the pillow under my head, something that wouldn't lie flat. There was a scent of hair-tonic on the pillow—Tony's?—that I kept dimly trying to break like a code which promised to make sense of everything.

Then the phone. I heard it first as the ripping in two of something with writing on it and reached across Sharon for whatever it was, whatever I was, knocking the receiver off the hook in the dark and feeling her move beneath my arm as I fumbled for it. It was Bebb's voice I pressed to my ear, Bebb telling me who I was: Antonio?

"That you, Antonio? Now listen real close. I got to talk fast."

He said, "The hour is at hand, Antonio. The powers of darkness are on the march, and time's running out. Here's what I want you to do. I'm in New York City, never mind where for now. There's things better not said over the wire."

He said, "There's a place in the park where they serve sandwiches and soda pop under beach umbrellas. It's down a flight of stone steps. There's a pond at the bottom has a stone angel in it. You know the place I mean?"

When I told him I knew it, he said, "If you can make it round four P.M. tomorrow, don't be surprised to find a certain person there can guide you to me. Can you make it, Antonio, Sharon and you both?"

I didn't ask him how he knew Sharon was back or if he knew also that at that moment I was leaning across her to get at the phone. I told him just that we would make it, and his relief was audible. I pictured him squeezed into a streetcorner booth somewhere with his black raincoat buttoned to the chin and the brim of his Tyrolean hat pulled down.

He said, "Meantime you tell Sharon Bip said not to worry about anything. Tell her we all of us just got to hold tight to Jesus."

Somebody else evidently said something to him then, and he must have covered the receiver with his hand as he turned to answer. All I could hear was a burst of muffled laughter. I don't know that I ever heard Bebb laugh before, and the incongruity of it stayed in my ears long after the harried tone of the rest had faded. That hushed and conspiratorial s.o.s. and then that solitary, fat man's laugh so rich and abandoned. It was as if beneath the secret of his whereabouts lay a deeper secret still which only by accident I had heard an echo of. Then all was gravity again as he came back.

"Hold tight to Jesus," he said, "because he's the only one there is won't never let you down." Then "Tomorrow four o'clock, Antonio. Meantime don't take any wooden nickles," and he hung up.

"It was Bip," I told Sharon. "He says we've got to hold tight to Jesus."

"Jesus who?" she said.

I had started to roll back to my side of the bed and tell

her the rest of what he'd said when she slipped one arm around my waist. She said, "A person's got to hold tight to something."

Sex education is known as Human Relations at Sutton High, and among those of us who are pressed into teaching it each year to small, glassy-eyed groups of freshmen and sophomores, the party line is that sex for sex's sake is at its best not much. If only your bodies meet and the human beings that happen to inhabit them don't, the chances are you'll only compound the problem you shacked up together to solve. It's not a bad rule of thumb as rules of thumb go, and by and large I'm willing to stand by it myself. But there are exceptions.

I didn't have the faintest idea who was inhabiting Sharon's body that first night she got back. The very familiarity of her outer presence beside me there only deepened the inner mystery, and she had no reason to be any better informed about me. So it was only our bodies that met that night, those two old reactionaries going off half-cocked as usual, and by all rules it shouldn't have added up to much. Except that it did. I suppose you couldn't say we made love together, being in inward ways too far apart for that, but at least we made a kind of stopgap peace together. Human relations notwithstanding, even the flesh has its own cloddish wisdom.

When we were through, I remember she said, "That one was on Bip," and when I told her about his smothered laugh, she said, "You never can tell about Bip. Maybe that's what he woke us up for."

CHAPTER THIRTEEN

THE RAIN HAD DWINDLED to a fine grey mist by the time Sharon and I arrived at the Bethesda Fountain in Central Park. The place was nearly deserted, the umbrellas taken in. Only one of the tables was occupied. There were two middle-aged Japanese sitting at it. One of them looked as though he might have been part of a U.N. delegation. He had on a Humphrey Bogart trench coat and a tweed golf cap with the visor unsnapped. The other was plumper and shabbier with a Daily News unfolded over his head like a small, peaked roof. They were sitting side by side facing out across the water. They both wore glasses and seemed to have their eyes closed. The terrace was littered with shallow puddles, and under one of the empty chairs a few pigeons pecked half-heartedly for crumbs. The whole scene had an oriental feeling—only the tops of the tall buildings visible in the distance, the two old friends, the single grey of water and sky. The only spot of color was the yellow plastic rain hat Sharon wore. We stood just inside the arch that the wide stairs descended through. From the refreshment booth farther back under the arch a scent of coffee floated out into the damp city air. On the chance that one of the two Japanese was Bebb's emissary, we walked to the edge of the basin where they could see us. Neither of them seemed to notice.

On the fountain, the angel was striding forward in a purposeful way with his head bowed. One hand was at his side as though to keep his long skirts from blowing, the other extended out over the pool.

A pigeon sat on one of the angel's outstretched wings, and under his stone hand the water lay flat and still. A paper plate floated upside down, an unfurled rubber filmy and vague as a dead fish.

Sharon said, "You sure he said four? It's nearly half past."

A young couple appeared down the stairs and stood in the archway looking out in our direction. The girl had a Bonwit's shopping bag and the boy a camera strung around his neck. There was something foolish and abandoned about them, like actors taking their bows to an empty house. After a while they came out and sat down at one of the tables.

Sharon said, "Maybe it's some kind of trap."

She had picked me up after my last class and driven me straight to the train where we couldn't find seats together, then the quick dash from Grand Central to the park so we'd hardly had the chance to exchange a word since the night before and didn't dare exchange more than a few at a time now for fear of missing what we'd come for.

"Maybe," I said, "only I've had a queer feeling right along there's been nobody following us."

The boy got up from the table and came over. He said, "Sir, I wonder if you'd mind doing us a favor and taking a picture. You've just got to line us up in the window and push that jigger down."

"Honeymooners?" Sharon said.

The boy said, "I guess you could call it that."

He went back to the table and sat down, and I crouched to my heels on the wet terrace in front of them moving the camera around to get the background right. What followed was pure Alfred Hitchcock—the missing finger on the stranger's hand, the old lady turning around and not being Dame May Whitty. Beyond the lovers' heads, standing on the balustrade above the archway, a solitary figure appeared in the viewer. He was wearing a green rubber raincoat that almost touched the ground and a porkpie hat. I couldn't make out his face very well, but I didn't need to. That great heap of a body lumping out in the wrong places as though it was several people gotten up to look like one, that scrawny neck—there was no mistaking him. It was Mr. Golden. He raised one arm and with a single backward sweep motioned us to follow him.

By the time we made it up the stairs, he had crossed the road and traveled a surprising distance away from us through the wet grass. The way the raincoat hid his legs, he never seemed to be running, but we had to rush to keep from losing sight of him in the mist. He didn't stick to the paths but took a crazy, zigzag route as if he was trying to shake us instead of lead us. Once we saw him clamber up a slippery outcropping of rock so nearly on all fours that he looked like a giant turtle. Once we had to dodge traffic to follow him across a road only to find that he'd doubled back to the other side and was heading off in a new direction. At a dip in the ground where several paths intersected by a drinking fountain, we lost him completely until Sharon spotted him up in the air beyond some shrubbery.

He was standing on the topmost rung of a slide in a children's playground, and I half expected him to hoot out *Ally-y all-y in come free*—the sense I had that he was playing with us, leapfrogging the hills and dales of Central Park like some enormous child. It must have been the way he set his fires, I thought, touching them off for the sheer sport of it, that great shambles of a man dancing around with his beautiful, withered smile lit up by the flames. As we ran toward the playground, he slid down the slide like a basket of laundry and bounded off through a gate in the fence. I remember him silhouetted at the far end of one of those brick-lined underpasses that smell of dead leaves and piss. I called out his name, the echo bouncing back and forth between the curved walls, and raising his porkpie hat, he waved it at us, then off again up the steep path beyond.

We had started out south from the fountain, but after all the backtracking and crisscrossing we ended up going north till we found ourselves entering the zoo. A cloud of pigeons clattered into the air as Mr. Golden plowed down an avenue of cages with a lead of about fifty yards. A llama was still gazing after him with a look of superb hauteur as we came along in his wake, a red fox pacing back and forth with his clever face always turned toward the bars.

When we reached the open plaza where the seals are, we saw Mr. Golden on the far side of the tank. He had bought a white helium-filled balloon that bounced above him on its string as he disappeared around the corner of the old armory. Starting up the stairs to the street level, we had just time to see him spring into the frontmost of several cabs drawn up at the curb and take off down Fifth Avenue with a sizzle of tires on the wet pavement. Sharon and I piled into the next one. FOLLOW THAT CAB I said.

Somewhere between Park and Lexington we lost him in the traffic. Sharon was for giving up, but I had the feeling she was only matching my classic charge to the driver with a classic of her own—the moll who turns chicken when the heat's on and has to be slapped back into commission. So we kept inching east through the honking jam of red taillights and glistening fenders until we ended up first in line at the light on Second. Halfway down to the next side street, a cab was double-parked on the avenue with Mr. Golden's head stuck out through the back window. He had his thumb in his ear and was wagging his fingers at us. A few blocks farther down Second he turned east, but we missed the light again and had to wait at the corner. When we finally made the turn, there was no trace of him so we kept going till we hit First.

The block between First and York was almost empty. There were tenements on both sides with fire escapes out front and bars at the lower windows. An armchair with the springs falling out stood abandoned by a litter basket as if the last inhabitant might have sat there evenings before he finally pulled out with the rest of them. There was a brownstone garage with a corrugated portcullis rolled shut and EAT SHIT chalked across it less as a call to action, I thought, than a kind of parting confession. The steam from a manhole cover flattened out in the moist air, and overhead the hazy sky had gone brown with the approach of dusk.

A few doors beyond the garage, the cab of Mr. Golden had drawn up with the motor running and its yellow flanks steaming as we cruised up behind it. The driver jerked his thumb toward the building across the street, then with a death rattle of valves shot off toward York. The building was a great windowless pile of sootstained brick with a sign on it that said *Bull's International Fire-proof Storage*.

It was like entering the great pyramid of Khufu and I wished we had Gertrude Conover with her memories as Ittu the Pharoah's ward to guide us. We passed several doors, but they were locked. The one marked Office had a bell beside it, but the sluggish buzz failed to raise anyone. If Mr. Golden had preceded us, he had left no trace. The corridor ended in what seemed to be a blank wall but turned out to be the latrine-grey doors of an elevator. The only sounds were the ones we made trying not to make any. Then as we stood there, Sharon in her yellow hat and I clammy as the sweat cooled between my shoulderblades, a dime-sized light above the elevator button came on red, and from deep below we could hear the rumble and slap of cables. I said, "We've still got time to go home."

Sharon said, "We came to see him, didn't we?"

It was less a reproach than a real question. Bebb on the skids, Bebb down and out in the fireproof depths of Bull's storage—maybe we didn't want to see him. I thought of the fatness of his laugh over the phone, pictured him bleary and unshaven with his eyelid at permanent half-mast. Maybe we'd better go home while we still had our illusions intact. The latrine-grey door shuddered, and as it started to slide open what we saw through the inner grille was that the elevator was empty except for the white balloon resting against the ceiling with the string hanging down. We got in and rode down as far as it would go.

"With trembling hands I made a tiny breach in the upper left hand corner and peered in," Howard Carter writes in his account of discovering the tomb of Tutankhamen. "Surely never before in the history of excavation had such an amazing sight been seen—objects, some familiar but some the like of which we had never seen, piled upon one another in seemingly endless profusion—two life-sized figures of a king in black, gold kilted, gold sandaled, the sacred cobra upon their heads . . . a heap of curious white oviform boxes, a beautiful lotiform cup of translucent alabaster, a confused pile of overturned chariots . . . Somewhere in all this magnificent panoply of death we would find the Pharaoh lying."

Sofas on sofas, chairs and tables stacked higgledy-piggledy with their legs in the air like sacrificial victims, translucent refrigerators, cardboard packing cases big enough to hold a Pharaoh each and coil upon coil of sacred carpet, lotiform lampshades, gilt frames, fire screens, old wardrobe trunks humpbacked and multi-stickered, headboards, bookshelves—we picked our way through a vast, dim basement down narrow paths piled higher than our heads with the debris of generations. If you'd dug deep enough, you would have come to stone knives, potsherds, the bones of extinct species. I'd brought the white oviform balloon with me from the elevator, and it floated above us like a cloud full of question marks.

Then, before we saw Bebb, we heard him, and I can hear him still as his voice came echoing toward us through the subterranean dusk. "Strait is the way and narrow is the gate which leadeth unto life, Antonio, and few there be that find it."

You think of Bebb squeezed into his gents' furnishings suit or buttoned up to his chin in his black raincoat. You picture his neck bulging out over his tight-fitting collar and that pint-sized hat on his head. But here was Bebb untrussed and overflowing, Bebb with the stays unloosed and the lid off. He had on a pair of loose-fitting paisley pajamas and a huge red dressing gown with satin lapels and a tasseled cord at the waist. His face looked firm and vigorous as though he'd just stepped out of a cold shower. His bald scalp was polished to a high sheen. When he spread his red arms to welcome us, he was like the sun rising.

He said, "Rejoice with me for I have found my sheep which were lost. Put rings on their hands and shoes on their feet and bring the fatted calf and kill it."

Sharon said, "This is some hideout you got here, Bip," and wrapping his arms around her he said, "Sharon honey, I'm through hiding. There is nothing hid which shall not be manifested nor anything kept secret but that it shall come abroad."

He took both my hands and said, "The winter is past, Antonio, and the sound of the turtle is heard again in the land." I suppose he could have gone on entirely in quotations from Scripture if he'd wanted to.

216

I said, "You're looking good, Bip," and Bebb said, "Antonio, you look like you've had a dose of monkey glands yourself."

He said, "Follow me."

We proceeded single file still deeper into the labyrinth of Bull's International Fireproof Storage, Bebb leading the way with the pajamas flopping about his ankles and Sharon and I following along behind, damp and disheveled by our chase through the park. Sharon said, "You better leave go your balloon. It looks like we escaped from the funny farm," and giving it its freedom, I watched it rise to the ceiling and stick there. We passed through several more acres of buried history.

What we came to finally was more of a cage than a room—three wire-mesh walls and a wire-mesh ceiling built out from the rear wall of the building like something to keep out rats. It was so much brighter inside than the rest of the basement that it took a few minutes to make it all out.

There was a large roll-top desk, a filing cabinet and some folding chairs. There was an electric hot plate on top of the filing cabinet, some coffee mugs and a bag of Hydrox cookies. A girlie calendar dated 1957 hung over the desk and beneath it a standing phone of an even earlier vintage. Hooked here and there through the wire walls were a number of hangers with clothes on them—an overcoat with a Persian lamb collar, a Mandrake the Magician opera cape, some double-breasted suits and a Chinese kimono. I pictured Bebb whiling away the days down there trying them all on. There must have been a whole MGM costume department stashed away somewhere.

The rear wall of concrete was decorated with a crudely

painted scene which from its resemblance to the murals that had burned up with Open Heart I recognized as the work of Mr. Golden. There were a lot of feather duster palm trees in it, a bright blue sky with birds flying across like black checkmarks, some overstuffed white clouds—a scene not unlike the ones on the rugs that Sharon sold at the novelty shop in Armadillo. Beneath this tropical paradise was a cot, and stretched out on it on his back with his raincoat folded under his head for a pillow and not even breathing hard was Mr. Golden. On his low-hung bolster of a paunch a small transistor radio was balanced, and he had it plugged into one ear by a cord. His eyes were closed, his expression serene.

Sitting down in the swivel chair at the desk, Bebb clasped his hands behind his head and gazed at us with the look of a parlor magician who's just taken fifty cents out of somebody's ear. He said, "Fats and me, we spent five years in a place no bigger than this. I'm going to be honest with you. In some ways it's been like coming home."

Sharon said, "Jesus, Bip, you can't hole up here forever."

I said, "That was some chase you gave us, Mr. Golden," and with his eyes still closed, Mr. Golden said, "I'm a nightwatchman that sometimes watches with his eyes and sometimes watches with his ears, but the point is I'm always watching. There's a woman calling in who says she's got a alligator pear pit with a plant coming out of it better than four foot tall."

That was the way our conversation began, and in many ways it is characteristic of all that followed. To the best of my recollection, our four statements followed in the sequence I've given—home, Jesus, chase, alligator pear—but you could rearrange them any other way, and they would hang together as well or as badly. Possibly chase came first, then alligator pear and home, and only then Jesus. We had moments, of course, when the sequence was as unalterable as knocking and opening, but it seems to me that much of the time we said what we wanted to whether it fitted in or not, and that's the disjointed way I will set it down here. Sharon and I, Mr. Golden and Bebb—each of us had a particular set of words to get across, and at the heart of each set was one special word so deeply buried in the others sometimes that you had to be a Howard Carter to dig it out without having it fall to dust in your hands.

Bebb, for instance. It took Sharon to explain to me his special word. I hadn't gotten it on my own, so lodged it was in everything else. She said, "He was telling us *goodbye*, you poor peckerhead. Couldn't you even tell?" It was days afterwards that she explained it, standing out on a potatofield in New Jersey as the sun started to go down, and I knew she was right though at the time Bebb was actually saying it I hadn't heard it. Goodbye is such a sad word, and by comparison all his other words in that cage seemed bright and hopeful.

Twirling and untwirling the tassel of his robe around his thumb as he spoke, he said, "Antonio, I've been in the ring for Jesus going on forty years, and I've been beat up something cruel. Spiritually speaking, I've been— why, this pitiful soul of mine, it's got lumps the size of an egg all over and a pair of cauliflower ears and a jaw on it looks like raw hamburg. I'm a walking grocery store the way the powers of darkness have worked me over all the way from Miami Beach as far north as Princeton, New Jersey, and they're not done with me yet. Only they're not the ones I'm scared of. It's the darkness in here I'm scared of," he said, tapping his chest with his tasseled thumb. "The shameful things a man does with his life. The shameful things don't anybody know about but him. I've been down for the count more times than you could shake a stick at. I'm not denying it. But the ref's never gotten farther than nine yet. Jesus, he's always propped me back on my feet somehow. He's always had me back in there slugging it out for him again."

I said, "Did you ever think of retiring from the ring for a while, Bip? I mean you're pushing sixty-five and there's nobody on your back a good lawyer couldn't square you with. Why not just get the hell out—you and Gertrude Conover take a trip somewhere. Think of all the places you've never seen—museum tours, South American cruises. . . ." I all but had the travel brochures out on the desk in front of him, and I remember the acceleration of my pulse as I spoke, my mounting excitement at the thought that if I could only persuade him to let go, we could somehow all of us let go. I suppose what I wanted Bebb to do was wash decathexis itself in the blood of the lamb.

He said, "Antonio, I've had thoughts like that myself sometimes. A man dreams dreams. This isn't the Ritz Hotel, but I've got Fats to bring me food and drink and keep watch nobody comes around asking embarrassing questions. I could be snug as a bug down here laying low till things blow over. The IRS, they've got bigger fish than me to fry anyhow and so's that insurance company I've got on my tail. When the heat's off, maybe I could take off someplace like you say." His eyelid fluttered shut as if to hold his dream in for a moment, like the smoke of a good cigar—he and Gertrude Conover watching the moon rise over the Acropolis, taking a boat trip up the Amazon.

220

"Why not just get the hell out, Bip?" I said.

He said, "Because getting the hell out, that's what hell is. This place is hell, Antonio. I've got to gird up my loins for the next round. I've got to move on."

"Where you going to gird up your loins to move to next, Bip?" Sharon said.

Bebb said, "Up. Holy Love, Open Heart, Love Feast," he counted them out on his fingers. "I've burned all my bridges. Up's the only place I got left."

Mr. Golden gave a little grunt and cradling the radio against him so it wouldn't fall, rolled over onto his side.

Bebb said, "He's awful big on those talk shows. Seems like the world's full of lonesome folks dying to talk."

Mr. Golden said, "The world's full of sickies. A man's sounding off how the people that hand out trick-or-treats with razor blades in them ought to have their private parts cut off with a razor blade."

Sharon said, "What's with this insurance company you've got on your tail?"

Bebb said, "Somebody wrote them a letter the fire at Open Heart wasn't any accident."

Mr. Golden said, "The good thing about fire is it burns your bridges, and a man's got to burn his bridges so he can move on. It's a rule of life, if a man don't keep moving on, he's good as dead. Every time you cross a bridge, burn it."

Bebb unclasped his hands from behind his head and stretched them high into the air. With the trace of a yawn in his voice, he said, "So when you expecting the baby, honey? You picked out a name for her yet?"

Sharon said, "I never said I was expecting any baby."

Bebb said, "I know. You weren't planning on saying it either."

Sharon said, "I'm not saying it. You're saying it."

Bebb said, "I kind of hoped you might call her after your mother. She'd set a lot of store by that, poor soul."

I said, "It's true? You're having a baby?"

Sharon said, "You tell him, Bip. You've got all the answers."

Bebb said, "It's going to be a girl, and she's going to name it Lucille after her mother. It'll have its father's eyes."

Sharon said, "It better have somebody's eyes."

"What if it's a boy?" I said.

Bebb said, "It's a girl."

"What if somebody'd been tailing you?" Mr. Golden said. "You think I was leading you all around Robin Hood's barn just for the fun of it?"

"It crossed my mind," I said.

Sharon said, "What if we'd have lost you?"

Mr. Golden said, "Where's your faith? Where's your ding-dong faith?"

"I don't have any," Sharon said.

Mr. Golden said, "Then you didn't have anything much to lose."

Bebb said, "Sharon, nobody that doesn't have faith ought to feel too bad about it. Even the ones that have it, it's not like they have it permanent, like a face-lift."

Mr. Golden had propped himself up on one elbow. He said, "Here today, gone tomorrow, that's faith for you."

Bebb said, "The Apostle Paul wrote faith is the evidence of things not seen. Now if the only evidence a man's got is something he can't see, you can't blame him if sometimes he—when a thing's not out where you can see it, sometimes you have a hard time believing it's there."

Mr. Golden said, "If a thing's not out where you can see it, there's a fifty-fifty chance it's not there, period."

"It's a chance you got to take," Bebb said.

"You think there's something there, Bip?" Sharon said.

She said, "Forget all the preacher talk. Just say it like it is. If you had to bet everything you've got there's something there, would you do it? When it comes right down to it, would you bet your tail, Bip?"

Bebb said, "Remember that thing your mother wrote before she passed on? She wrote what she was washed in, it wasn't the blood of the lamb. It was the shit of the horse. Show me a son of Adam doesn't have days he feels like that."

"Would you bet your tail, Bip?" Sharon said.

Bebb said, "Sharon, there's been days I wouldn't even bet my green stamps."

"This day, now," Sharon said.

Bebb drummed his fingers on Mr. Golden's desk. There was a clipboard with a bunch of inventories in it, and he worked his finger in under the clip till it was caught there. He said, "When the time of testing comes, I'll just have to say, Savior, let thy grace be sufficient. Jesus, take pity on this wore-out old tail of mine that's all I got left to bet with."

Mr. Golden said, "Flying saucers have landed." He was frowning with concentration, his hand held up for silence and his transistor still plugged into his ear.

223

"This lady was walking home from the pictures after dark when she saw something she took for a fire hydrant. It had a little round hat on it and it didn't come up any higher than her knee. Then the hat commenced to glow red like the end of a cigar when you take a pull on it, and she could see it had a queer kind of face to it like a balled up handkerchief. Just before it took off, it said something. Just as plain as day she heard it. It said, 'Don't be afraid.' Soon as it said it, it shot up like a rocket."

"Think of it," Bebb said. "A creature that size come all those millions of miles just to offer a word of comfort."

Mr. Golden said, "They're all heart, those small-size ones."

Bebb was smiling. "All heart and a yard wide," he said. "Sometimes wider."

Mr. Golden had lovely white teeth, but when he returned Bebb's smile, you could see all the back ones were missing. His face had a puckered look like a hand that's been in hot water too long. He said, "The big ones too. They'd give you the shirt off their backs if they had a shirt."

Bebb said, "If they had a back."

Mr. Golden said, "They come in all sizes and shapes and flavors like ice cream though there's some you couldn't tell from humans unless you were one of them yourself. You could tell then easy enough."

"If you felt like telling," Bebb said.

Mr. Golden said, "They're the same breed of cats as the angels of Scripture. They've been paying us visits since the beginning of time."

Bebb said, "They carry messages for the Almighty

down through all the moons and stars and Milky Ways of outer space."

Mr. Golden said, "There's not a doubt in the world about it."

Bebb said, "Not if there's an Almighty anyway."

"Right," Mr. Golden said. "Not if there's an Almighty and he has messages to send out."

"Like Having a wonderful time, wish you were here," Bebb said. "Or Keep in touch. Love to everybody."

"Or Don't be afraid," Mr. Golden said.

Bebb said, "Don't be afraid for the terror by night or for the arrow that flieth by day."

"Our God is a consuming fire," Mr. Golden said, "but don't be afraid of him either. It's just if we won't burn our own bridges, he burns them for us. It's a rule of life a man's got to move on."

"I don't know as I ever happened to see one myself looked just like a fire hydrant," Bebb said, and I remember still the sound of their laughter—Bebb's like wind whistling down a chimney, Mr. Golden's like somebody cracking kindling across his knee.

Mr. Golden said, "A yellow dog that answers to the name of Ed slipped his collar in front of the Public Library on 42nd and Fifth. It doesn't bite. There's a reward out. It's five dollars; no questions asked."

He seemed to be listening to his radio and talking at the same time. He said, "The man that runs the show, he says not a yellow dog runs off but Guess Who's eye is upon him."

Mr. Golden got up off his cot and stretched. His bulk was mostly width, from shoulder to shoulder, hip to hip.

225

In terms of thickness he was oddly flat as though, like a playing card, if you looked at him edgewise, you'd see almost nothing. He passed around the bag of Hydroxes.

He said, "I wasn't always a mole like you see me down here now better than twenty feet underground and more. It used to be I flew the wide blue yonder with the best of them, wheeling around up there in the clouds with my wings stretched out like a red-tail hawk. You take your roughest ocean, up there it looks like the wrinkles of old age. It looks like you can pick up whole cities and put them in your trouser pocket."

Bebb said, "They used to call him Josephine back then. Remember 'Come, Josephine, in my flying machine'?"

"*Up, up, a little bit higher!*

Watch out! The moon is on fire," Mr. Golden sang the old song out in a voice that was unexpectedly high and sweet. "The things I've been called in my time you wouldn't half believe."

Bebb broke his Hydrox in two and gave half each to Sharon and me. He said, "You take it. If I lose my figure, what have I got left?"

Mr. Golden said, "Technically, I was ground crew, a grease monkey, but on test runs they shoved me the stick fast enough. Inside and out, nobody in the outfit knew those ships better than me."

Bebb said, "Antonio, they figure I'm through. That miserable little Connor of the IRS and Virgil Roebuck with his combat shoes and those fingers of his that's all over nicotine—even down here in the bowels of the earth I've heard the echo of their rejoicing. Ever since they broke things up at Alexander Hall, there's been dancing in the streets of Princeton, New Jersey. Back

226

behind bars with Bebb. Well, I'm not behind bars yet. I've still got me an ace or two up my sleeve."

He had gotten up to offer coffee around and stood with his back to the wire-mesh wall, his red bathrobe and polished scalp bright against the dim cavern that loomed behind him. Lucille had a theory about certain mysterious elevators which, if you knew their secret, took you down to levels deeper than the deepest basements where people from outer space met to lay plans, and I thought how if she could have seen Bebb and Mr. Golden there in the vaults of Bull's Storage, it would have confirmed her wildest suspicions. As Bebb stood there like a routed general on the eve of a great come-back, it crossed my mind that hidden among all these acres of junk behind him there might be batallion after batallion of God only knew what—fire hydrants, angels —ready to follow him to victory.

I said, "Bip, the first thing you need is a good lawyer. You can't just—" and raising his hand, he interrupted me.

He said, "Antonio, we're past all that, Fats and me. Wrangling things out in court, having them rake up a lot of stuff that's over and done with and better to leave lay. I'm through trying to fight them on their own ground where they're the ones know every hill and valley of it."

Mr. Golden said, "When you got wings, why stick to the ground, period? Ever hear of a bald eagle scrapping it out on his feet?"

Bebb said, "All I've done up till now, it's been small potatoes. A soul here, a soul there. . . . I reached out far as I could. The unchurched multitudes I tried to catch with the mail order ads of Gospel Faith College. The great whore of the North I set up Open Heart to wean

227

away from the cup of her fornications. The Pepsi generation, how I made to stay them with flagons and comfort them with apples for I was sick with love, Antonio, and I don't know as I'll ever get over it. None of those things ever come to as much as they should of maybe because I never gave much as I should of to them. I thought small, and I reaped small. Sharon, the time's come to think big. This may be the last round coming up, and your old Bip's going to shoot for the moon."

"Up, up, a little bit higher!" Mr. Golden sang with chocolate Hydrox blacking out most of his teeth. "Watch out! The moon is on fire!"

Sharon said, "Do me a favor, will you, Bip? This time keep all your buttons buttoned."

Bebb said, "What God hath joined together, let no man put asunder. That's number one. Number two is like unto it. What Bebb hath joined together, let no man put asunder either. I joined you two together. Way back in Holy Love days I fixed the whole thing up in ways you never knew. Antonio, first time I ever laid eyes on you, I could see you were right for each other. You were a tree without apples. Sharon, she was apples without a tree. She was the apple of her daddy's eye, but what kind of future's that for a girl? She needed a branch to grow on same as you needed her to put out leaves and fruit on the shiftless branches of your life. Without you'd had each other, you wouldn't have either of you amounted to spit."

He said, "Why, if you couldn't stand the sight of each other, that's one thing. If you treated each other like dirt and went around saying cruel and spiteful things and cheating on each other every chance you got, that's one thing. Sometimes maybe a divorce is made in heaven same as a marriage even though it don't say so in Scripture. But you've been through thick and thin together, and it's made you the best friends either one of you's ever like to find again. Even if you split up and get married off each one to somebody different, you'll be forever phoning each other long distance and trading the kids back and forth. Antonio, he'll be coming round every time there's a birthday or somebody's took sick. They'll all of them say isn't it something how those two get on so friendly even so.

"If there's one thing makes me want to puke, it's a friendly divorce, "Bebb said." If it's got to be, give me a divorce that's hateful. When you're friends, stay put. So what if it's not all moonlight and roses? What is? Stay put because if you don't, you'll spend the rest of your life looking to find each other in the face of strangers."

Sharon said, "All my life I listened to you, Bip. Even down home this winter, everything I did I could hear you quoting Scripture about it."

"Don't listen to me," Bebb said. "Listen to your own self."

Sharon said, "It got to where sometimes I thought maybe the reason I ran out on Antonio was because you picked him for me just like you said."

Bebb said, "Sharon, you'd have picked him anyhow. Gertrude Conover, she'd say it was on account of there was some other life you used to love him in. It's not doctrine, but who knows? Nobody's got a corner on the God's truth, and there's nobody has the right to dump on somebody else's version of it."

Sharon said, "What is it makes people want to dump on you, Bip? Your whole life they've been dumping on you."

Bebb released the clipboard far enough to get his finger out. There was a red line across the knuckle. "Jesus never let on it was going to be any different," he said. "It goes with the territory."

Sharon said, "Far back as I can remember, they were dumping on you. Right from the time they picked you up in Miami."

She said, "I always dreamed you'd be like Oral Roberts someday. I wanted them to run your picture on TV and name a college after you. Only every time you almost had it made, somebody dumped on you. How come, Bip?"

"I took some crazy chances," Bebb said. "Sharon, the way I figured it, if a man was to lay bare all the hurt and shame in him out where folks could see it, might be somebody's come along someday who'd make it right." You could see he'd forgotten Mr. Golden and I were there, only Sharon.

He said, "Take what happened down there in Miami, for instance. Those kids. Talk about your angels, why the eyes those kids had, they were the eyes of angels if I ever saw one, and their kid faces and their bare feet and the way they were hollering around out there in the sunshine—they were having them a time like all the good times a man ever had when he was a kid himself rolled into one. A *good* time, Sharon, a time with goodness and fun and bare feet skittering all through it. I was watching them play niggerbaby back of that seafood place, and it come over me all in a minute. I had this feeling if just one split second those kids would have turned those eyes they had onto me the shameful way I was laid bare in front of them and not gone and mocked at me or tore off home, just looked at me with all that fun and beauty they had in those eyes of theirs, why I'd have walked away from that place a saved sinner.

"It was a fool thing to do, a crazy chance," Bebb said, "and I never two seconds running held it against anybody things went and turned out just like they did."

I'd only seen Sharon's face wet with tears twice before—once just after Bill was born and once when she read the long letter Lucille wrote Jesus on that paper of hers that had flowers blooming all over it. Both those times it seemed to me her tears had more to do with just her face than with whatever was going on inside her face like the tears if you smell an onion or Bildabian hits a nerve, but this time she looked as though they were rolling down on the inside too.

She was sitting beside Bebb with her hand resting between both of his on his knee, but she withdrew it when he finished speaking and pushed back a strand of hair. The act of twisting around to see her at such close range next to him bugged Bebb's eyes out so that his face looked dangerously overinflated. Reaching out to take her hand back again, Bebb raised it up and as though he suddenly had an unbearable toothache pressed it against the side of his face like a poultice. Or else it was her hand where the unbearable pain was, and the poultice was his plump, white cheek. He didn't say anything for a while, just sat there with his eyes bugged out and Sharon's hand pushing his mouth crooked where he'd pressed it to him.

Finally he said, "Honey, you know what's the last word of all the millions of words there are in Scripture not counting the Amen at the end, which one it is that comes at the tail end of the whole shebang?"

Sharon shook her head.

Bebb said, "Well, it's 'Come, Lord Jesus,' Just as plain and straight as that. I always figured it put pretty near the whole thing right in a nutshell. Just 'come.' "

Sharon said, "All I can say is he better come on the double then.

"If he's coming," she said.

He in his bathrobe, she in her raincoat with her head resting against his shoulder—I don't suppose the light in that cluttered cage of a room changed in the slightest, but the way they were sitting there propping each other up, it was as if they were watching a sunset.

On the wall behind them the palm trees stand stiff and motionless as the clouds turn pink. The checkmark birds become a flock of spoonbills. They are flying back from a long day's fishing on the flats. They circle around once or twice through the tinted sky, then float down to settle for the night in the place where Sharon and Bebb are sitting.

From my first meeting with Bebb years earlier, the picture I remember best is at the entrance to the Lexington Avenue subway. I had walked him there in the rain, and half way down the stairs he turned and looked back at me over his shoulder. He had on his black raincoat and Happy Hooligan hat, and he said, "All things are lawful for me, but all things edify not. One Corinthians ten." Oddly enough, the picture I remember best from this final meeting is something like it except that in this one Bebb is going up instead of down.

When it came time for Sharon and me to leave, he led us to a handier elevator than the one we'd arrived by, a large freight elevator so packed with furniture there was barely room for two of us to squeeze in together up front. He said he wanted to see us safely on our way so Mr. Golden and I waited below while he and Sharon took the first ride up. The only door the elevator had was a folding grate you could see through, and that is the last picture of him I have kept.

Over his pajamas he is wearing the overcoat with the Persian lamb collar, but he has on that same original hat. He is looking neither to right nor to left but straight ahead through the grating of the door. His mouth is snapped shut on its hinges, and as the elevator starts to move, I think I see his trick eyelid flutter, but maybe this time it is a genuine wink. The elevator rises slowly—first his head disappears, then his Persian lamb collar, then those two plump fists hanging stiff at either side. Finally all that is left are his feet in what I suspect are the same black shoes I mentally tied for him while he said the Lord's Prayer over the remains of poor Lucille laid out in a Houston funeral parlor. Then nothing is left but the empty shaft with the cables looping down like shroud-lines. As things turned out, it was the start of a record-breaking flight.

CHAPTER FOURTEEN

WHEN Brownie flew on from Houston in a cloud of after-shave, he brought John Turtle with him, and my heart sank at the memory of the abominations he had committed at the funeral of Herman Redpath and at the thought of what he might go on to commit now in that potato field north of Princeton where we all gathered—Sharon and Gertrude Conover and I, Tony and his brother Chris, Charlie Blaine and Billie Kling, Nancy Oglethorpe, and Anita Steen of all people, Anita Steen looking the most stricken of all and in a dress for once instead of her usual slacks. She wore the rusty black dress and black stockings of an Italian peasant, her face puffy with grief. I hadn't even realized she'd known Bebb, but she had apparently, from the days when she used to come to the house to teach Sharon guitar.

She said, "Listen, religion's not for Anita Steen, and he knew it, but we always got on anyhow. Maybe it's because we were both queer as three dollar bills," and then the wrinkles of grief started to shoot across that fierce, orphaned face like a cake of ice when you hit it with a pick, so when she asked if she could come along with Sharon and me, we agreed to drive her down with us from Sutton.

Brownie did his best to reassure us about John Turtle. He said, "John Turtle is not here in his official capacity as Joking Cousin because Mr. Bebb was never a member of the tribe, dear. He's here to pay his respects like the rest of us, and I don't look for any trouble from him."

And Brownie was nearly right. John Turtle didn't interrupt the prayers with blasphemies or carry on indecently during the Scripture readings, and he didn't take a leak in the coffin either as he had in Herman Redpath's because of course there wasn't any coffin, just that sprawl of blackened debris with one corkscrewed wing jutting up and the neat furrows scorched the color of toast in streaks that shot out starwise. The only trouble he caused, if you could even call it trouble, was after Brownie had finished and we were all standing around like a ruin, and before anybody realized what he was up to, John Turtle had kicked off his saddle shoes and moved as far in toward the wreckage as he could without hurting his bare feet on the shattered hardware.

He was wearing a double-breasted checked suit with built-up shoulders, and his black hair was greased down so flat it looked as if he'd painted it on. With his arms crooked at the elbows, he held his fists up around his ears, threw back his head, and did a dance. It seemed to me a rather restrained dance with a lot of bending over double in it and straightening up again, the legs moving mostly from the knees down, the feet never leaving a circle not much bigger than a steering wheel. He didn't sing any of his songs while he did it or make any other sound, and after a few minutes we almost forgot to watch him the way we might have forgotten to watch a black crow pecking around for potato bugs.

But then he left his small circle and came toward us with a crouching step, his legs wide apart, his arms curved out to the side and wobbling like a crab's claws. His gold-framed teeth glittered as he swayed from side to side on his haunches, and then suddenly he leapt forward and with the delicacy of Rudolph Nureyev seized Gertrude Conover by the waist from behind and raised her off the ground. You might have thought they'd rehearsed it.

If Gertrude Conover was taken aback, she gave no sign of it but rose up in his grip as light as a bird, her expression unchanging as she gazed out straight ahead, her black pumps dangling in the air. The Joking Cousin held her there maybe two feet off the ground, that small woman with not a feature or a blue hair out of place. He circled around with her a few times, his bare feet padding softly up and down through the scorched furrows. It was as if he was searching for just the right spot, the right vantage, and when he found it, he straightened out his arms so that she was raised that much higher still and stopped dancing then, just held her there as far as his arms would reach like a man at a parade hoisting a child to see the elephants pass by.

Her dress had gotten hitched up in the process, and I

remember how her white slip showed, beneath it her thin, beige legs. I remember the little exclamation she gave as though what she could see from up there was both a surprise and an end to surprise, the way she brought her hands together palm to palm in front of her face like a diver.

Nancy Oglethorpe's beehive, the grey crew cut of Anita Steen, the fedora Charlie Blaine wore in fair weather and foul because of his sinuses, we were the skyline John Turtle raised her to see beyond—beyond us and the wreckage we'd gathered by, to the flat acres stretching out behind it, to a blue silo dazzling in the sun, to the horizon where swollen grey clouds were crowding each other like elephants. Like the time I stood out by the compost heap looking up at Sharon's lighted window the night she came home from Armadillo, it is one of those frames where all of us who were there go on standing forever.

"Widow lady, oh my," John Turtle said, his cheek pressed tight against Gertrude Conover's behind. "Window lady, oh my." Considering all he might have done and said, I figured we'd come off remarkably well.

"My dear, have you ever been to a Princeton reunion?" Gertrude Conover had said that morning out on the terrace of Revonoc with an espaliered quince spidering out on the wall behind her. "Let me tell you I have lived through a great many of them. They are Walpurgisnacht. They are Vanity Fair. Well, they are a disaster. I remember when Harold Conover was still alive going with him to the twenty-five year tent one evening. There were two elderly men at one of the tables pouring

237

pitchers of beer over each other's heads. They were both of them bishops. Suburban housewives with brand new permanents and too much lipstick. People's children in little T-shirts with tigers on them throwing up and getting lost. And my dear, the P-rade. The P-rade is the gaudy climax of the whole thing. Matadors, Mickey Mouses—each returning class is dressed up to look like something different, and they all carry comic signs and bottles of one thing or another. They come from the far corners of the earth.

She said, "Naturally Leo Bebb chose the P-rade just the way he chose the Pharaoh's court in days gone by and just the way he will choose who knows what spectacular arena in days yet to come. If there are to be days yet to come for him. I like to think perhaps he has burst the fetters of his karma once and for all and can slip off now into cosmic consciousness like a drop of water slipping back into the ocean. It's only selfishly I don't like to think that," her blue curls bobbing in the spring breeze, the Pharaoh tying back some red roses across the lawn by the swimming pool. "Selfishly, I don't like to think of never running into him again. Even at his bluest he was . . .

"Leo Bebb was always good company," she said.

The color blue. Red roses for a blue lady, as the old song goes; the blue hair of Gertrude Conover; the wide blue yonder where Mr. Golden had winged it with the best of them in his time; Bebb at his bluest. As though I'd been there myself I can see him appearing like a bolt out of the cloudless blue sky over Nassau Street. The band in their ice cream white flannels and orange blazers. The old grads with their hearing aids and straw boaters. The young grads gotten up to look like Martians, like castaways. I see the flash of the trombones, the revolving blue lights on the cars of the cops blocking traffic, hear the bum-boom of the big drums, all that.

Then *Come Josephine in your flying machine*—coming in over the squat turrets of Alexander Hall and the Presbyterian Church a low-flying spit-and-glue flivver laying balloons like eggs, hundreds of them, and leaflets, LOVE IS A FEAST, with a shot of Bebb on each. It was the same shot Sharon said made him look as though they were taking his temperature rectally, his eyes popping out of his head, his mouth clamped tight on a cry for help.

It buzzed the whole length of Nassau Street from Palmer Square to Jugtown and back with the engine roaring like Armageddon and the wings a-flap, so low that in many places the marchers scattered and children clung to their mothers' skirts. They say you could feel the wind of the props, that dogs ran wild, that Charles Wilson Peale's Washington fell to the floor in Nassau Hall and cracked its frame.

I see Fats Golden at the stick like the Red Baron—his scarf streaming out behind him, his leather helmet, his goggles, that lovely, wind-swept smile. I don't see Bebb because he is swamped in balloons, the whole fuselage stuffed with them—they must have spent days blowing them up—Bebb himself a balloon as he shovels them out into the sky.

On the return flight when they hit Palmer Square for the second time, Mr. Golden must have given it everything he'd got. They say you could see rivets popping, seams straining, sweat breaking out on the scarred silver belly, as it hovered for a moment like the sun at Gideon, pulled itself together, then shot straight up into the wide blue. At about three times the height of Holder Tower it

239

leveled off and spoke—two streamers spilling out from the tail in a long line, two twenty foot pennants trailing out behind in tandem, on one of them HERE'S TO JESUS, on the other one HERE'S TO YOU.

Gertrude Conover said, "It was his parting shot, his One for the Road, circling around up there over the town the better part of an hour doing all kinds of crazy stunts, climbing and swooping and what have you. They found out the plane had been stolen from the Princeton airport, and there were troopers out there waiting for them to land. They called me to find out what I knew. I knew absolutely nothing. The last time I saw Leo Bebb was at the *débacle* at Alexander Hall. The last time I spoke with him was when he phoned me late one night just a day or so ago. He said he'd left his red preaching gown in the back seat of the Lincoln and would I have it dry-cleaned for him. He said that portable television he keeps in his room wasn't working properly and asked if I'd get the repair man up before the guarantee expired. They seemed queer things to be calling up so late about. I believe they were his way of letting me think he was planning to come back. I knew he wasn't, of course."

I said, "He'd burned his bridges behind him."

Gertrude Conover said, "His friend Clarence Golden burned them for him. That remarkable man came to see me one day. I'd never even heard his name mentioned before, and there he was strolling across the lawn with his hands in his pockets like my oldest neighbor. I recognized him almost immediately. He was one of the great eighteenth century *castrati*, a man by the name of Serafico Veluzzi. I was myself a provincial *contessa* visiting in

240

Rome at that period, and more than once I heard him sing so beautifully in St. John Lateran that the Pope himself was in tears. Serafico sat on this very terrace and told me I was not to let Leo Bebb come back here even if he wanted to. With the sweetest smile in the world, he told me that if I did, he would personally notify the Internal Revenue people and the Borough Police to come get him. He told me he'd seen to it he couldn't go back to you in Sutton either. It seems he was the one who wrote that anonymous letter to the insurance company about the fire there to make sure that sanctuary too would be unavailable. He said, 'We've got to keep him from getting sidetracked this time, Mrs. Conover,' and then he went drifting off across the lawn again like a cloud of steam. What I wouldn't have given to have heard him do just a bar or two of the *Miserere*. They say that once or twice even the statue of the Virgin was seen to wipe her eyes."

Here's to Jesus . . . Here's to you . . . trailing circles through the blue sky as Gertrude Conover watched from Gouverneur Road. The police waiting at the airport. The P-rade getting underway again. Then a spasmodic hiccoughing from deep in the vitals of that antiquated machine—a belch of tobacco-colored smoke from the exhaust, a long expectoration of flame. It fought for altitude, stalling and rattling itself to pieces, and set out on a mad, zigzag course roughly north. Like the Keystone Cops when the steering wheel comes off in their hands, I picture Mr. Golden and Bebb squeezed into the cockpit with what's left of the balloons, and the controls gone haywire, Ptah-Sitti the priest and Serafico

241

Veluzzi. I picture them with their arms wrapped around each other, their Red Baron goggles clacking together as the green world wheels and turns upside down. I picture those two old cons locked in fiery embrace as the world hurtles up through the blue air to embrace them.

What I want to picture next is this. They bale out. Their chutes pop open, and swinging side by side in their harnesses they float slowly down through the sky like toys. They hit the ground together in a tangle of ballooning silk and scramble to their feet. I see them then from up where the abandoned plane is burning to death, two small, round figures, Tweedledee and Tweedledum, tearing off across the acres of potato land. They are already half way to the horizon when the plane hits.

There was no evidence that any such thing took place. Nobody saw them come floating down, and no chutes were discovered on the ground afterwards. There were several witnesses to the crash, and all of them agreed that while the plane was still high in the air, it was gloved in flame and fanned to fury by the long, fast fall. The only evidence for their escape was the negative evidence that there wasn't the slightest trace of anything that could be identified as either Bebb or his friend in the wreckage afterwards: not so much as a button or a tooth let alone a charred porkpie hat thrown clear or a partly melted lapel button with Holy going across and Love coming down through the single O. But that was not considered significant since there was hardly anything else in the wreckage that could be identified either. The fire was so intense and its destruction so complete that some said it could have been caused only by somebody's soaking the old crate with gasoline and then touching it off with a match. That is not incompatible with the escape theory, of course, and might even be used to support it—Mr. Golden touching it off precisely in order to account for the absence of any identifiable remains. But no one ever advanced such a theory officially, and even I advance it only in a tentative and wishful way.

In any case, it was because there was no body to bury or even any ashes to scatter with the assurance that they weren't just the ashes of leftover balloons that Brownie suggested he hold the service at the site where, if anywhere, the dust that had once been Leo Bebb lay. The farmer who owned the field gave his permission with the understanding that we keep it small. He didn't want his potatoes trampled any more than he had to, and the rest of us were just as glad, not wanting a horde of former Love Feasters or any more trouble with the authorities. So just the handful I have already listed came, and Brownie kept things short and, needless to say, sweet. Dear Brownie. He must have had his store teeth especially buffed up for the occasion. I have never seen his relentless smile so bright.

He started off with *I am the resurrection and the life,* then read two or three psalms including the twenty-third, and when he came to the part about preparing a table before me in the presence of mine enemies, I remember wondering with what homiletic ingenuity he would have explained away that always rather discordant and to me unedifying note. I suppose he would have said something to the effect that the table was a kind of smorgasbord to which the psalmist had every intention of summoning his enemies too as soon as he got around to it.

He read the part where Jesus says that in his father's house there are many mansions, and I could not help thinking of it as rather like the Red Path Ranch outside of Houston with all those flatroofed stucco buildings and the new Holy Love Herman Redpath had built for Bebb to look like the Alamo, not to mention John Turtle's Tom Thumb golf course, Bea Trionka's exercycle, the greenhouse, the swimming pool, and so on—something there for every taste. There was no eulogy, just a prayer which Brownie had written specially with lots in it about fighting the good fight and death where is thy victory and how when the heavenly city comes down at last, there will be no sorrow or pain in it because God himself will wipe away the tears from all our eyes.

I don't know for sure that anybody wept at the service. Out of the corner of my eye I could see that Charlie Blaine had his handkerchief out, but it may have just been his sinuses, and Nancy Oglethorpe's eye-liner ran some, but I had seen it run on other occasions when she was at her most cheerful. I noticed Tony's brother Chris standing there pale but dry-eyed in a beautifully cut gabardine suit and thought how with the exception of Gertrude Conover he could probably already buy and sell us all. Sharon was beside me, but the way her long hair fell all I could see was the rim of one ear and the bridge of her nose, so I couldn't tell about her. But she had already said goodbye, after all, in the basement of Bull's International Storage when Bebb had tried to explain to her about Miami Beach, when they had sat there at sunset and watched the spoonbills home.

Brownie came up to shake our hands afterwards. He said, "What the Lord taketh away with one hand he giveth back with another. I understand you're expecting a blessed event, dear," and when he had moved away to shake some other hands, Sharon said to me, "There's one thing I've got to put you straight on, Bopper. It's not on account of the baby I'm willing for us to give things another try, and I hope it's not on account of the baby you are either. I wasn't even going to tell you about it till Bip pulled the rug out. And there's something else about that baby I've got to put you straight on too, about who that baby is," and just as she was getting ready to tell me, I reached out and laid my hands over her mouth.

I said, "Let me put you straight on something instead. It doesn't matter who that baby is. Maybe it matters to God, but it doesn't matter to me. Maybe it ought to matter to me, but it doesn't. So don't you let it matter too much to you either."

She moved my hand away as far as her cheek and said, "It wasn't his fault. I made him stay. I didn't know but what I was pregnant anyhow so it didn't seem like that way it made much difference. It was New Year's, and I was feeling so low in my mind. He was too. He was having this nothing vacation with Charlie and Billie. I couldn't let him go home alone. So maybe it's your baby, and maybe it's not. I'm not even sure myself, if you want to know the truth."

I said, "Well anyway, at least it's all in the family," and what she said was, "That Bop"—not That *Bip* for once but That *Bop*, with the same mixture of admiration and disbelief, saying it about me as though there was somebody else there to say it about me to as she stood among the scorched star-points slowly shaking her head. That Bop.

Nobody was sure whose baby it was, and when it finally came and was a girl just as Bebb had predicted, we named her Lucille although what we ended up calling her was Lucy. My nephew and I looked enough alike in a general kind of way—dark-haired, dark-eyed, like organ grinders—so that even if she'd turned out to look

245

like one of us, it could just as well have been a form of looking like the other. The way it worked out, she didn't look like either of us. She looked like Sharon—the same somber face, the same giveaway smile.

If Tony had any suspicions that she might have been his, he never let on that he did unless perhaps by the fact that soon after she was born, he gave up his job at Sutton High and moved in with Chris in New York as though that small geographical gesture would clear him in everybody's eyes including his own. The best thing that happened to him in New York was that he started seeing a good deal of his old classmate Laura Fleischman there, and when they were married about a year later and I stood up for him as best man with Sharon and the baby among others looking on, I thought how it would take God himself to sort out the tangle. But the point is that it was a tangle which somehow bound us life to life as though what we'd variously found in each other's arms was maybe not the home we'd been after but at least a place to get our bearings by.

On our way back from the wedding reception in the wall-to-wall living room of Mrs. Fleischman, Sharon put it this way. "It's like the man says, Antonio," she said. "The family that lays together stays together," and as she said it, I could almost hear that gusty, smothered laugh of Bebb's the night he rang us up in bed.

I have never dreamed about Bebb since the afternoon of Brownie's service, and if in one way I'm sorry about that because it would be nice to catch a glimpse of him again, in another way I'm just as glad because like all the others you run into that way, I suppose he would give me the brush-off, indicating that he had miles ahead of

246

him still and no time to stop and palaver with old friends. But if I do not have dreams about him anymore, I still sometimes have daydreams.

When the Joking Cousin put his hands on either side of Gertrude Conover's waist and lifted her up as high as he could reach, she could see a good deal farther than the rest of us, of course, and in my daydreams it's her eyes I see through, which is the only reason I can think of for why John Turtle called her Window Lady. Beyond the blue silo and the tree-line at the edge of the field, beyond the horizon itself, up and over what King Lear called "the thick rotundity o' the world," I see where it is that Bebb and Mr. Golden escaped to after safely baling out.

It is a tropical isle. There are palm trees and pink beaches on it and jungle pools where in the daytime brown-limbed natives swim and at night the beasts pad down on velvet feet to take their ease and drink. The natives have made Bebb their king. What else could they do with him? I see him naked as the day he was born only even more so if possible because this is a nakedness of his own risking. Night after night he presides at the great tribal feasts. The food is laid out in heaps—parrot-colored fruit to eat which is never to thirst, wine made of yams and citrus and sassafras root to drink which is never to hunger. Bebb himself is a great pile of fruit glinting the color of pearl by the light of the moon as he dispenses himself. Mr. Golden also is there like an oddly shaped swarm of fireflies, the keeper of the flame, and of their kingdom there shall be no end unless that day should come when it seems time to end it, and against that day there is always the flame that Mr. Golden keeps, another bridge to burn for the sake of another bridge to cross.

Which brings me finally to decathexis and myself. I will not pretend that something didn't end for me during that sad time when Sharon sent me packing or that the life that was left me wasn't a life I was ready enough to let go when that time came. Call it my youth that ended, a capacity for ignoring irony like Stephen Kulak, a taste for certain flavors of hope. Did I let it go because it had ceased to work for me, or did it cease to work for me because I had let it go? I don't know the answer to that, but I let it go anyway, and why not? A man has the right to let go the life he was born with and never asked for in the first place. Better to let it go and admit you no longer feel what you used to feel than to go on keeping up pretenses like old Metzger, thumping three times on the wall as if the death that approaches is the death of something that isn't already dead. In any case, I let it go, that first and original life that comes with the territory, and if once and a while I feel regret, I no longer feel remorse.

But the second life is another story. Out of the wreckage of things I picked up a kind of marriage again, a daughter who by one route or another at least has my blood in her veins, a capacity if not for rising above irony like the saints, at least for living it out with something like grace, with the suspicion if not the certainty that maybe the dark and hurtful shadows all things cast are only shadows. This second life is the one I chose for myself, and this time there will be no decathexis if I can help it. Because I have made this bed, I will sleep in it, and this time I will not let it go until the Shadow itself wrests it from my grasp, or if there is any truth at all in some of the more rotund and apocalyptic utterances of Leo Bebb, not even then.

FREDERICK BUECHNER

Frederick Buechner was born in 1926 in New York City. He was educated at Lawrenceville School and Princeton University, where he graduated in 1948 after two years in the army. In 1950 he published his first novel, A Long Day's Dying. After teaching English at Lawrenceville, during which time he published his second novel, The Seasons' Difference (1952), he attended Union Theological Seminary. In 1958 he received his Bachelor of Divinity degree and was ordained a Presbyterian minister. In that same year his third novel, The Return of Ansel Gibbs, was published to wide acclaim. From 1958 to 1967 he served as School Minister and chairman of the religion department at Phillips Exeter Academy. During that period he w.ote his fourth novel, The Final Beast, and two volumes of meditations, The Magnificent Defeat and The Hungering Dark. In 1970 his novel The Entrance to Porlock was published, and in 1971 Lion Country, first of the novels about Leo Bebb. Its sequel, Open Heart, followed in 1972. In 1973 he published a work of non-fiction, Wishful Thinking: A Theological ABC. He is presently writing in Vermont, where he lives with his wife and three children.